Knights of the Magical Realm
Warriors Gone Wild
By
Tina Gerow
Linda Wisdom
Dakota Cassidy
Brit Blaise

Triskelion Publishing
www.triskelionpublishing.net

Triskelion Publishing
15327 W. Becker Lane
Surprise, AZ 85379 USA

Printing History
First e Published by Triskelion Publishing
First e publishing August 2006
First printing by Triskelion Publishing
First paperback printing November 2006
ISBN 1-933874-40-6
ISBN 13: 978-1-933874-40-1

Cover design Triskelion Publishing
Cover model: Andrei Claude

Other Titles by Tina Gerow

Available now

The Maiden series
Stone Maiden
Fire Maiden
Ice Maiden (2007)

Into A Dangerous Mind (2007)

Fantasy Quest
By
Tina Gerow

Dedication

To all my online gaming friends who like to spend time in worlds very much like the one I've created here–especially the Ascension Guild, my online family. Special thanks to my son Darian, aka Oopec, my sister Amy, aka Daira and my brother in law Doug, aka Dynar.

And of course, to my very own warrior gone wild – Lerik, aka my husband Jon.

Chapter One

"Can I buy you a drink, and we can discuss the rest of our lives?"

Astiria Petrey huffed out a heavy sigh and snapped her book shut before glaring up at the newest intruder. He leered down at her. Ken-doll bronzed skin and plastic-looking muscles bulged out from under his ridiculous shirt decorated with small chili peppers. A tiny blue Speedo peeked out from under the shirt before giving way to unnaturally bulky thigh muscles.

"Not. Interested." She enunciated each word carefully and searched his flat vacant eyes for any sign of understanding. Or even humanity.

"That's only because you haven't met *me* yet." He flashed a too white smile, which threatened to blind her even through her sunglasses before he sat on the edge of her beach chair and snatched the book from her grasp. "*Stone Maiden*?" He glanced at the back cover before looking up again. "Gargoyles, angels and cowboys?"

Her temper sparked. She loved to read paranormal romances, and this one allowed her to combine two of her favorite things—reading and gargoyles. All her coworkers and friends teased her incessantly about the collection of both gargoyles and romance novels littered across her desk at work and her entire house. She definitely didn't need more grief while on vacation, and not from this bad caricature of an action hero.

"What kind of thing is this for a beautiful woman to read, when she should be more interested in what's right in front of her face? Me." He smiled and flexed a bicep that looked like it might explode right off his arm at any moment.

She grabbed her book back, brushing down the edges where he'd bent them, and then pushed to her feet to glare at him. Anyone who didn't take care of books lost even more respect in her eyes—not that he had any to begin with after his poor behavior. "As I already said— not interested! And even if I was illiterate and couldn't read, then I would still have much better things to do with my time than waste it talking to someone who obviously eats steroid Pop Tarts for breakfast."

He stood and reached for her, confusion swimming in his eyes. He must not be used to hearing the word 'no' very often. "Don't be like that, sweetheart."

She sidestepped his hands and anger flowed hot and heady. "If you don't turn and walk away right this second, I swear I'll tell every woman on the beach that fully hard, you aren't much bigger than a Vienna sausage!" She held up her hand, pinkie finger extended, hopefully illustrating for him in case he didn't get the reference.

His eyes widened as understanding dawned. He opened his mouth, but before he could speak, the manager of the resort neatly intervened.

"Mario, why don't you leave Miss Petrey to her reading? I'm sure there are others on the beach who would love to see you." The manager's blue eyes twinkled with amusement behind the lenses of the Harry Potter glasses perched on the end of his nose. "I do apologize, Miss Petrey."

"Well, at least you keep saving me from them. I'm beginning to think there are a never ending stream of vacuous pretty boys frequenting your private beach."

He chuckled. "This is the Caribbean, Miss Petrey, and the Fantasy Quest resort. They all come here to meet beautiful women sitting on beach chairs, sipping drinks and hoping to meet a man to make their vacation more memorable. You are one of the few who come alone, who wish to remain so."

She bristled at his comment, slightly mollified he'd referred to her as beautiful, even though she knew being nice was part of his job description. Someone with plain brown hair, plain brown eyes and a body that wouldn't be caught dead in a bikini, didn't exactly fire men's passions. Hadn't that been exactly what her ex-husband had told her when he left her for a younger, more attractive woman after Astiria had worked and slaved to put the bastard through medical school?

She stifled a sigh and squared her shoulders. No, men weren't interested in a woman with brains and personality unless they looked like a super model, so she wasn't interested in them. Besides, her sister and brother in law had bought this trip for her birthday and practically forced her onto the plane. Amy and Doug had come here on their honeymoon and had raved about it ever since. A free vacation was hard to pass up, no matter where it was.

She just hadn't counted on such persistence from the local herd of men. "All I want to do is relax, walk barefoot on the beach, have a few drinks and read my book." She didn't realize she'd said it aloud until the manager answered.

"Miss Petrey, again, I truly apologize. Why don't you go inside, relax, and order some room service? There will be a beautiful view of the coming storm from your room since it faces the ocean."

"Coming storm? But it's sunny and..." She trailed off as the sky darkened as if triggered by his words. "Wow, storms come up fast here." Grabbing her towel, she shook it off to remove any excess sand.

"Your profile mentioned a certain fondness for computer games, Miss Petrey. We have several, which are free to our guests. It might help you pass the time while we ride out the moods of Mother Nature."

A hotel manager suggesting computer games while at a beautiful resort in the Caribbean? Something about the entire situation, including the manager, struck her as very odd, but she couldn't quite put her finger on it. *You're on vacation at somewhere called Fantasy Quest! Of course, they are going to take your preferences into account. You need more drinks and much more relaxation.* She laughed at herself. "Thank you. I'll have to check that out. But after the storm. I don't want to fry the computer in my room if the building takes a lightning hit."

He smiled, his blue eyes still twinkling. "We are fully insulated from any such happening. Feel free to play. After all, if it weren't storming, most likely, you would be staying here on the beach."

She started at his strange wording, and the shiver of unease that slid down her spine, but she shrugged it off. "Thanks, I'll keep that in mind."

*****

The door to her room closed behind her with a click she ordinarily wouldn't have noticed. Nerves? It made her pause until she shook off her unease and dropped her towel. She deposited *Stone Maiden* onto the overstuffed leather loveseat recliner by the bed, giving it a silent promise to return. Before she could kick off her sandals, a brisk knock sounded.

"Room Service!"

She shook her head again. In the two days she'd been here, room service had been unnaturally quick and she'd never once ordered. She might find it irritating if they didn't have an uncanny knack of knowing exactly what she wanted. Hand on the doorknob, she paused. *If I could order anything I wanted, it would be chicken Marsala with veggies on the side, parrot bay and diet coke for the drink and tiramisu for dessert.* "Get that one right," she muttered under her breath in challenge before pulling open the door.

"Good evening, Miss Petrey." The waiter pushed

his cart inside and unloaded several silver domed plates onto the table next to the balcony door.

"Good evening. What's on the menu tonight?" She crossed her arms over her chest and allowed a smug smile to crease her lips.

He lifted the first domed lid and the scent of garlic and Marsala wine wafted out to tease her senses. *No freaking way!*

"Chicken Marsala with a side of steamed vegetables." He pulled a bottle of Parrot Bay out from under the linen-covered cart. "Here's a nice bottle of rum and the mini-fridge is fully stocked with soda." He nodded toward the mini fridge before setting the rum and a full bucket of ice onto her table. "And of course, dessert."

"Let me guess. Tiramisu?"

"Yes, ma'am." He smiled. "Can I get you anything else?"

"How do you do that?" She stared at him in open awe.

He shrugged. "This is the Fantasy Quest resort, Miss Petrey. We pride ourselves on giving you your fantasy."

Her stomach rumbled as if to remind her that delicious food was waiting just for her, and here she stood contemplating how it had come to be. She pressed a tip into the waiter's hand and thanked him as he left.

It had to be her sister's doing. Amy had probably provided them a detailed list of her preferences. Astiria shrugged and headed back toward her food. As much as she loved to cook her own food and experiment with new recipes, she could get used to all her meals being provided for her.

The open drapes showed her the darkening sky and the oncoming storm the manager had predicted. Rain fell in the distance, dappling the clouds and the far horizon with streaks. She clicked on the small lamp next to the bed to chase back the deepening gloom and pulled a purple stuffed gargoyle from her suitcase. She hugged it tightly before setting it on the other side of the table, just behind the tiramisu.

Over the years, men hadn't always been reliable, but her trusty stuffed gargoyle always had been. That's why he always got to accompany her on vacations and they didn't. Besides, he never needed his own plane ticket and definitely didn't hog the covers.

"So what do you make of this place, Max?" She made herself a rum and diet with extra ice and sat down to enjoy her meal. Garlic and spices broke over her tongue, carrying with it a truly irresistible aroma. "Mmmm." She laughed at herself when the sound came out almost orgasmic. "Don't look at me like that, Max. A girl's gotta have vices, right?" Max's perpetual evil grin made her smile.

When she savored the last bite of chicken, she pushed her plate away and decided to save the tiramisu for later in the evening. "Well, Max. It's dark and gloomy outside and I'm not in the mood to watch television, and I'm too keyed up to read. Why don't we check out the computer games the manager and even Amy raved about? Although why they would even think about computer games on their honeymoon is totally beyond me!"

She tucked Max under one arm and grabbed her drink before heading to the far side of the room where the wireless keyboard and mouse sat on a honey-toned desk. The 42" flat wall-mounted TV monitor doubled as a computer monitor, which allowed her to sit on the loveseat recliner where she'd dumped her towel and book earlier.

After moving her things to the bed, she balanced the keyboard on her lap and the mouse next to her on the second seat, since it rolled easily over the butter-smooth leather. The tiny end table gave her a perfect place for her drink and of course, for Max, who overlooked the proceedings with his usual evil glee.

She pressed the power button on the top of the keyboard and the monitor flared to life. A gold embossed border surrounded the Fantasy Quest logo that emblazoned everything she'd seen so far at the resort. Background music flowed through the surround sound speakers making her think of every action adventure movie she'd ever seen.

"Welcome to Fantasy Quest Resort, Miss Petrey. Would you like to try our online role-playing game, Fantasy Quest?" The computer monitor's voice sounded suspiciously like the manager's, but being a project manager in technologies, she knew voice scripts were easily made. It just seemed like a lot of effort to make one with each guest's name on it.

She shrugged. "I must be really predictable. How did this thing know I didn't want to check email?" She reached for her mouse to click 'Yes.' A self-proclaimed computer geek, she played several online games regularly. She wondered briefly how this one would stack up against her familiar favorites.

A video clip flowed over the screen to the blare of processional trumpets. Several different characters–wizards, mages, warriors and what appeared to be a paladin fought a group of fire-breathing dragons and flying griffins. However, these weren't digitized people, these were actual actors playing out the parts on screen for her enjoyment. The video clip disappeared, replaced by a 3D paper doll woman.

"Please choose features for your character, Astiria."

She started at the use of her name, but then if the hotel's systems could call her by her last name, it was a small leap to have it interface with this hotel-hosted game to use her first. But the paper doll woman made her do a double take. Again, this looked like no digitized construct, but like an actual woman who had been photographed and inserted.

"Wow, maybe they need a technologies project manager, Max. Can you imagine living here year round and getting to play games for a living? Especially with this technology!" She glanced over at the grinning gargoyle. He'd never answered her, thank God, but she did always leave him conversational room—just so she'd know when she'd finally lost her mind.

"But it looks much more advanced than what I'm used to working with. Hell, I'd even take a pay cut if they'd be willing to train me. Especially if I get a beach view year round." She paused to take a swig of rum and diet soda. "But the Ken doll men have to go. The only men I'm interested are ones I create in my imagination." She chuckled at her own joke and returned her attention to the game.

Used to this sort of preliminary game set up, she breezed through defining her physical options. She chose a high elf, with delicate pointed ears and long red hair rioting around her in sexy waves. *Much better than my own boring brown hair!* With quick clicks of her mouse, she chose sea green eyes, a tall athletic frame, still curvy enough to catch a man's attention, but not so much it would get in the way of a good sword fight. For profession, she chose an assassin with healing abilities, and clicked on the default options for clothing, knowing it didn't matter. She would have to buy armor within the game, the starter clothes were just to keep her character from being naked.

"That was quick," she told Max as she clicked on 'Save.'

"Please choose features for your consort, Astiria."

She choked on a mouthful of her rum. "Consort?" She glanced over at Max, but he only continued to smile, seemingly enjoying her reaction. "What kind of game is this?" She chuckled. "Pretty scary when the only place I'll be getting lucky is online with a 'consort' I built from scratch."

"Please choose features for your consort, Astiria," the computer repeated.

"Don't rush me," she said as she studied the options. "If I'm going to build a consort, he's going to be so good, I'll be wishing he'd come to life."

As if in response, thunder boomed and a bright flash of lightning blazed across the sky, causing her to jump and slosh rum onto her shirt. The lights in her room flickered, but as the manager said, the computer seemed unaffected. She sat her glass down on the end table and looked around the room.

"You'd think if they could insulate the computer hardware that they could do the same for all their electronics." She shrugged. She worked with computers, but didn't really know if overhead lights could be protected in the same way. But as a project manager, she only knew enough to speak intelligently on the subject — she had tech leads for all the deep down information.

"Do you require help choosing features for your consort, Astiria?"

She jumped. She hadn't expected the computer to be so persistent. "All right. Keep your shirt on." She glanced down at the keyboard on her lap. "So to speak."

She clicked through the options choosing a human warrior with a muscular build, eyes the color of melted dark chocolate with hair to match. The hair was shoulder length, and could be pulled back with a leather thong as needed. When she finished, she looked up at the screen and caught her breath.

The man staring down at her seemed very real. There was even a real man's hunger in his eyes she hadn't seen in a long time. One that spoke of passion, possession and that said he'd already seen her naked and planned to do so many more times. Goosebumps marched over her body in a quick flowing procession, causing her to shiver. Heat pooled low in her stomach and her nipples suddenly tightened with need.

A flesh and blood man had never caused this kind of instant physical reaction. "Damn, I really need to buy better toys!" She shook off the strange reaction and moved her cursor over the 'Save' button. Glancing back at him, his dark eyes burned through her skin until she thought she would spontaneously combust right here in the chair. Almost without conscious thought, her finger slowly depressed the mouse button.

"Thank you, Astiria. You have chosen Lerik, the Warrior, as your consort."

"Lerik." She rolled the name around on her tongue. It seemed to fit him somehow. "I'd definitely like to do more with Lerik than just choose him."

A small progress bar flowed across the screen and then Lerik disappeared. She blinked at the sudden loss and inhaled, realizing that when he'd looked at her, the air in the room had seemed thin and in sparse supply. Leaning back in her chair, she concentrated on getting enough air back into her lungs.

"Please answer the following questions honestly, Astiria. Honest answers will complement your gaming experience."

She sighed. "As long as you don't ask me my weight or something equally horrendous, I think I can do honest." She scanned down the list of questions frowning at several. Most were simple such as hobbies and food preferences, but they also asked about allergies and even a few very personal questions.

"Do you need help answering the following questions honestly, Astiria? Honest answers will complement your gaming experience."

She threw back her head and laughed. "Damn,

Astiria. It's just a game, why are you letting yourself get nervous over a few questions. Just answer them." With a fortifying drink of rum and diet, she quickly clicked her answers down the list, being honest, but trying to get it over with as quickly as possible.   Then the very last question stopped her like a fist to the stomach.

44. HOW DO YOU LIKE YOUR SEX?
A) GENTLE & SLOW
B) HARD & FAST
C) A TOTAL POSSESSION OF BODY MIND AND SOUL THAT MELDS
YOU TOGETHER WITH MELTING PASSION.

A slow persistent throbbing began between her thighs as she read option C again.   Her imagination quickly supplied several vivid images of what such an option might look like, and she considered breaking out her toys before moving on with the game. "With my luck, Max, the computer voice will ask me if I need any help with that too.   And unfortunately, I probably do."   She scrubbed her hands over her face and slowly clicked on C.

"Thank you, Astiria. Your world is being created."

Arousal still flowed through her body and she swallowed hard against the sudden need.   Her clothes were now scratchy and rough against her sensitive skin and she wished Lerik would come to life and try A, B & C with her—repeatedly. She might go home limping, but it would be well worth it.

Suddenly craving comfort, she reached over and closed her fingers around Max's front paw, pulling him over to sit on her lap facing her. "What do you think, Max? Do you think I could handle an entire week with a real live man who doesn't cheat, doesn't want me for my money or anything I can do for his career, but just wants me?   A man who is sensitive and caring, but not a doormat. Someone who sees the real me and wants me anyway. Someone who could…love me. The real me." She whispered the last few words, almost afraid to speak them aloud. She blinked and then refocused on Max. "Do you think a man like that exists?"

"Welcome to Fantasy Quest, Astiria." She glanced up at the screen in time to see a lush view of a deserted beach complete with slowly lapping waves kissing the picture-perfect shoreline. Stars twinkled overhead reflecting their diamond-like lights off the water. The scene was so beautiful, it caused something inside her chest to tighten with longing. She hugged Max to her chest and inhaled the tangy scent of the ocean breeze.

Her eyes widened as that same breeze ruffled her hair. Holding onto Max for dear life, she reached down beside her until her hand buried in cool white sand.

Chapter Two

"Holy Hell! Where am I?" She squeezed Max to her chest, thankful that wherever she was, his comforting bulk came with her.

"Ouch! Astiria squeeze too hard!" Max squirmed, loosening her grip.

Astiria squealed and tossed Max into the air as if she'd just found a live snake in her lap. When he landed with a thud in the sand and began sputtering and spitting, his long purple tongue hanging out, she closed her mouth and studied him closer.

"Max?" She scooted to her knees, the warm sand digging into her bare skin. She reached out a tentative hand to stroke Max's head. His fuzzy purple fur was warm under her touch.

He turned toward her, a pout on his thick gargoyle lips. "Yes, is Max. Why Astiria throw me? Max hurt his nose and got icky sand on tongue!" He extended a fuzzy purple tongue until it hung to his toes and he pointed out tufts of sand still sticking to his appendage.

Dear God, I've finally lost my mind. At least Max came with me into insanity! Just go with it–when in Rome…

Astiria took a deep breath before continuing. "Max, I'm so sorry. You just startled me." She grabbed his long tongue and helped him brush the remaining sand away. "You've never moved or spoken before and…" Her mind went blank. *What do I say to my stuffed animal that has suddenly come to life?*

He rushed into her arms like an affectionate child, burrowing his fuzzy head against her middle. She couldn't help but cuddle and comfort him since just having him close kept her from hysteria over her current situation. "Astiria forgiven. Astiria take good care of Max, always."

She picked him up so she could look into his face and he rewarded her with the mischievous evil grin he'd always worn since the day she bought him. "Do you know where we are, Max? And how we got here?"

He nodded enthusiastically, his entire body participating in the movement. "Yes, Max knows. Max from Verrath."

Her shoulders relaxed in relief that at least someone who was on her side knew where the heck they were. "Verrath?" Astiria wrapped her mouth around the unfamiliar word. "Is that where we are now?" When he nodded, she continued. "How did we get here?"

"Astiria chose consort and we come to where he is. Lerik good and strong. He give Max bananas!" His long tongue licked a path from one side of his cavernous mouth to the other, slobbering all over Astiria's fingers in the process.

"Wait. You said I *chose* a consort, but in the game I *created* someone out of my imagination." She set him in the sand and rose to rinse her hands off in the water gently lapping against the beach. She splashed some onto her face in case it might wake her up out of this dream. The cold water stung her skin, and she winced as Max bounded beside her, playing and splashing in the shallow current.

He laughed as he picked up a snail from the sandy bottom and crunched down on it loudly, as green snail juices dribbled down his chin. "Game is only a portal between this world and that. Lerik always good to Max. Sent me to Earrath to find his consort."

Earrath? Astiria rubbed at her temples as she figured out what Max meant. "You mean Earth — right?"

"Yes, Earrath. That what Max said." He scrubbed a fuzzy hand over his face to remove the slimy snail juice and jumped into Astiria's arms.

She squealed and then realized what she wore–and what it covered, or not. The thin white cotton top clung to her now wet breasts, which stuck out like happy full torpedoes under her sodden shirt. She set Max down and pulled the shirt away from her wet skin so she could look down at her new anatomy.

"Oh, my God! I can not believe I've got stripper boobs!" *I wonder if everything I chose for my 'character' came with me?*

Max perched on her shoulder. "Max want to see!"

She hastily closed her shirt. "Uh, never mind. Hey, Max? Do I look different than I did when we were back at the Fantasy Quest resort?"

Max's purple head nodded so fast she thought it might pop off his body and roll around on the sandy beach. "Yes. Astiria look like game profile now. But Max like Astiria either way. Even with stripper boobs."

Heat suffused her face and she bit her lip. *I'll have to remember to watch what I say around Max from now on!* She returned her attention to the rest of her newly renovated body. Her legs were long and athletic under her thin white cotton shorts, her ankles and bare feet, dainty and petite. She grabbed a strand of hair and pulled it in front of her face for an examination. "Yup, definitely red."

Taking a deep breath, she closed her eyes and reached both hands around to her grab her ass. "Oh my God, Max! I'm a freaking hottie!" *Maybe there are some perks to this particular delusion after all!*

Max stepped tentatively forward and touched a single outstretched claw to Astiria's leg. "Astiria no hot."

"Sorry, figure of speech." When Max opened his mouth to ask, she shook her head. "Never mind. How about you take me to see Lerik?"

He did a happy jig in a circle around her feet. "Lerik give Max bananas!"

A sensual shudder flowed through her as she remembered some of the questions she'd filled out on the questionnaire. *I wonder what Lerik will try and give me...*

Max's oversized head whipped around, his lips opened in a wide grimace and he bared what appeared to be hundreds of needlelike teeth, a low feral growl escaping from deep inside his throat.

"What is it?" She whispered and knelt down beside the gargoyle.

"Goblins..." he said through gritted teeth. "Max hate goblins!"

As if the words had conjured them, they were suddenly surrounded by half a dozen of the ugliest four foot nothing men she'd ever seen. The stench from the newcomers caused her eyes to water.

Each of them wore clothes so caked in dirt and grime, there was no hope of ever identifying the color the garment had originally been. Ragged scars criss-crossed each being's skin, and she resisted the urge to laugh–a nervous habit. *Must be all the rage for the well-dressed goblin.*

"Fresh meat, we claim you in the name of the lord of Marsoon!" Each goblin drew a wicked looking sword and pointed it at them.

"You be sorry, goblin. She belong to Lord Lerik." Max's small frame stood in front of Astiria reminding her of a loyal terrier.

She opened her mouth to protest that she didn't belong to anyone, but another quick look at the goblins made her close her mouth. If she had to choose, belonging to Lerik sounded like a much better deal.

One of the goblins stepped forward. "Once she's properly declared, no one will question Marsoon's claim." He stabbed the air in front of him with his sword as he opened his fly and leered at Astiria. "Take them, and save the gargoyle for dessert."

With startling clarity, the meaning of 'declared' hit

her like a blow to the gut. Before she could decide what to do, Max darted forward to sink his teeth deep into the leader's leg as Astiria was grabbed from behind. Panic surged through her and her knees threatened to buckle beneath her.

A flash of sunlight glinted off the leader's sword as it came down in an arc headed directly for Max's neck. Anger and fear for Max burst through her and she kicked her foot back, surprising her captor and loosening his grip. "Max!" She rushed forward, blocking the arc of the sword with her shoulder and knocking her fuzzy purple rescuer free.

Pain sliced through her as the sword hit her shoulder, driving her to her knees. She let instinct and adrenaline take over. Her hand darted forward toward the goblin's exposed crotch and her fingers closed around his bulging privates. Using all the strength she could muster she squeezed and them twisted. A pain-filled squeak filled the air before the goblin crumpled before her, clutching his injured manhood. She bolted to her feet, worry for Max twisting her insides, as she cradled her useless left arm.

Suddenly a large silvery column of light vortexed around her and the pain in her shoulder disappeared. A quick look confirmed her suspicion that it was healed. *I'll be damned, I must've made a new level in the game. Most games give a healing boost whenever that happens.* A tingling inside her palm made her rub her hand against her thigh before whipping around to look for Max.

When she turned, she saw him expertly weaving in and out of the goblin's legs and easily avoiding their sword thrusts. *That's what I get for assuming he can't take care of himself!* She refused to stand by and be the helpless damsel in distress. She picked up a handful of sand and thrust it into the face of the nearest goblin.

*****

Lerik paced his chambers, his boots stomping a flat line in the rushes from the man-sized fireplace and back to the door. The door his consort should already be entering through. He scowled and resisted the urge to yell for one of the servants to see if his consort had arrived yet. However, since he'd bellowed for the servants on and off for the past few hours, they'd found ways to make themselves scarce.

"I've waited patiently for far too long. Where the hell is she?" A man of action, he decided he could wait no longer.

"Oopec!" His voice boomed across the castle and he heard scuttling, like all the servants shuffled into hiding at his call. He scowled again. He was the lord of this castle, he could damn well call anyone he pleased! Before he could rip the door from its hinges in preparation for giving one of the servants the same treatment, a stocky wood elf scurried in through the door, his small round spectacles slipping down his nose.

"Yes, Lord Lerik. You called?"

"Yes…"

"Nay, my Lord," Oopec cut in neatly. "She has entered the portal to Verrath, but has not arrived at the castle gates." Oopec craned his neck to look up at Lerik's chest and raised one thin dark eyebrow. "And bellowing and scaring the life out of everyone will bring her no faster."

"Damned insolent elf!" He glowered at the elf, using his superior height and bulk to tower over him. When Oopec merely gazed back patiently, he ground his teeth in frustration. "I'll have your pointy ears removed and served to me for breakfast."

"Yes, my Lord. Buttered and boiled or fried in eel oil? I'm here but to serve you."

Lerik resisted the urge to laugh at the witty

comeback, reminding himself that he didn't like insolent elves, even though this one had been with him for nigh on twenty years since he was but a lad. Finally, he sighed and shook his head. "Why do I put up with you, Oopec?"

"Probably because you scare everyone else in the realm but me, my Lord."

Lerik threw back his head and laughed. "You're probably right." He slapped the elf on the back–a blow, which would send any other being flying across the room. However, elves were sturdy stock–especially wood elves– and Oopec didn't budge.

"My lord, if you're finished berating me for the day, there is something I should bring to your attention." Oopec pushed his glasses back up to the bridge of his nose and blinked up at Lerik.

"What is it, Oopec? Spit it out."

"The portal, my Lord. Your consort and Max came through the portal near Castle Marsoon."

Rage boiled in Lerik's veins as all the ramifications of the news flashed through his mind. Marsoon was the lord of a particularly bloodthirsty goblin clan who enjoyed raping their victims before boiling them with vegetables and serving them for the evening meal. And not only his consort was in danger, Marsoon and his minions didn't much differentiate between men, women, animals and any other creature as long as it breathed and could be eaten later.

"Don't just stand there, elf! Ready my horse!"

"Strikyr is already saddled and waiting, my Lord."

Minutes later, Lerik rode his horse across Verrath, dread warring with anticipating surging through his body. He'd waited an entire lifetime for this woman, he'd not allow Marsoon or any of his goblin clan to lay one claw on her–or Max. The little gargoyle had served him well, venturing into Earrath to befriend his consort. A brave little creature, Lerik would reward him with an entire

moat full of bananas for his loyalty. Few warriors had
braved the trip to Earrath, let alone a tiny purple gargoyle
without clan or kin.

Stryder's hooves thundered over the grassy plain
and the first tang of ocean air tingled over Lerik's tongue.
He reined the spirited horse to a slow gallop as they
started up the last hill before Castle Marsoon came into
view. It wouldn't do to alert Marsoon or his minions that
they had company.

When he crested the hill, the dark ominous castle
speared up from the sand, obstructing part of the view of
the ocean. Lerik searched the beach for any sign of Max
and his lady and his breath caught in his throat as he spied
them.

Max loped next to a fiery-haired siren with curves
that could threaten a man's sanity. She wore a simple
threadbare cotton tunic and short trousers held up by a
frayed piece of rope. The material was so thin, her coral
nipples and the lava colored curls at the juncture of her
thighs showed like a beacon, causing his mouth to water
with anticipation.

She turned to face him as if sensing his presence
and their gazes locked, shaking him to his toes.
Awareness burned through him, like none he'd ever
experienced. It wasn't purely sexual, it was an awareness
that the woman whose soul he read behind those brilliant
green eyes was destined to be his. When her cat eyes
darkened with desire, his body reacted and he shifted in
the saddle, his soft leather trousers, suddenly too tight and
confining.

Out of the corner of his eye, the movement of Max
scenting the air caught his attention. Both he and the
goddess before him shifted their gazes toward Max in time
to see the fuzzy purple gargoyle bare his sharp teeth in a
menacing growl.

"Damn!" His woolgathering had put his consort in

danger. Reaching over his shoulder, he pulled his long sword from its sheath and flicked the reins causing Stryder to spear forward. His gaze combed the surrounding beach for any sign of the goblins.

Guttural grunts from the side were the only warning he had before three of them jumped at him, knocking him from his horse. Years of fighting to survive allowed him to keep his sword in his hand and land without impaling himself, or injuring Stryder. He rolled as he landed, coming up into a fighting crouch and striking out with his foot, sweeping his three attackers off their feet.

Stryder reared into the air stomping one of his attacker into the sand.

"More fucking goblins!"

Lerik's brow furrowed at the sweet female voice. Apparently, his consort could curse like a common serving wench. He turned his head to see how she fared and the sight made his mouth drop open in shock. She kneed one goblin in the crotch and when he crouched to grab his tender bits, she elbowed him in the face, causing a spurt of green blood from his nose. Meanwhile, Max had set about taking large bites out of any goblin ankles that came too close to his lady.

Pain sizzled through Lerik's head and as if from a distance, he felt himself fall to his knees in the sand. Only years of hardened battle and instincts had him swinging his sword out in a wide arc until screams of pain accompanied slight resistance as his sword met goblin flesh.

He turned his head to check for more attackers and the world swam in front of him. Then Max was licking his face in large enthusiastic motions.

"Must heal Lerik, Astiria," Max said in between slobbery licks. "Must leave Marsoon before more goblins come!"

Max words sounded very far away, even though the fuzzy warmth of the gargoyle pressed against Lerik's chest.

"I don't know how to heal him, Max. On the computer there's a button I click to heal someone. Can we get him onto his horse like this?"

"Astiria must! She choose healer in game options. Here in Verrath, Astiria can heal." Max's weight moved off his chest and cool feminine hands settled over his forehead, beating back the pain. "Put hands on Lerik. Picture him healthy inside Astiria's head."

"Shit! Why couldn't I have chosen something I actually know how to do in reality?"

Lerik's lips quirked at the curse, and then she moved her hands over his skin leaving behind a trail of liquid heat that had nothing to do with healing. His erection strained against his already uncomfortable trousers and he groaned.

"Crap, Max. I hurt him."

Lerik opened his mouth to explain, but no words came out and she swam unsteadily in his line of sight.

She puffed out a breath fluttering her red mass of hair and then repositioned her hands and closed her eyes. Lerik allowed his own eyes to drift closed as a familiar warm tingling of magical healing teased at his senses. It wasn't the full healing rush he was used to from other healers–it was obvious that this was her first time using her new powers. However, as his headache cleared, he was able to open his eyes without the world spinning.

His consort still knelt over him, her eyes closed, sweat beading over her forehead while her lips silently chanted unknown words. Lerik pushed himself up to a sitting position and grabbed her wrists in his.

Her green eyes popped open, widening in shock as he dragged her forward into his embrace. A small squeak broke from her throat as his lips closed over hers. Fissions of fire flashed between them as he dipped his tongue inside the plush paradise of her mouth. She tasted of ale and something he couldn't quite identify.

Lerik swallowed her moan as she buried her fingers into his hair, dislodging his leather tie and spilling his hair over them.

Tentative at first, soon she met his tongue thrust for thrust and plastered each of her full curves fully against him.

A small growl from Max brought him out of the haze of passion, as if he'd surfaced from a very deep lake. He reluctantly pulled away from her, holding her at arms length. When she opened her eyes, they were the color of the deepest green leaves in the enchanted Forest of Baltaise. Her well-kissed lips tempted him, but he quickly reminded himself that they would have a lifetime to finish such things.

"Thank you for healing me…Astiria."

*****

Gooseflesh marched over Astiria's skin at the exotic pronunciation of her name from that sensuous mouth. Her thoughts were still so scrambled from the mind-numbing kiss, she was amazed she still breathed. As if of their own accord, her fingers reached up to trace the tingling warmth still lingering on her lips.

She considered herself an experienced woman. She'd dated extensively before marrying her asshole ex-husband. But, never in all those years had a man's kiss affected her anywhere in the remote universe of this one. She allowed her gaze to travel over every inch of him. The man who'd captured her attention and her hormones on the computer screen stood before her in the flesh. And oh, what a wonderful specimen of flesh it was.

"Come, we must return to my castle. We aren't safe here."

Castle? My God, I made myself a laird or some other type of clan leader. Which means he probably has an ego to rival his... Her gaze traveled down to the enormous bulge straining to be free of his pants.

Lerik turned a confused gaze toward Max. "Do you think she's still weak from the healing, Max? I know it was her first time using her powers." He looked back down at her. "She does speak our language, does she not?"

Astiria's ire at being talked about in the third person pushed aside her still-raging hormones. "Of course I speak your language!"

Max wrapped his purple arms around Lerik's leg. "More goblins, Lerik. Must take Astiria and go."

Lerik, not bothering to reply to Astiria, nodded and then reached down, hefting her over his shoulder like a giant bag of potatoes.

"Hey!" When, two steps later her view became Max sitting on a rounded black horse's ass, she recovered her wits. "Damn it! I'm perfectly capable of sitting up."

As if he hadn't heard her words, the horse beneath them shot into a gallop, jouncing her breasts against Lerik's muscled back with every pump of the horse's powerful legs. She beat her fists against his back. "I should have created you with some manners, you barbarian!"

Her behind stung as his large hand swatted her. "We can discuss all this later, when you are safe, Astiria. And I'm no barbarian, I'm human. The barbarian's are even worse than Marsoon, the Goblin Lord."

"Let me down, you ass!" When she received no response, she turned a pleading gaze to Max who held on tight to two fistfuls of saddle blanket, to keep from being dislodged. "Max, how do I get out of this place? How can I go home?"

Unmistakable hurt suffused Max's features and

Lerik's muscular body stiffened beneath her.

"Astiria belong here with Lerik and Max. Earrath make Astiria sad." Max smiled up at her wanly. "Here, Astiria be happy. Saile the Seer has ordained it."

Max's crestfallen expression coupled with the hard truth deflated her anger. Even before she'd met the asshole-ex husband, she hadn't been happy. Not that she was ready to accept that this fantasy world was real. However, if she could truly be happy here, why not give it a chance–even if it was only in her delusional mind? After all, if an overbearing man was the only negative–okay and groping goblins, what did she have to lose? She braced her elbows against Lerik's back and endured the rest of the bumpy ride in silence.

Chapter Three

Lerik dismounted his horse with Astiria still thrown over his shoulder. She'd stopped yelling at him, but her silence unnerved him more. Especially since she'd asked Max how to get back home. He clenched his free hand into a fist. Damn it all. *This* was her home, even if she didn't know it yet.

He strode past Oopec, noting the elf's raised eyebrow. "Reward Max with all the bananas he can eat, and send some suitable clothing to my chambers for my consort!"

"Thank Lerik! Thank Lerik!"

Then the only thing he heard was the scrabbling of Max's claws against the rushes strewn over the stone floor. He continued past gaping servants and muted whispers until he reached his chambers. Once inside, he closed the door and bent down to gently set Astiria on her feet.

She pierced him with a mutinous glare and his fingers itched to reach out and touch the delicately pointed ears that peeked from beneath her tumble of fiery hair.

"As I was trying to say when you tossed me over your shoulder without a word, I'm perfectly capable of sitting and walking all on my own." She crossed her arms just under her generous cleavage, stretching the thin fabric tight against her breasts and displaying her large coral aureoles to perfection. His mouth watered at the sight. When he raised his gaze to hers, her sculpted eyebrow rose in accusation.

The edges of his lips twitched as he covered a sheepish smile at being caught staring. "My apologies, Astiria. Your portal entry put you in danger. My only intention was to save your life so we would have a chance to discuss the niceties at our leisure." He crossed to the table beside the fireplace and pulled out a chair. "Would you like to sit and we can talk? Or would you like something to eat?" He resisted the urge to stare down at her nipples again.

The intensity of her glare increased to lethal and she humphed before crossing to the chair he still held out. "If I recall correctly, I healed you, therefore saving *your* life, so I don't appreciate being treated like a bag of potatoes."

Stunned, Lerik opened and closed his mouth as he realized the truth of her words. As a master warrior, he was extremely hard to kill, but with the entire force of Marsoon, it was definitely possible, and if she hadn't healed him, he was sure Marsoon and every goblin available would've taken advantage of the opportunity. "It seems I spoke too hastily. My apologies again, Astiria." He bowed at the waist.

She shot him a suspicious look from under her lush lashes. "First let's start at the beginning, like how I got here?" She sat and studied him expectantly.

Lerik took the chair opposite her and drank in her beauty. He would've welcomed her no matter if she looked like Oopec's backside. The seer sought him a consort as a soul mate, not as a trophy. Besides, physical beauty was as fleeting as the blacksmith's sober spells. He'd spent his life having beautiful women throw themselves at his feet, but the contents of their minds and hearts had been as lacking as their beauty was abundant. However, in his consort, he'd found both, and he was grateful to the universe for its abundance.

When she cocked her eyebrow at him again, he realized he'd been staring and hadn't answered her question. "Forgive me. I've imagined you for many seasons, but to finally gaze upon your beauty is a fine treat indeed."

She huffed out a frustrated breath, her beautiful green eyes narrowing. "Cut the crap and tell me how I got here."

He wasn't sure why she seemed so irritated at the compliment, but offered her a comforting smile. He must remember that she'd been thrust into a strange world. Surely, she was frightened and confused and it was his duty as her consort to help her acclimate. "You were brought here through a portal between Earrath and Verrath. Certain places in both our worlds overlap and in the right circumstances allow people to cross over whose destinies lie in the other plane."

"Great, my insanity leans heavily toward the overdone sci-fi novel."

"Sie Fie?" His brow creased at her strange words.

She waved his question away. "Never mind, just thinking out loud. How does Max figure into this? I've had him for four years and he's been my constant companion. How does he suddenly become a major player in this world?"

Lerik's fingers itched to reach out and touch the creamy smooth skin covering her long neck, but he held himself in check–for now. "Max volunteered to go into Earrath to find my consort. He befriended you, protected you and brought you to me when the time was right."

She leaned back in her chair as even white teeth gently bit into her ripe bottom lip. The succulent flesh pillowed around her teeth and he had the sudden urge to run his tongue over the bite, to sooth it.

"Look, Lerik. Can I be honest?"

"Always, Astiria. There will never be anything but truth between us." He leaned back in his chair, mirroring her, happy that she seemed to finally be accepting her situation.

"Great, good to know." She laid both her palms on the table and leaned forward as if taking him into her confidence. The actions pressed her large nipples flush against the thin cotton. "My sister, Amy, and her husband bought me a vacation to Fantasy Quest resort. One minute I'm playing an online game and the next, I'm sitting on an actual beach here in..." She paused as if searching for the right word. "Verrath," she finished. "When the game asked me to create my consort, I *created* you." She made a sweeping gesture from Lerik's head all the way to his boots, pausing at his groin.

She's just as affected as I am. She just won't admit it. Such coyness in a consort... He smiled at the thought of breaking through her barriers and burying himself inside her lush bounty.

When she pierced him with an expectant glare, he nodded to show he'd heard her. "Correct. The Fantasy Quest resort is one of the portals on the Earrath side others before you have used. However, you and I have been destined to be together long before either of us walked our respective worlds. When I became of age, our Saile, our seer asked me to describe my perfect consort, and I described you."

Her gaze turned icy. "No doubt you specifically requested the red hair, stripper boobs and all," she muttered.

His brow furrowed. Why would she be concerned if he requested certain things? And what exactly were 'stripper boobs'? "Actually, I requested no specific physical attributes at all. There were many other qualities I held essential beyond hair color and a lush body, even though I'm quite happy with the ones presented."

A sudden flush darkened Astiria's cheeks and she appeared almost sheepish.

He smiled as her obvious display of guilt. "So, tell me, Astiria." He leaned closer and let his gaze roam over her full lips before meeting her green gaze. "What attributes did you request for me?"

*****

The temperature in the chamber suddenly rose dramatically and Astiria was sure it was due to the fire in her cheeks. This irritating man actually made her feel shallow. She squared her shoulders and leveled her best glare his way. "Let's just say the only ones the game actually came through with were the physical ones. You're obviously lacking all the important attributes I requested." *There, see how you like it tossed back at you!*

Amusement lit his dark chocolate eyes and he leaned forward to capture her hand in his. "So, my looks please you, then." He made it a statement.

Damn, he had her there. She'd just admitted that physically, he was her ideal. Double damn! She refused to give him that much power — especially since he wouldn't be looking at her with quite so much unbridled passion if she'd popped through the portal in her real body. *Won't anyone ever want me for myself?!*

She sighed. Even as her pride smarted, she acknowledged that she didn't want to blow this chance. For once, she actually looked beautiful, and there was a slavering man around who thought so too. What was the harm in enjoying this reality until her mental breakdown healed enough to drag her back to her regular life and body?

"Are you having that much problem deciding?" An adorable dimple winked at the side of his sculpted lips that threatened to melt her into a puddle of boneless goo. He stood and held his arms out at his sides. "Take another look to help you decide." He turned in a slow circle, allowing her plenty of time to admire her...creation.

He stood before her, well over six feet of muscular perfection. His form fitting leather pants did wonderful things to such sculpted anatomy and her mouth literally watered as she imagined tasting every inch of skin hidden by them. She swallowed hard before meeting his gaze.

"You're reasonably attractive, I guess." It wouldn't do to feed his ego too much. She was all too familiar with pretty-boy men.

He threw back his head and laughed, the full rich sound reverberating all the way to her core. "I like you already, Astiria. A woman who isn't daunted by my looks, someone who can stand up to me and be my equal." He grabbed her hand and laid a warm kiss inside her palm, causing gooseflesh to march over every inch of her. "Someone worthy to be my consort."

She shook her head as his final words seeped through her sexual haze. Someone worthy...in other words, a matching good-looking book end. In her real body, she was sure she'd never hear those words unless the man had an ulterior motive. The asshole ex had taught her that lesson well.

Tears burned behind her eyes and she blinked them away furiously. *For now, you are the attractive woman, Astiria. What will it hurt to see what life would've been like if you'd been born gorgeous?*

The idea took root and her lips slowly curved as she imagined all the things she would do as someone who knew they were irresistible to the man before them.

"That's a dangerous smile you're wearing, Astiria. What thoughts are passing through your mind?" Amusement danced in his eyes as he studied her.

"I'm thinking if you can stop treating me like the damsel in distress, I might enjoy being your...consort." She stood and took a few steps forward until only a whisper of a breath remained between them. "What exactly is involved in being each other's consort?" She allowed all her fantasies to blossom inside her mind, and the passion and excitement to show in her expression.

Lerik's eyes turned molten as he slowly leaned down toward her.

She allowed her eyes to drift closed and she

shuddered as his breath feathered across her lips.

Knock! Knock!

The loud noise startled her, and she jumped back like a guilty child caught stealing candy.

Lerik growled low in his throat before calling, "Enter!"

A stocky man with pointed elf ears and glasses perched on the end of his nose entered the room carrying a handful of clothing. Standing straight, he only came up to Astiria's chest and all his exposed skin looked like…bark. Her brow furrowed as she sifted through her online gaming knowledge until she found a match. *Wood elf, highly intelligent, stubborn and loyal. Deadly in a fight.*

"My Lord, Lerik. I brought a wide assortment of clothes for your consort to pick from." The strange elf turned toward her and bowed at the neck before meeting her curious gaze. "If these aren't to your liking, my Lady, I can accommodate whatever you wish."

"Astiria, this is my steward, Oopec. He's trustworthy as well as discrete, but has a horrible sense of timing and irony."

Astiria almost laughed at Lerik's pained expression. "I like you already, Oopec. It's nice to meet you."

He smiled and took her hand in his, placing a quick chaste kiss on the back, pointedly ignoring Lerik's scowl and warning growl. "Finally, someone in this castle who has manners."

"Damned, insolent elf!" Lerik's murderous glare seemed to bounce off the wood elf harmlessly. "I'll have your pointy ears removed and served to me for breakfast."

"Yes, my Lord. Buttered and boiled or fried in eel oil? I'm here but to serve you."

At Lerik's resigned sigh, Astiria knew this was a familiar exchange between them. "Anything else, Oopec, before I have you hung and your entrails fed to the birds?"

"Yes, My Lord. Marsoon and a contingent from the Verrath council are at the front gates claiming Astiria was willingly declared to Marsoon and that you've kidnapped what is rightly his."

Lerik sighed. "What is Marsoon up to now? He must know Astiria would never willingly declare to him. His proof must be false."

"I know not, My Lord, but might I suggest you consummate things between you before meeting with the council?"

Astiria's mouth fell open at the word 'consummate,' even though she'd been perfectly willing to do just that only minutes before. "Does someone want to fill me in on what the hell is going on?"

Lerik opened his mouth to reply, but Oopec cut in, causing his master to grind his teeth and mutter. "Lord Marsoon–and I do use the term 'Lord' loosely since he's a rapist and a cannibal–is claiming that you have willingly declared to him. Meaning you have shown intention to become his consort by either word or deed. Thus my suggestion that if Lord Lerik's claim is indeed reality, Marsoon's lies and trumped up proof will hold less weight."

Her eyes rounded at his description of Marsoon and she swallowed hard, glad that Lerik had gotten her away from there quickly. "His lies and trumped up proof shouldn't hold *any* weight!" She took a deep breath and switched into project manager mode. Hysterics wouldn't help her solve the problem, only logic and information would. "Exactly how would Lerik's claim become reality?"

Lerik yanked the wood elf backwards before he could speak again and stepped in front of Astiria, gently laying his hands on her shoulders. "We can officially declare before an empowered witness or we can sexually consummate."

Her blood turned to lava inside her veins at the last option, and her cheeks burned. If Oopec would've waited another ten minutes to knock, the 'declaration' might be already made. Her raging hormones obviously voted for the latter option. However, even in a fantasy world, her mind overrode her baser instincts, and focused on the safer option. "What happens if the council believes Marsoon's lies?" The fear lacing her voice hung heavy inside her ears.

Lerik's expression darkened. "Then we go to war. I'll never let him take you from me."

"My Lord and Lady," Oopec interrupted. "The best course is still the declaration."

Lerik didn't spare a glance for the wood elf, but kept his gaze steady on hers. "I regret that we don't have many options, Astiria. I would've preferred you to get used to this world, and to me before asking you to...declare." He ran the pad of his calloused thumb over her lips causing her to shiver. "But even so, I will do what I must to protect you from Marsoon. Would you be willing to verbally declare intent to become my consort?"

Panic skittered through her system. It sounded suspiciously like getting engaged, but if her other choice was to be given to a rapist-slash-cannibal, the dream man standing before her definitely seemed like the way to go. She took a deep breath before answering. "What do I say?"

Lerik visibly relaxed and turned his head toward Oopec, who stepped forward and whipped a leather-bound book from the pocket of his tunic. He wet the tip of his finger before flipping pages until he found the correct one.

"According to council law, you must just state aloud your intent and name the other party."

Sounds easy enough. She swallowed hard. *Here goes nothing...* "I declare my intent to become Lerik's consort."

Oopec pushed his glasses up his nose. "You must use his correct address. He is addressed as 'Lord Lerik."

"Jeesh!" She rolled her eyes toward the ceiling. "Fine, I declare my intent to become *Lord* Lerik's consort."

A shimmering column of golden light surrounded her, reminding her of a transporter beam from Star Trek.

"I, Lord Lerik, accept Lady Astiria's declaration."

The golden light expanded to encompass them both, and the tiny hairs on her arms stood on end as if teased by a gentle summer breeze. Then Lerik's lips were on hers and the entire world was forgotten. Only the feel of his muscled body pressed against hers and those wonderfully talented lips and tongue were of any concern to her. A soft sigh filled her ears, and she realized it had come from her. Lerik swallowed the sound greedily and deepened the kiss, demanding more, as her traitorous body screamed for option two.

The heat from his body pressed through her thin cotton outfit and it was almost as erotic as being naked while he remained fully clothed. His erection pressed against her stomach making her whimper with need. She ground herself against him and when he growled with pleasure, gloried in the feminine power she held over this gorgeous man. Her breasts were sensitive and heavy with need and moisture pooled between her thighs. Lerik's large hand closed over her ass pulling her tighter against him and her heartbeat galloped in anticipation.

Oopec cleared his throat, interrupting them. "Excuse me, Lord and Lady? The council still waits."

Nooooooo! Her mind spun in frustration as she battled her way through the sexual haze back into this reality.

Lerik pulled back slowly, his eyes still darkened with passion. His gaze lingered on hers for a long moment before he released her and stepped back. "I regret to admit the elf is right. We *will* continue this another time."

His dark promise zinged through her and straight to her groin and she bit back a groan.

Oopec cleared his throat and pushed up his ever-slipping spectacles. "May I also suggest the Lady Astiria avail herself of some of the clothing I brought before we meet the council?"

His words threw a cold bucket of water on her traitorous sexual urges and heat burned her cheeks as she realized how close she'd come to screwing Lerik right here on the floor...or against the wall, or wherever he'd led. Not to mention, she wouldn't have cared if Oopec stood and watched, as long as he hadn't interrupted.

She cleared her throat, hoping her voice didn't sound husky with arousal. "Thank you, Oopec. Clothes sound like a good idea."

Chapter Four

Astiria stepped into the large council chambers and tugged at the collar of the unfamiliar dress. All sound stopped at they entered and hundreds of pairs of eyes swiveled to openly study them. Lerik stood at her side, a comforting presence cutting through the tangible tension swimming inside the room. He squeezed her hand and she clung to him like a lifeline.

How strange to remember that she'd never laid eyes on him before a few hours ago, and now her immediate future depended on the fragile bond they'd forged between them.

Oopec scurried just ahead of them, clearing the way toward the center dais, where a large throne-like chair sat covered in sapphire blue material. Flopped into the elegant chair was a barrel shaped goblin, twice the girth and breadth of the goblins she'd fought earlier. His mouth curved into a cruel line as his cold eyes looked her over, as if he examined a piece of property he was considering buying. His attention made her shiver in revulsion. Small flies buzzed around him, feeding off the stench that billowed around him in a visible cloud.

Lerik placed a possessive hand around her shoulders, pulling her close to his side before he turned his gaze toward the intruder. "Remove your carcass from my chair, Marsoon, before I have to burn the chair just to get rid of your foul smell."

The goblin smiled revealing several rows of black, rotted teeth. "Once you are reveled as a thief and a liar, I'll possess everything that is yours, including this hideous chair."

Lerik's face darkened with anger and every being in the room took an involuntary step back, while Astiria leaned closer, drawing comfort from the warm hard muscles playing just under her fingers. Marsoon's pudgy face blanched, but he continued the stare down with Lerik.

"Enough!" Silence reigned as a man no taller than Astiria's knees stepped forward waving a long gnarled staff to part the sea of goblins. Flowing white hair and beard merged and trailed the floor, almost completely covering his black robes. His royal blue eyes were stern, yet kind. They settled on Astiria and it seemed as if he saw through to her very soul. She resisted the urge to squirm under the close scrutiny and instead lifted her chin and squared her shoulders.

Lerik nodded his head, an obvious sign of respect for the little man. "Welcome to my lands, Council Master Ocam." His grip around her waist tightened slightly as if steeling her against the next few minutes. "Please meet my declared, Astiria of Earrath."

Grumbling arose from the goblin hoard and Marsoon glared at them with open hatred, but no one interrupted. Astiria wasn't sure if they were cowed by Lerik or by Council Master Ocam. Unsure of the etiquette of the situation, she bowed her head in the same manner Lerik had. "A pleasure to meet you, Council Master Ocam."

A smile split his wrinkled face revealing perfect white teeth. "Welcome to Verrath, my dear. I'm sorry it must be under such circumstances."

Marsoon pushed his bulk from Lerik's chair leaving a large dark stain against the once pristine blue fabric. "If you're done with the niceties, Ocam, hand over my property and mete out punishment so I can begin to enjoy my new...holdings." His lecherous gaze raked over inch of Astiria making her skin crawl.

A pointed look from the Council Master silenced the goblin, but he continued to scowl and grumble under his breath.

Kind blue eyes turned back toward her. "I realize

you are unfamiliar with our culture, but as in any civilized society, ignorance of the law cannot be an excuse."

She stepped forward out of the circle of Lerik's comfort and gazed down at the small man. "Council Master, I am declared to Lord Lerik. I did nothing to declare myself to…" She gazed at Marsoon, searching for the correct words. Finally she settled on, "anyone else."

Marsoon's grin widened. "If that was *nothing*, I can't wait to try out *something*."

Unease trickled along Astiria's spine. The goblin master's glee seemed to indicate that he knew something she didn't. But even as crazy as she might be, she'd definitely remember having sexual contact with someone or declaring as she'd done with Lerik.

Ocam waved a hand in the air leaving behind a shimmery circle of silver light. "Show me…" The circle swirled into a picture of Astiria and Max on the beach when they were attacked by goblins.

Heat filled Astiria's face as she watched herself reach out and grab the goblin's privates and twist hard. *Oh no… They can't interpret that as sexual contact, can they?*

"Freeze!" Ocam's words stopped the picture and a collective gasp rose from the crowd.

Lerik pulled Astiria close as if ready to protect her from every being in the room if necessary. "It's obvious she was defending herself from being attacked, *not* declaring!"

"The law is clear. *Any* sexual contact is considered a declaration." Marsoon licked his lips as he spoke, revealing a slimy green tongue. "And since I own my minions, any sexual contact with them is considered a declaration to me." He wrapped bony fingers around Astiria's free arm and pulled. "I demand my declared be returned to me at once."

Without thinking, Astiria kneed him in the groin and watched him crumple to the floor yelling something about foreplay. "There's some sexual contact for you, you slimy bastard." She pulled out of Lerik's grasp and glared around the room, suddenly angry at the entire populace of Verrath. "You can't be serious! I was fending off a rapist and avoiding becoming their evening meal, not feeling him up. What kind of world do you people have here, anyway?"

Ocam laid a comforting hand on her arm. "My dear, as I said, our culture is very different from what you're used to, but ignorance of the law is no excuse."

She took a breath to rant some more, but he held up a hand, deflating her arguments.

"However, there are other laws that apply to this situation." Ocam shot a meaningful look around the room, which silenced even the murmurs. "Not only is she officially declared to Lord Lerik through a vow, but neither declaration may be legal. Astiria, please hold out your hands, palm up."

Confused, she slid a look toward Lerik. When he gave her an imperceptible nod, she acceded.

Ocam snapped his fingers and a small blue stone appeared instantly cupped in his hand. He waved the stone over her open palms spreading a warm tingling sensation. When the tingling receded, she noticed a large number two on one palm and a number three on the other.

Well that explains why my palms kept itching! That's where the numbers change when I level inside this world.

"As all assembled can see," Ocam stated loudly as he secreted the blue stone back inside his voluminous robes, "Astiria is a level two healer and a level three assassin. By the laws of Verrath, she has not yet become of age and is therefore still a ward of the Council, in absence of parents inside this world."

Marsoon's angry growl reverberated around the room, but a narrowed gaze from Ocam silenced him.

"As I was saying, Astiria must complete the

coming of age quest in order to make her own choices within this world. This will also help her understand our ways."

"A quest? What do I have to do to complete this quest? And what level do I have to be to make my own choices inside Verrath?"

"My dear, you must reach level ten to be considered a full adult in our world. However, you may choose a companion and a protector to help you with the quest if you wish. They will be able to advise you, but parts of the quest are your own to complete."

Astiria chewed her bottom lip. She'd expected quests when she sat down to play, but being inside the game was a much different prospect. She couldn't be sure, of course, but if getting hurt in the game was painful, dying in the game seemed very permanent. Would she be kicked back to earth, or just be found dead in her hotel room back at Fantasy Quest Resort?

Not that she really had any choice, if this quest would allow her to get away from Marsoon, then all the better. She glanced up at Lerik, his face unreadable, and resisted the temptation to trail her fingers through his dark silky hair. There was definitely attraction here, and she'd wanted an adventure.

"What happens if I don't complete the quest?"

"If the coming of age quest is not completed within a lunar cycle, the first declaration will be found valid, and any remaining declared will have to dual to win their suit."

Lerik's words echoed through her mind again. *Then we go to war. I'll never let him take you from me.*

"Choose your companion, Astiria."

She spoke the first name that popped into her mind. "Max."

A shimmery column of light appeared in front of her and Max materialized within the column. The little gargoyle looked around confused, a banana still held in his grip. "Astiria!" He jumped into her arms and pressed his fuzzy head against her chest, burrowing close. She hugged him back as the familiar comfort he always brought flowed through her.

Ocam cleared his throat. "Max, Astiria has selected you to be her companion for her coming of age quest, do you accept?"

Max's purple face lit up with excitement. "Max does, Max does. He keep Astiria company and guide her on quest."

"Thank you, Max. Now, Astiria, choose your protector."

Heat sizzled through her veins as she thought the name before she spoke it. "Lord Lerik, my true declared." Couldn't hurt to make it known she was *not* Marsoon's, and what her willing choice would be.

A column of light shimmered around Lerik reminding her of her declaration up in his chambers–not to mention the aftermath. Heat suffused her cheeks as his hungry gaze roamed over her.

"I'll not have my property…er…declared running around Verrath with Lerik. I don't trust him!" Marsoon stomped his foot causing a cloud of dust from his clothes to powder in the air around him, nearly engulfing Ocam.

The little man snapped his fingers and the dust disappeared. "Quiet, Marsoon. It has always been the choice of the quest seeker to choose their companion *and* their protector." He turned toward Lerik. "Lord Lerik, do you accept the role of Astiria's protector on her coming of age quest?"

Lerik's chocolate eyes gleamed with satisfaction. "I do."

Ocam raised both arms, after disentangling one hand from his floor-length beard. "The quest begins at dawn. If anyone impedes the quest for any reason—" He turned a steely gaze toward Marsoon. "They will be held accountable with the full force of the council."

Marsoon grinned, making the hairs on Astiria's nape rise to attention. The goblin didn't seem like the type to give up without a fight–the more underhanded the better.

*****

The first day of the quest dawned early, with heavy rain battering everything in its path as if seeking to destroy every bit of life. Astiria shivered inside her new leather armor, pulling her fur-lined cape tighter around her and cuddling Max close. Between the body heat from the horse she rode and the fuzzy gargoyle, it was almost bearable. She silently thanked Oopec for the thigh high leather boots, shorts and tunic, which lovingly hugged her every over-generous curve, while still allowing her freedom of movement. Not to mention the fact that they held in her body heat.

When she'd first laid eyes on the garments, she'd backed away in horror until Lerik had convinced her this was appropriate apprentice armor for an assassin. *Somehow wearing sexy armor when you're playing a computer game is much different that doing it up close and personal!*

She spared a glance for Lerik. He rode his black stallion just ahead of her, but through the thick curtain of rain, she could just make out his form under the fur-lined cape. His mood had been dark since Ocam had decreed that they spend the night separately to appease Marsoon. Apparently, if she and Lerik gave in to their 'joining instincts,' as Ocam called it, Lerik was guilty of some sort of statutory rape.

She sighed and shifted in the saddle. What good was having this killer body to play in when she couldn't even play doctor, and a few other professions, with the sexy warrior she was 'declared' to. *Man, I really need to get better at this fantasizing stuff, because so far, it sucks!*

Lerik's horse, Stryder, stopped short in front of her, and she guided her mount up beside them. A large thatch roofed cottage rose through the downpour. A servant ran out to grab their reins while they dismounted.

Inside, the air held a thick haze of incense. Some exotic spicy scent that reminded her of far off lands tickled her nose.

"Enter, Lady Astiria."

Astiria peered through the haze. Against the back wall, a large *something* sat against the far wall, lying on a huge chaise lounge. The sultry voice issued from the middle of three bald heads. Each face was beautiful and totally unique, although neither female or male. Its body resembled a large octopus and what appeared to be several dozen sinuous arms tipped with two opposing protrusions she assumed were fingers.

Lerik and Max immediately dropped to their knees and bowed their heads in a sign of respect. Heat burned Astiria's cheeks as she realized staring open-mouthed at the seer probably wasn't the best protocol.

An amused chuckle echoed around her. "No one here will chop off your head for breaches in protocol, Astiria. Come forward and we will talk." Three long grey limbs gestured toward the kneeling men. "Leave us. My servants will provide for you while Astiria and I speak."

Lerik's dark gaze caught hers and his quick smile reassured her. "As you wish, Saile." Max scrambled up onto Lerik's shoulder as they left the cottage.

"Please sit. We have much to discuss and time is short."

She took a chair near the seer and gazed around the bare room. Nothing here showed that this cottage was even inhabited except for the three smoking piles of incense, the chaise lounge the seer reclined on and the simple wooden chair where Astiria now sat.

"I have no need of material things here. My

purpose is to see and that I do best with no distractions."

Can she…he…it, read my mind?

"I can, and I am both and neither if that helps. I have no need of gender. As long as Verrath exists, so do I. I can see beyond the veil of our world and even into yours."

A chill ran down Astiria's spine. "Did you bring me here? Into Verrath?"

The three faces smiled. "You brought yourself, Astiria. Only a pure desire can open the portal."

Her brow furrowed in confusion. "I didn't desire to come here."

"Didn't you? You allowed yourself to dream, and you entreated the universe to see if your perfect man actually existed."

Her words to Max back at the resort flowed through her mind. *"What do you think, Max? Do you think I could handle an entire week with a real live man who doesn't cheat, doesn't want me for my money or anything I can do for his career, but just wants me? A man who is sensitive and caring, but not a doormat. Someone who sees the real me and wants me anyway. Someone who could…love me. The real me."*

A sigh escaped her. "Okay, let's say that I buy this. How will I ever know if Lerik cares for the real me in this…" She gestured toward her body. "I don't look anything like this back on earth!"

"Your wish was for a man that would see the real you. The real person has little to do with their physical attributes unless they allow it to define who they are."

"That sounds great in theory." Astiria pushed to her feet to pace to the door and back. "But if I'd popped into Verrath in my normal body, I doubt even Marsoon would be fighting over me right now!" A sudden headache pounded at her temples and she closed her eyes and rubbed her fingers against both temples. A large shimmery column flowed around her and both palms itched until she rubbed it against her cloak. "What the hell? I didn't do anything!"

"You healed your headache and starting on your quest earned you another adventure level. As you are probably aware, early leveling is quicker than that in later levels. The first ten are all about learning who you are, as is your coming of age quest."

"What am I supposed to learn? I already know who I am."

"Do you? You've spent your life feeling uncomfortable in your own skin. You must come to terms with yourself before you can expect to have any type of relationship with others."

Stunned, Astiria just stared at the three serene faces before throwing back her head and laughing at the absurdity of the situation. "You're kidding–right? This isn't therapy, this is a quest. Don't I have to kill so many creatures, or bring back certain artifacts or something like that?"

All three faces smiled, the barest movement of the lips. "You will journey to the middle of Verrath to the main portal. Once there, you will step through. If you have completed your quest and you know who you are and have made peace with yourself, you will be recognized as an adult in Verrath and will be able to make your own choices."

"And if I don't succeed?"

"You will go back to your life in Earrath and Lord Lerik will be tried and found guilty of failing to protect you during a coming of age quest."

A lead ball settled inside Astiria's stomach and nausea tossed it mercilessly. "What happens to Lerik and Max if I fail?"

"In the end, they will both die."

Chapter Five

Lerik tethered the horses and led the way toward the first quest. The challenge was different for everyone, and he and Max would only be able to watch–if part of the challenge didn't include isolation. Frustration flowed through his veins quickly turning to anger. Astiria was his declared, he should be able to protect her in any situation! He chopped through the dense foliage in front of him with his sword, turning some of his emotions into action.

"What was your quest challenge, Lerik?"

Her sweet voice brought him back to the present and he smiled back at her. "I had to kill several goblins and then scale a sheer cliff to retrieve a golden statue."

Her beautiful brow furrowed. "That sounds pretty hard for a low level warrior."

Lerik smiled at the concern in her voice. "It was a difficult quest, but the statue was stolen from Gargoyle Island. It was the talisman of the Queen and it ensured them prosperous crops and fair weather." He shrugged. "I promised to get it back."

"Gargoyle Island?" He grinned at the excitement in her voice. Max had told him of her host of gargoyles at both her home and work. "Will we get to visit there during the quest?"

Lerik laughed. "We won't know until we go through each portion of your quest. But someday, we'll go. I think you'll enjoy meeting the Queen."

"Isn't that Max's home?"

Max scurried up Astiria's shoulder to perch just under her waterfall of red hair. "No! Max's home is with Astiria and Lerik."

She absently scratched behind his ear sending him into gargoyle ecstasy. "Don't you like to visit your parents or your siblings?"

Max shook his head and Lerik stayed silent. It was up to the tiny gargoyle to tell her about his past, it was not Lerik's place. "Max's family killed during goblin raid. Lerik save Max as baby gargoyle. Max's place with Lerik, and now with Astiria."

She pulled Max from her shoulder and hugged him to her generous bosom. "Max, I'm so sorry. I didn't know. We don't ever have to visit there if it causes you pain."

Admiration for his declared flowed through him. On one hand, she was tough and resilient and on the other, she was sweet, caring and loyal.

Max turned his head away so he could draw in a labored breath. "Astiria's stripper boobs suffocating Max!"

A blush darkened her cheeks, but she loosened her grip on Max, and once again Lerik wondered what exactly stripper boobs were–especially since the mere mention of them always seemed to embarrass her. However, Max intervened before he could ask.

"Max loves Gargoyle Island. Good snails and other creepy crawlies for snacks!"

Astiria made a face that showed she disagreed with Max's choice of cuisine.

"Let's make camp there by the stream." He dismounted Stryder allowing the horse to drink from the stream while he unloaded their supplies from the saddlebags. "Max, do you think you can find some wood for the fire?"

He turned to see Astiria already dismounted and unloading her own bedroll and supplies. Their eyes met and his heart skipped a beat at how right the connection between them felt. Astiria was his, and once this quest was done, he'd make it known to the entire universe.

In the next instant, he closed the distance separating them, and they reached for each other greedily. When his lips met hers, he swallowed her sigh and gently explored her lush mouth as she melted against him. She moaned inside his mouth and he swallowed the sound as she threaded her fingers through his hair and pulled him closer, igniting a slow burn everywhere their bodies touched.

Loud crunching from behind them startled them both and he instantly pushed Astiria behind him, his sword at the ready.

Max stood over Astiria's bedroll, pulling out a never-ending stream of scorpions and poisonous snakes, stuffing them greedily into his mouth.

"What're all those creepy crawlies doing in my bedroll?" Astiria sounded more irritated than scared and he smiled at his declared's bravery.

Max burped and turned to look at them. "Max see squirming in bedroll, so opened and notice munchies. Plenty for dinner." He held them up in offering.

White hot rage burned through Lerik and he ground his teeth in frustration. "Marsoon! I knew he would try to thwart us, no matter what Ocam threatened him with, but Astiria could've been killed."

Astiria laid a comforting hand on his arm. "But I wasn't, and Max seems perfectly content. Why don't we build the fire and we'll figure out sleeping arrangements later?"

He turned to face her and pulled her into his embrace. "You can share my bedroll tonight."

Her green eyes darkened with desire and color rode high in her cheeks. "We can't consummate our declaration, Lerik. Ocam said that was off limits until I reach level ten."

He smiled down at her. "Then we'll both have to practice some creative restraint. Besides, Ocam said it was just actual 'joining' that was forbidden. Everything else is still in bounds, unless you'd rather I kept my distance..." He trailed off leaving the thought hanging in the air between them.

"I just don't want to be defaulted back to Marsoon." She poked him in the chest for emphasis. "But this is your world and I trust you to know what's fair game, and I think I'm up for playing a few innings if you are." The saucy look she threw at him from under her lashes turned his blood to lava.

His hand snaked out pulling her tight against him and he enjoyed her little squeal of surprise. "I'm not sure what these innings are you speak of, but I think we understand each other all the same." He ran a calloused thumb over her bottom lip, enjoying her resulting shiver. "We also need to catch some dinner and you may be able to gain a few levels finding us some gourmet fare." Before she could answer, he fused his lips to hers until Max's loud crunching made them both laugh and step apart.

"Okay, Lerik." She smiled up at him, her cat green eyes twinkling. Let's go play assassin and allow Max to eat in peace."

*****

Astiria crouched behind a tree and tried to remember everything Lerik had tried to teach her about hunting in the last hour. All she'd managed to do so far was cut herself with her dagger. But on a bright note, she gained a healing level, which brought her up to level four as both a healer and an assassin. *Only six levels to go before I can lock Lerik in his room and not let him out for a week.* Arousal tingled through her body and she purposefully pushed it aside in order to concentrate on the task at hand.

Movement in her peripheral vision startled her, but her body acted on instinct, her twin daggers suddenly flying through the air and finding both marks. She turned to see two small hares pinned to a tree, her daggers protruding from their necks. "Holy shit! I did it!" She resisted the urge to jump up and down in celebration since it would scare the rest of the local prey away.

A twig cracked behind her and she whirled, her hands held out in front of her in a defensive posture. Pink tendrils of power flung outward and hit Lerik square in the chest knocking him back a few steps. He shook his head as if to clear it and then a wry grin twisted his lips. "So, you've figured out your stun spell, have you?"

Astiria looked down at her hands and then back up at Lerik. "Oops! I'm sorry, did I hurt you?"

He stepped forward and took her hands in his, she wasn't sure if it was to keep her from spelling him again or just to touch her. "I'm a master warrior, a low level stun will only startle me for a few moments, but remember that spell well, it will be enough to allow you to escape if you get into a bad situation."

It's a good thing I didn't have the daggers in my hand when he startled me or I might have ruined a prime piece of male flesh!

Kneeling, she pulled her daggers from the carcasses and handed the animals up to Lerik, which he deposited in a leather pouch tied to his belt. Unease prickled along the back of her neck and without thinking, she turned, still crouched and let her daggers fly. Another small hare and a gnarled goblin were shoved backwards against another tree as her daggers pinned them fast through the throat. "What the hell is the damned Goblin doing here? They aren't supposed to interfere!" A shimmery column of silver light flowed around her and her palm itched. She absently rubbed it against her thigh.

"Marsoon isn't much for rules. I knew he'd be a problem." Ignoring her level, Lerik closed in on the dead goblin before she could even force herself to move. He pulled a small blue stone from his tunic and pressed it against the goblin's head. The stone strobed blue and white and in the next instant, the goblin disappeared.

"Where'd he go?" She pulled her dagger from the tree and replaced it in her hip sheath.

"Ocam knew Marsoon would cheat, so he gave me this stone to send back any minions we find. Call it a collection of evidence that will keep you from being defaulted, as you put it, back to Marsoon."

"Damn! I haven't even done the quest pieces yet and we've already had two incidents from Marsoon. I'd really like to kick that guy's ass!"

Lerik smiled wolfishly and pulled her into his arms for a soul-searing kiss. "For some reason it fires my blood when you curse like a serving wench."

Still breathless from the kiss, she couldn't muster enough outrage to be angry with him. "Remind me of that once I reach level ten, will ya?"

"Most definitely, my declared. But right now, we should probably go and cook dinner."

*****

The warm glow of the fire relaxed Astiria and she took a large bite of roasted hare, ignoring Max's crunching in the background. Apparently, her bedroll had been spelled to have a never-ending supply of Max's favorite delicacies. She shuddered, glad *she* hadn't slipped into the bedroll—she'd most likely be dead or at least extremely sick from the poison. Somehow, when all this was over, she vowed to make Marsoon pay for all the trouble he'd caused both her and Lerik.

"I'm a bit concerned that we haven't had word of your first task by now." Lerik's chocolate brown eyes glinted in the fire light.

"Is there supposed to be a note or a messenger or something?" Unease snaked through her causing her to rub her hands over her forearms to chase away the gooseflesh.

Lerik chewed and swallowed before answering. "Usually this clearing is where the message is received. Not always, but usually."

"So should we wait here until it arrives?"

"No, we must move forward. This is a world of magic, the message will find us wherever we are. Mayhap the lateness of the message is part of the trial. I don't think Marsoon is strong enough to waylay Ocam's magic."

Astiria thought over what the seer had told her and sighed. It was entirely possible that there would be no actual quest tasks, and that this entire trek up to the portal was to ensure she'd made peace with herself. But since the seer had advised she couldn't share that information with Lerik or Max, she kept her council and bit into the hare, letting the spicy flavor of the ale they had basted it in burst inside her mouth.

She chewed deliberately as her thoughts turned back to her conversation with the seer and she frowned. She'd spent her entire life not quite sure who she truly was and now in a handful of days she was supposed to suddenly smack her forehead and have some grand epiphany? And yet, if she didn't, Lerik and Max would die for failing to safeguard her. What choice did she have but to move forward and trust that things would work out all right in the end? After all, her confidence had already improved along with her assassin and healing abilities. The only thing holding her back was her fear that Lerik only wanted this body she'd borrowed and not the true woman beneath.

She smiled grimly as an idea formed. If Lerik knew the real woman underneath the hot body and stripper boobs, and accepted her faults and all, then maybe she could put her fears behind her. Hell, it was worth a try, wasn't it?

"Astiria, what troubles you? You seem sad."

She glanced up from where she'd been staring into the fire, her half eaten hair suspended part way to her mouth. "Sorry, I was just thinking." Laying the food aside, she licked the juices from her fingers and smiled when Lerik's eyes darkened in response. If he ever could truly accept the real Astiria, then maybe she could be truly happy here, whether she was insane or not. She was sure there would be no lack in the horizontal extra-curricular activities department.

"Lerik, do you think we can take some time on this trip to get to know each other?"

His seductive smile zigzagged arousal through her veins, arrowing straight between her legs.

She shifted in her seat against the fallen log and held up her hands to keep him for reaching for her. "I meant talking. You know, getting to know each other–hopes, dreams, favorite colors, that sort of thing."

His rumbling laugh answered her. "I would like that as well, Astiria. I know much about you from speaking with Max, but I realize you haven't had the same time, what with recent events. What would you like to know?"

"You grilled Max about me?" All thoughts of her plan fled before her under the curiosity of what Max told Lerik.

"He told me of your love of reading and of gargoyles."

Heat flooded her face at the blatant revelation of her secret vices to this Adonis sitting before her.

"I didn't know about it when I sent Max, but it seemed to work out well for all. Saile, the Seer, promised that whomever I sent would be successful since we were destined to be together." He took a last swig of ale from the pouch on his belt before stretching out his long legs before him, crossing them at the ankles. "Max also told me how unhappy you were in Earrath and of your past with the one you call, 'asshole ex-husband.'" His eyes darkened with sudden anger and his fingers tightened into fists. "It is a good thing I did not go into Earrath, for he would've paid dearly for treating you so callously."

Shock slapped Astiria like a sudden open hand and she decided to study her boots so she wouldn't have to meet Lerik's gaze. "I can't believe Max told you all of that."

Firm fingers found her chin and gently raised it until her gaze was captured by his. "There is no shame in your past, Astiria. We all have one, even I. He was not worthy of you."

The tenderness she saw in his eyes threatened to shatter her into a million pieces, and sudden panic surged through her. The small clearing closed in around her and she had to get away somewhere where she could breathe. She bolted to her feet and when he reached for her, she pushed her palms forward and the now familiar pink tendrils of her stun spell snaked out to hit him squarely in the chest. His grip loosened and before he had time to recover, she turned and fled into the darkened forest.

Her feet had a mind of their own and carried her until her adrenaline ran out. Then finally, mercifully, she collapsed in a bed of pine needles on the forest floor and cried until sleep took her.

*****

Astiria woke to the sounds of soft snoring beside her, mingled with the soft shushing of the wind playing through the tops of the pines. Even before she opened her eyes, she recognized the warm fuzzy lump she cradled in her arms as Max. She sat up slowly, careful not to wake her tiny protector and came face to face with Lerik, who sat watching over her.

She knew she should be embarrassed for her behavior last night, but she was too spent from crying to feel anything. Instead, she walked toward him, relief washing through her when he opened his arms and allowed her to sink into his embrace.

He smelled of forest and man and she inhaled,

imprinting the scent into her memory. Grabbing two handfuls of his tunic, she allowed the comfort her offered to seep into her, until she found her voice. "I'm sorry, Lerik." She wasn't sure he heard her whispered words until he kissed the top of her head and stroked her hair.

"There is no need, Astiria. I realized that my intrusion into your past overwhelmed you. I have no excuse but that I have waited for so long for a woman like you. A woman who is caring, and loving, yet strong and resilient–a woman who is a force to be reckoned with and who can love me for something besides how I look or what I have…"

She stiffened in his arms and leaned back to look at him. Could it be true? That this man had the same fears she herself had? Instead, she asked, "How can you know any of that about me after only a few days?"

He traced a calloused thumb over her bottom lip and searched her gaze. "You were brave under attack from Marsoon's minions and even braver before his lies. You were willing to stop and heal me in the desert when you were still in danger, and you've shown nothing but tenderness and honestly toward both Max and myself, not to mention my damned opinionated wood-elf, Oopec."

She opened her mouth to protest and he placed a finger against her lips to silence her.

"I realize you and I are both attracted to each other's outer forms, but attraction either increases or decreases as you get to know the inner person. And with each passing moment, I want you more, until each breath is labored when I'm in your presence."

His words hit her like a blow, and she thought back over the past few days. She'd found out that while Lerik could be stubborn, demanding and domineering, he could also be sweet, sensitive, vulnerable and playful. And he was right. The thought of leaving him tore her heart out. She had to find a way to complete her coming of age quest and keep Lerik and Max safe. Without thought, her lips found his and a gentle slow burn ignited between them. She threaded her fingers through his hair, dislodging the leather thong capturing his silky mane as his arms tightened around her, his fingers kneading her flesh.

The kiss broke and Astiria leaned her forehead against Lerik's. "I'm scared, Lerik. I'm scared of the same things you are. Scared that no one, not even you, can love the woman underneath. But you make me hope and I think we need to stop wasting time and get me leveled."

He chuckled, the sound reverberating through her body, tightening her nipples and causing her to sigh. "You're right, of course, my Lady. Shall we?"

Chapter Six

For the rest of the day, they trekked on toward the main portal, through jungles, through forests, through valleys and around lakes. Astiria practiced with her daggers and then with a short sword Lerik had brought and managed to hit level ten in both healing and her assassin skills just as the sun touched the horizon, bringing dusk.

As the silvery column of light disappeared, elation flowed through her and she threw herself into Lerik's embrace. "I did it! I really did it!"

"I had no doubts you would, Astiria. As I've said before, you are a fighter. *My* fighter."

She grabbed his tunic pulling him down for a searing kiss, which smoldered and turned into something more tender and infinitely more precious. She'd reached level ten and was now a fully sanctioned adult by the terms of Verrath. She wasn't about to waste time making her first adult decision. "I want you, Lerik," she whispered against his lips.

His dark chocolate eyes opened and his searing gaze captured hers. "Are you sure?"

"For once in my life, Lerik, I'm absolutely sure. I want you...only you..."

He swallowed her last word inside his mouth as his lips captured hers and he crushed her body against his. The heat from his skin burned through her and she slipped her hands beneath his tunic, tracing the muscular planes of his chest. He growled deep in his throat and picked her up, tossing her over his shoulder like he had the first day they'd met. Only this time, she laughed, a sense of freedom flowing through her like heady wine.

He pulled his bedroll from his saddlebags and spread it out over the soft sand of the lakeshore before gently setting her on her feet, her breasts rubbing against him all the way down. She reached back behind her neck to untie the top of her assassin leather armor, letting the leather fall away, to reveal her breasts, the nipples peaking as the early evening air brushed over them.

Lerik's breathing came in harsh pants and an obvious erection strained at the front of his pants. "You're so beautiful, Astiria. I want to see all of you."

She slipped off her boots and then a few more opened ties allowed everything she wore to slide off her to pool around her feet. His molten gaze raked from her face, down over her breasts, to the patch of dark red hair between her thighs and then all the way down to her bare feet. He seemed rooted to the spot, as if she might disappear. The vulnerable look on his face almost undid her.

Stepping forward, she pressed herself against him, laughing when his erection hardened impossibly against her stomach. "Am I going to be naked all by myself, or are you going to join me?"

As if her words had snapped his invisible chains of his control, he crushed her to him, his hands everywhere at once and she allowed the fire of his need to consume her. The soft leather of his tunic and trousers against her naked skin felt forbidden and erotic and she moaned as the material scraped over her heated flesh.

Lerik pulled his tunic over his head, dropping it to the forest floor before capturing her lips once again. The springy hairs on his chest rasped over her engorged nipples, causing a surge of moisture between her thighs and she groaned in frustration and the clothing still between them. Her fingers fumbled with the laces on his trousers until his erection sprang free into her hand. She wrapped her fingers around the width of him, her other hand, cupping the soft sacs below. Lerik growled and in the next instant, she found herself on her back on top of Lerik's bedroll, with his muscular body pinning her to the earth.

He gave her no time for thought or action before his lips and hands began a thorough inventory of every inch of her body. He scraped his teeth over a sensitive spot just above her right breast while his roughened hands explored her hip and stomach before sifting through the springy hair at her juncture. Heat spiraled through her as she traced the hardened muscles of his back and shoulders.

Another impatient growl and he captured her hands over her head as if her explorations had threatened his hard won control. His mouth closed over her breast as his fingers separated her feminine folds and delved inside. Sensations broke over her, threatening her sanity and she couldn't form coherent thoughts, could only feel. Her hips bucked against his fingers, while she struggled against the iron grip of his hands, wanting to touch him, wanting to drive him as mad as he drove her.

He only continued his slow attentions, slowly thrusting his blunt fingers inside her as he switched his attention to the other breast, sucking and laving until she thought she would scream. His erection lay heavy against her hip and she longed for him to replace his fingers with it. "Please..." She tried to say more, but the words wouldn't form under the onslaught of the sensations. His thumb found her clit and slowly rubbed while he continued his slow torture with each thrust of his fingers. Her internal muscles clenched around him and she bucked her hips seeking the release that he held just beyond her reach.

His bit down on one swollen nipple, pushing her over the edge, molten sensations flowing through her, stealing her breath. When her mind cleared, he was kneeling between her knees, his large hands cupped under her ass. Before her fuzzy mind registered what he was up to, he lowered his dark head and his tongue laved over her in one long swipe. She gasped and then he traced circles with his tongue on the soft underside of her clit, the sudden rush of arousal through her system almost sent her flying off the bedroll. But Lerik's strong hands anchored her, her world narrowing to the fire each motion of his mouth brought.

When her breathing hitched, coming in short choppy pants, he shifted and slipped inside her. She gasped at the very full feeling of him inside her at last, and her heart melted when she looked up to see an almost reverent look in his dark gaze. He captured her mouth in a slow sensual dual of tongues, matching the rhythm set by their bodies. She reveled in the sensations of his springy chest hairs rasping against her sensitive breasts, while the scents of pine needles and earth rose thick around them.

The world spiraled down until it only included the two of them and this stolen moment of bliss. Astiria gave herself up to it, needing to meld her soul with Lerik's in a way she didn't quite understand. She wrapped her legs around his waist, changing the angle and making them both groan at the deep penetration. Sweat beaded on Lerik's brow and she smiled as she wiped it away and nipped at his lower lip.

"Astiria..." He whispered her name as he drove into her with new urgency.

She grabbed his muscled ass in both palms to pull him fully inside with each thrust. The familiar tightening deep inside her womb heralded the beginning of her orgasm. "Let me feel you cum inside me, Lerik. Make me yours..."

He growled against her lips as his urgency increased and he pistoned into her, driving her over the edge. She contracted around his thick shaft as pleasure flowed through her like warm honey. But he didn't stop, he reached back to wrap one large hand around the back of her knee, bending her leg so he could drive himself deeper inside of her.

She moaned and reached out blindly grabbing the edge of the bedroll along with some pine needles, trying to anchor herself against the intense invasion. "God, yes! Lerik, please…"

"Look at me, Astiria." His words came through gritted teeth as if he fought a hard battle for his control. "I want you to watch me while I fill you with my seed."

The possessive words drove her over the edge and with the first contraction of her orgasm, his hot seed spilled inside her, filling her with warmth and love.

Love?

She pushed the thought away and ran her hands through Lerik's hair, enjoying the weight of his body on hers. *There will be time for thought later. Now, there is only Lerik.*

*****

Max's growl brought them both out of their reverie and Lerik rolled off her, grabbing his sword and brandishing it over her. Fumbling through her discarded clothes, she palmed both her daggers and looked around them for any sign of a threat.

Max bolted through a space between two trees, his teeth still bared. "Goblin army almost here. They march toward portal."

"The portal?"

Lerik scowled and pulled on his trousers, tunic and boots. "If they can stop us before they enter the portal, you will be unable to complete the quest. You've reached level ten, but you must enter the portal to finish it."

Astiria shrugged into her armor, pulling on her boots as she jogged up the hill after Lerik. "How far is the por…" Her words trailed off as she reached the top of the hill and saw it.

The portal pulsed in front of her looking like a writhing sphere of ectoplasm. It briefly reminded her of an old cartoon where a small white blob of goo called Shmoo was the main character. However, where Shmoo was cute, this portal looked as if it would swallow her whole, and according to the seer, it just might.

"You must go through now, before they come."

Taking a deep breath, she turned to Lerik. "No matter what happens…"

He closed the distance between them, cutting off her words with a savage kiss that scrambled her senses. When he pulled away, her eyes burned with unshed tears that threatened to overwhelm her.

"I love you, Astiria. That is all you need remember."

Sounds of horses riding hard broke through the stillness of the forest, reminding her to hurry. But small fingers of doubt prodded her and she threaded her fingers through Lerik's silky fall of hair, and pulled him close until his breath whispered across her lips. "Lerik. No matter what happens, please remember that I love you too. Always."

His triumphant smile was enough to melt any woman within ten miles. This time his lips were gentle, a mere brush of flesh upon flesh, which threatened to crumble her shaky resolve. *Damn it! I know myself and I'm happy with who I am now. So, why am I so worried about this?*

"Astiria, portal turning colors!"

Max's words broke her out of her thoughts. If she didn't step through the portal, Marsoon would stop her and Max and Lerik would be in danger, not to mention she couldn't officially finish her quest and come of age in Verrath, which would also condemn them. It was time.

She ran her thumb across Lerik's lips and smiled

up at him, memorizing his every feature. Then she turned to Max and held out her arms. He scrambled up, throwing his tiny arms around her neck. "No worry, Astiria. You belong with us in Verrath."

She brushed a kiss over his fuzzy cheek before handing him to Lerik. "Well, guess we'd better get this over with so we can go plan our joining." Her words would've sounded confident if her voice hadn't wavered. Damn.

Lerik's eyes darkened with desire, causing a surge of moisture between her thighs even as her nipples budded to tight peaks inside her leather armor. "I look forward to it, Astiria."

Without looking back, she squared her shoulders and stepped through the portal.

A wrenching sensation caused a surge of dizziness and nausea and she took deep breaths against the onslaught. She opened her eyes and saw *Stone Maiden* lying on the bed where she'd left it in her room at the Fantasy Quest Resort and her world came crashing down around her.

*****

Knock! Knock!

Astiria heard the knocking as if from a great distance. There had been several knocks in the blur of days she'd sat inside her room trying to find a way back to Lerik and Max. She'd ignored them all. Earrath...or Earth, was no longer her world. The magical world of Verrath called to her and she knew each day she spent away withered her soul a little more.

She'd neither eaten nor slept since her return. Her time had been spent leveling up in the game, in case that would trigger the portal once more, bargaining with God and trying to recreate the night she'd been sent to Verrath. It had been lonely here without Max and unbearable without Lerik, but she refused to stop until she'd found a way to return.

The sound of the plastic hotel key sliding into the lock and the door opening registered somewhere in the back of her mind, but she refused to spare a glance. Her eyes were firmly fixed on the computer screen and Lerik's strong form, where he was currently battling a dragon. She hoped that meant he was still alive and hadn't been executed yet for failing to protect her. Bitter guilt rose up like bile coating her throat.

"You look like total and complete crap, Sis."

The voice of her sister Amy wrenched her away from the computer screen and she looked up. She blinked a few times to make sure she wasn't hallucinating, but the amused blue eyes of her sister still stared back at her. Amy's long blond hair fell in a waterfall to her shoulders and as always, she reminded Astiria of a happy porcelain doll.

"Amy? What are you doing here?"

Amy took the keyboard from Astiria's lap and set it on the couch beside her and then sat on the bed facing her. "I figured you might need some help. When I went through this, I was alone, and I always wished for someone to be there for me. Come on, we need to get you cleaned up and you have to eat."

Jumbled thoughts tried to gel inside Astiria's tired mind, but failed. "Someone to be there?"

"Yes, I met Doug here, remember?"

Understanding slowly dawned, shocking her to the core. "Doug is from Verrath?"

Amy nodded, a smile that spoke of warm memories curving her full lips. "I won a free vacation, and I have a feeling I spent mine much like you spent yours. Anyway, Doug was a Master Wizard Lord inside Verrath and he gave all of that up to come back with me."

Amy's words hit her like a splash of cold water and for the first time in days she realized her mouth was dry and tasted like she'd slept in a sewer, not to mention her eyes were gritty and tired. She rubbed at her eyes with both fists and when she opened them, Amy was there with a glass of water and two aspirin.

"Drink and take these and we'll find you some food. You have to eat."

She took the pills and then the tears began. They poured down her face in a steady warm stream. "I've lost him, Amy. I failed. Even now, he and Max are probably on trial to be executed for failing to protect me."

Amy sat down next to her on the love seat and pulled her into a comforting embrace. Sobs wracked Astiria's body as her sister gently rocked back and forth riding out the storm. When the sobs slowed and the tears were gone, she pulled back, suddenly empty and spent.

"Are you done feeling sorry for yourself? I'm supposed to be the younger sister *you* comfort, remember?"

Astiria couldn't help a watery laugh. "I guess this is role reversal for us." She looked up at her sister, studying her as if for the first time. "Thanks, girl. I'm glad you're here."

Her head throbbed from lack of food, lack of sleep and her heart hurt from lack of Lerik, Max and Verrath. She shook her head. "I would do anything to get them back. I feel like part of me has been ripped away." A memory of her sister's words trickled through her sleep-deprived brain and she sat up straighter. "Wait! You said when you went through this, you were alone. You mean you went to Verrath, right? When you stepped through the portal, did it bring you back here?"

Amy's smile widened and she nodded.

Adrenaline surged through Astiria's veins and she grabbed her sister, resisting the urge to shake her. "How did you find Doug again?"

"You are declared, I assume?"

"Yes, but…"

Amy cut her off. "You are declared and you completed your quest. You are now an adult citizen of Verrath. As such, you can claim the rights of citizenship, to visit…or to stay. I went to stay, and ended up only visiting, but I have a feeling your decision might be different. As my declared, Doug decided to come back to Earrath…Earth, with me."

Astiria sucked in a breath. "Why didn't you ever tell me?"

A blush flowed up Amy's neck and into her cheeks. "You were married to the asshole-ex at the time. Even though you weren't happy, you wouldn't be able to declare to anyone in Verrath if you were married here. Besides, would you have believed me?"

A smile curved her mouth for the first time in several days. "No, you're right." She took her sister's hand in hers. "I love him so much, and I miss Max. I have to go back. I've fallen in love with them and with Verrath, I'll whither and die here without them."

Tears glistened inside her sister's eyes and she reached out to caress Astiria's cheek. "I know, Sis. Tell Lerik hello for us and don't worry, we still visit."

"You know Lerik?"

"Of course, Doug was the Lord of Lerik's castle before he came here. Lerik is his younger brother."

Shock sucker punched Astiria. "I'll be damned! I can see the resemblance now that I know about it." Doug had sandy blonde hair and blue eyes to Lerik's dark hair and dark chocolate eyes, but the rugged good looks were the same and the smile now that she thought about it.

She stood and impulsively hugged her sister before grabbing her book, *Stone Maiden*, off the bed. She smiled at Amy. "I'm determined to finish this book some day."

Amy nodded. "The author lives in Verrath, Tina Gerow lives in the large castle out on Gargoyle Island.

You'll have to visit her there."

Astiria shook her head. She'd think about that later. Right now, all that mattered was getting back where she belonged. She held her arms wide. "All right. As an adult citizen of Verrath, I request to go there, to be with my declared, Lord Lerik!"

When she opened her eyes, she stood in a large room surrounded by stacks of gold, chests overflowing with diamonds, rubies, emeralds and dozens of other precious stones. She turned to find Council Master Ocam watching her.

"Welcome home, my dear."

"Ocam! Where is Lerik?"

He smiled, his kind blue eyes crinkling. "Patience, Astiria. You've completed your quest, now you must choose your reward. And might I suggest you clean up and put on a joining dress before seeing Lerik? I can send Oopec to attend you when we are finished here."

"Reward? What are you talking about?" She caught sight of herself in a large gilded mirror hanging behind Ocam and her elation died. She was back in Verrath, but this time she'd brought her normal body. How would Lerik react to that?"

"The riches of Verrath are at your disposal my dear, or pretty much anything you can imagine– any one wish. What is it you would like for your quest reward?"

A slow smile curved her lips as an idea formed. She turned back toward Ocam. "How creative can I be?"

*****

Once she was bathed and dressed, thanks to Oopec's help, Ocam clapped his hands and she found herself standing on the dais in Lerik's throne room surrounded by what looked like the entire population of Verrath.

"Now that Lady Astiria has arrived, let the joining commence!" Ocam stood in front of them, ready to officiate.

She turned and caught her breath as she saw Lerik standing next to her in a royal blue tunic with Max at his feet.

"Lerik!" She rushed forward until his strong arms closed around her. Contentment and happiness flowed through her and she wished they could stay like this all day. He gently pulled back enough to see her face.

"Welcome home, Lady Astiria." He smiled, his grin almost wolfish and predatory. "I love the wavy sable hair and look forward to exploring this new body at my leisure…"

She sighed with relief as she realized how she looked really didn't matter to Lerik either way. "I kept the stripper boobs as my quest reward, I hope you don't mind."

His grin widened. "I think I finally understand what these 'stripper boobs' are, and I'm most happy with your decision.

Finally, she was totally accepted for her real self–body, mind and soul–okay, along with some perkier boobs. She laughed out loud. She was home. "I look forward to a very leisurely exploration of each other, say the next seventy or eighty years?"

Lerik rumbled a laugh. "Here in Verrath, that is just the honeymoon period, my love. We have centuries ahead of us."

Then his lips covered hers and she lost herself in her very own warrior gone wild.

Guarding the Hellion
By
Linda Wisdom

Prologue

Favors were a part of Brady Hayes' life. Over the years, he'd called favors in, and he'd owed them. He'd really preferred calling them in, because owing them-especially to someone like Shar, Lord of the Underworld-could be pure hell, pardon the pun. And you just didn't blow off Shar. Not if you wanted to remain intact. The last guy who blew Shar off was shipped home in a million tiny boxes tied in neat little bows with the guy's guts. Nope, not a pleasant prospect at all.

Which was why Brady was down here in the intense heat and darkness in response to Shar's command. He tried not to make eye contact with the woman seated behind the reception desk. She had to be as tall as him, and he was a hefty six-foot-four who could take down a tank on a good day. He noted her skin was pale as chalk while he was a deep tan from his stint working in the Middle East. Her flat black hair showed no gleam of health and her lips and nails matched her hair. It amazed him she wasn't sweating buckets in the black leather dress that fit her like a condom. She kept looking at him as if he *was* dinner. He didn't think she was thinking of a few sexy little nibbles, either. More like she wanted every damn course including dessert! He kept his eyes trained on the coffee table in front of him while vainly trying to ignore the severed fingers that wiggled inside the ebony wood.

"There you are, Brady." The tall, portly man in a charcoal wool suit straight from Savile Row that appeared at the inner office door looked more like a stockbroker than the typical, everyday Dark Lord, but Brady knew better than to underestimate him. The guy had balls of sulpher. "Come in, come in. Hold my calls, Morticia," he instructed.

"Morticia? You're kidding, right?" Brady followed him into a large rock-walled office that felt a good fifty degrees hotter than the reception area.

"Better than her real name, which is Annabelle." Shar gestured for him to sit and took his place behind a mile-long desk hand carved from ebony. "Thank you for coming so swiftly."

"You said I owed you one." Brady didn't think it was a problem to remind the man exactly why he came so quickly. He wondered if anyone had the guts to tell Shar he resembled the actor who played Elwood in *The Blues Brothers.*

"Still, I appreciate it." He beamed, which was downright scary. The man didn't seem to understand that smiles should be happy, not horrific. "I have a job for you."

"A job," he repeated, getting that sinking feeling in the pit of his stomach.

"I used the term you owing me a favor because I knew you would respond to my summons faster, but I am more than willing to pay you for your time. What I need here is the best and you're the best in your business." Shar grimaced. He fisted his hand and struck his chest. "I apologize. Lunch is just not settling right today." He released a belch that rocked the room. "There, that's better. Now, what I need is your services as a bodyguard."

"But you have something like a thousand bodyguards down here already," Brady pointed out. There was no way he would stay down here on a daily basis. He'd melt to nothing in no time.

"I need someone to watch over a family member." He grimaced and belched again. "That's the last time I have Renalda's bloodworm pie for lunch," he muttered. "I chose you because I require someone discreet for this job. And while you are rough around the edges, you are excellent at what you do plus you know how to keep your mouth shut when it is necessary."

Brady shifted in the chair that seemed to conform to his body with every move he made. "Sure, I do private security sometimes, but your people," he paused wondering if it was PC to call them people since by no stretch of the imagination had they ever been human, "they might be better for whatever you want."

"They wouldn't be at all suitable for this kind of work." Shar leaned back and pressed his fingers together, the tips resting just under his rounded chin. "I'll be honest with you, Brady. While my private security guards are excellent at what they do, they are used to coping with situations Below, not up above. They aren't equipped to handle a situation like this one even if it's nothing major. I just feel a human would blend in better. And since you have the skills, I immediately thought of you."

Danger, Will Robinson! Danger! clanged inside Brady's head. *The only reason he thought of me was because I owed him that damn favor and he knew I'd have no choice but to do whatever he needed.*

"What do you need me to do?" He had visions of riding herd over the Hounds of Hell or worse.

Shar smiled. "It has to do with my baby sister, Raven."

"You have a sister?" *Okay, not too tactful a way to put it. Even Dark Lords could have family.*

"Actually, she's my half-sister." Shar glared at a pile of paperwork that magically appeared on a corner of his desk. The papers immediately burst into flame. "The politics down here have become unbearable." He rested his arms on the desk, hands laced together. "You could even consider this a vacation. My half-sister is visiting an island resort in the Pacific and I would like you to look after her."

Brady stiffened. "That sounds more like a babysitting job."

"Not babysitting, I just want you to keep an eye on her and keep her out of trouble. And make sure no one bothers her." Shar made a face, which for him meant his face shifted in multiple directions as if it was fashioned from warm wax. "Raven has a mind of her own. She doesn't realize that the mortal world isn't like it is down here. I'm willing to allow her this time away, but I still want to know that she will be all right up there. I know you will keep an eye on her, but of course, she can never know I hired you. The consequences, well, she does have a temper." He tapped his fingers on the surface of his desk. A slip of paper silently floated upward. Shar handed it to Brady.

The number of zeroes he looked at was enough to quiet any misgivings he had about the assignment that literally could be from hell. His smile was a lot more affable.

"When do I start?"

Chapter One

"Hello, baby," Brady murmured, watching a shapely redhead stretched out by the swimming pool.

He tried to ignore the nasty tingle on his butt, but he wasn't having much success.

It was bad enough Shar insisted on marking him, but did he have to mark him *there*? Brady's argument that Raven would recognize the mark on his wrist for what it was met with a "That can easily be taken care of", and next he knew the mark was burned into his ass. Shar's argument that it was purely for Brady's protection was bullshit, but no way you could argue with a Dark Lord and survive being torn limb from limb after losing said argument. Plus since there were no photographs of Raven, he was assured the mark would help him find her. He was also promised the mark would be removed once his assignment was over.

He had to admit if he was supposed to protect a woman there was no better place to do it than at this exclusive resort set on a remote Pacific island. After a little judicious bribery alerted him to his charge's presence on the beach he sauntered out to the thatch-covered beach side bar that bisected the pool and beach, and settled on a stool. From there, he had a good view of both areas along with an even better view of the bikini-clad beauties lying out by the pool and stretched out on chaise lounges arranged along the white sandy beach. A few interested looks sent his way indicated they wouldn't mind getting to know him better. Too bad he was on the clock.

Brady thought of how he'd recognize the woman. According to Shar, the mark Shar branded him with would alert him.

"Who do we have here?" He viewed the beach area through his dark glasses. So far, every brunette he gazed at didn't create even a tingle from the mark. Convinced he found the mysterious Raven, he studied a dark-haired woman with pale skin that looked as if a dose of sun would set her on fire. Nada. He wondered if the mark wasn't doing its job. "So what the hell is the Dark Lord's baby sister doing out here in the sun and sand?" he muttered. "You'd think she'd prefer some dark ugly dungeon." He grinned at a shapely redhead in an emerald green thong bikini. "Still, who am I to complain?"

As his gaze again swept the length of the beach, he noticed a feminine figure making her way out of the water. He moved on since he was convinced she wasn't the one. The intense tingle on his ass soon grew into an all out burn. He swung back to the woman he'd first dismissed until the tingling burn warned him he was looking in the right direction. The longer he looked at the woman, the stronger the burning sensation.

"No way," he muttered, staring at the woman walking up to the registration desk. "Holly shit! I'm expected to babysit Malibu Hellion Barbie!"

His mental computer noted that the object of his scrutiny was probably around five-foot-ten, with long legs it was all too easy to imagine wrapped around his hips. The lean body of a disciplined swimmer and the tan of someone who didn't believe there was such a thing as skin cancer. Did Dark Lords' sisters have to worry about skin cancer? To further confuse him was a wealth of sunny blonde hair tied up in a perky ponytail worthy of Gidget. The body that inspired more than a few fantasies rolling around in his head wore a turquoise and white bikini and he could see the glint of a blue stone nestled in her navel. She didn't look to be more than her mid-twenties, but for all he knew she could be thousands of years old. But what surprised him the most was the surfboard she carried up the sand.

Brady picked up his Jack Daniels on the rocks and downed it like medicine. Considering the way his heart stopped when he saw her, he felt he needed something to jolt it back to working again. She was not at all what he expected.

Why did he feel as if Shar was enjoying some insane joke at his expense?

*****

She was free!

Raven couldn't remember the last time she'd felt this free and alive. She finally stood up to her brother and took back her life. No more Shar looking over her shoulder, telling her what she could and couldn't do, and explaining she had to remember he was a politician and she had to act accordingly. Then there was that long and boring speech about fulfilling their family destiny.

For a glorious month, she didn't have to attend tedious business functions with her brother and endure polite sneers and side-glances because she didn't fit the preconceived notion of what a Dark Lord's relative should look like and act. That she was going to be the political pawn her half-brother planned to use to further his own objectives.

Yeah, like she was going to wear black and look pasty faced the rest of her existence.

It took a lot of bargaining on her part, but she managed to talk her protective older brother into allowing her to leave Below and venture into the mortal world. Before, she'd only seen it on viewers and experienced it in fantasy rooms. Once here, she quickly learned it was nothing compared to the real thing. And now that she was here, she didn't intend to ever go back. As far as she was concerned, someone else who was better at it could take up the family duties.

She was staying up here in the sun and she was going to have the life she should have; one where she didn't have interfering–even if well meaning–relatives who totally cramped her style. Plus, Shar and her mother had plans that involved her settling down with the mate of their choosing. They talked about how some marriages were not only successful politically but personally, too. After all, look how well Shar's marriage worked out.

Oh, right. It was a well-known secret that Shar's wife Matthis, was fooling around on him.

She wasn't going to allow her family to dictate her future the way they had her past.

She stopped at the spot where she'd left her towel and beach bag on a chaise lounge and dug her toes in the sand lifting her face to the sun.

This was exactly where she belonged.

As Raven stood there, enjoying the warm of the sun stealing through her body, she couldn't miss the sensation that someone watched her. It wasn't anything unsettling, more a heated exchange that sent her pulse racing. She set her surfboard down by her chaise and towel and made a casual sweep of the area to see if she could find her secret admirer.

It turned out not to be too difficult. And what she saw she liked. Very much. He looked to be several inches over six feet, which went very well with her lean five-foot-ten. Muscles that she gauged didn't come from a gym, short-cropped brown hair and one of those little beards that should make him look like a university professor but made him look hot instead. She saw a jagged scar run up the outside of one leg to hide under the hem of his khaki cargo shorts. She flirted with the idea of wondering just how far up that scar traveled. He looked incredibly fit otherwise. Extremely fit. No, amazingly sexy with an olive-green t-shirt that stretched over a broad chest. At first sight, she would assume he was a soldier here on leave, but she couldn't imagine a regular soldier could afford an exclusive resort where a week's stay typically cost the price of a small car and that was just for the room.

She was positive it wouldn't take much to find out. The nice thing about being a Dark Lord's sister was the powers she had. But she didn't want to use her powers. And as tempting as he was, she told herself she didn't want a man, either.

She came here to lie on the beach, soak up the sun, surf and see how many umbrella decorated drinks she could down in one evening. Sex wasn't on her to-do list.

Still, a sweep of her eyes in that direction gave her a new look at the man, sprawled in the tall cane-backed stool that because of his height was more like a chair. His legs spread out in front of him making him look like some sort of Grand Poobah. As if he expected the serving girl to approach him on her knees and service him. Dark glasses covered his eyes, but she was certain he watched her with such intensity she could feel it like a layer of heat covering her skin.

And this heat was nothing like the heat at home.

Determinedly turning her back on him, she picked up her towel and dried her arms and shoulder then bent over to dry her legs so that he had a perfect view of her ass.

No reason not to give him something to look at.

*****

Whoa Mama! Brady almost choked on an ice cube. Luckily, the burning from the mark disappeared as soon as he acknowledged his charge. Considering the way his dick stood at attention, he was amazed that Shar trusted him to watch over this incredibly sexy woman when the Overlord insisted Brady was there to keep her safe. But who was going to keep her safe from Brady?

"Raven is young and isn't well versed with the outside world. I'm also worried about someone taking advantage of her," Shar had told him.

"Are you talking physical danger?" He didn't even want to think what would be after any of Shar's relatives or if bullets could stop them.

"I'm in a political battle down here, Brady," Shar said pompously. "Some factions don't agree my vision of what we need to do next. While I would hope Raven would help the family in our agenda, she has this crazy idea of going up to the human world. She has this crazy idea she needs freedom to do her own thing." He shook his head in frustration. "I'm certain once she has this vacation she'll come to her senses and do what is right for the family."

Brady wondered if he wasn't getting stuck with some bratty teenager who was prone to temper tantrums. "I still say you'd be better off using your own people."

"That wouldn't work well at all. They don't do well among humans." The Dark Lord grimaced. "There have been incidents in the past that are best not repeated."

Brady thought of the Shar's private guards he passed as he was escorted to Shar's office. Each one a healthy six-foot-eight inches of pure muscle, soulless eyes that could see even through pitch-black, hooked nose that could track down anything living or dead, razor-sharp teeth that could probably tear steel apart. Yep, definitely not creatures to let loose on unsuspecting humans.

"You see..." Shar hesitated, "the time will come when Raven will have to assume her duties down here. It won't be long before she can no longer ignore family obligations"

"So you're letting her out to sow her wild oats, so to speak," Brady said.

Shar beamed "Exactly. Perhaps it will be easier for her once she truly comes to realize her destiny is down here. Many of us go through this time where we think life is better up there, but it doesn't take us long to realize we need to be with our kind. But while she's away, I need to know she won't make any undesirable alliances. I know what can happen during this *time." He coughed uncomfortably. "But if you're there, you can befriend her in order to watch over her properly. She'll have her time away and come back ready to work for the family."*

Brady wasn't sure he liked the idea of anyone having to live down here even if this Raven had obviously grown up here. Still, Shar offered a lot of money for what sounded like a simple job. "Just tell me where to catch up with your sister and I'll make sure she's kept safe and sound," he assured the creature.

"Oh yeah, I'm only too happy to keep the lady under observation," he murmured, lifting his glass to catch the bartender's eye. In seconds, he had a JD on the rocks sitting before him.

This was the cushiest job he'd had since, well, never.

Feeling a twinge in his thigh where a knife had sliced in too deep, he stretched out his leg. At least the bastard with the knife wasn't going to cut anyone ever again. When he looked up again, his charge was missing.

Fuck!

"Hi, Mike, could I have a Tie Me To The Bedpost, please?"

Brady didn't need the burning sensation across the mark to warn him who stood nearby. He looked up and found Raven standing at the end of the bar. The drink name fostered all sorts of fascinating images, all of them having to do with the two of them naked, silk scarves and massage oil. If he wasn't careful, he was going to explode here and now. He shifted to give his aching balls a little more room.

"Sure thing, Rae." The bartender left Brady without hesitation and mixed the drink quickly, adding a bright orange stirrer in the whiskey sour glass before handing it to her.

She offered Brady a brief smile and concentrated on her drink.

There was never a better opening. "Interesting drink name." Okay, not scintillating conversation, but he was never one for small talk.

"The gift shop has a tropical drink book and Mike's letting me try every one of them," she replied, edging up onto a barstool.

"Are you going through it alphabetically or by the most interesting names first?" he asked, intrigued by her vacation hobby.

"Nah, she's trying the fun sounding ones first." Mike grinned. After catching a look in Brady's eyes, he quickly moved on to another customer at the other end of the bar.

"You do pretty well with that board out there," Brady commented. "No offense, but aren't long boards pretty heavy for someone as lightweight as you?"

Raven grinned. Brady couldn't believe that this beach babe grew up in the Underworld where the color black, pale skin and red glowing eyes were the norm. No way anyone would assume she was related to Shar.

"The good thing is once I'm out on the water the waves do all the work for me. I'm just out there for the ride. As for when I'm back on land, it takes some muscle to bring it in. I consider it a good upper body workout." Her comment immediately brought Brady's gaze to her tits. She ignored his less than subtle perusal and sipped her drink. She smiled and nodded. "This is definitely another one I like. I'm Rae." She held out her hand.

Brady found her skin warm from the sun but not moist like Shar's skin had been. He didn't miss the small shock that zipped along between their hands and judging from the slight widening of her beautiful blue eyes, she felt it too. He silently applauded her for not jerking her hand back.

"Brady. So are you here for the surfing, Rae?"
Damn, he might be better at this small talk than he thought
he was.

"Sun, sand and relaxation. What about you?"

Since he'd planned on striking up a conversation
with her as soon as he could, he had his story prepared.
But now that he'd met her and gazed into eyes he could
drown in, he wished this meeting wasn't deliberate. He
wished they could have run into each other in a bar, talked
a bit, he'd invite her out for dinner and maybe there was a
chance more would happen. They were going to be there
for a month, so there was hope. Instead, in case Shar had a
way of watching, he was determinedly keeping his eyes on
her face and not on her barely covered breasts. *Was there a
chance she was tanned all over? He wouldn't mind finding out.*

"I'm here on some R&R. I've been overseas a lot
and wanted some downtime," he said, knowing his vague
answer would imply he was in the military instead of his
usual gig as an independent contractor. He sorely needed
the sharp bite of the JD he sipped. Since he'd quit
smoking, he needed something to keep his hands busy.
Hell, he felt like a hormonally challenged teenager. Was
there something about Raven that gave off some sex
pheromones? He wouldn't be surprised given the way
bartender Mike hovered around them. Except, all he'd
have to do is look at the sunny blonde sitting nearby and
he felt his tongue hanging out and his dick all ready and
willing to dive into action.

Down, boy, he mentally admonished his randy body
part. *We don't want to be pulled down into some demon world,
do we? We're here to protect Raven, not fuck her.*

Except at that moment, Raven leaned forward,
resting her forearms on the bar, which gave him an even
better view of what looked like a perfect set of tits. Not so
large they'd smother him and not so small, he'd never find
them. Nope, just the right size for him.

She still watched him in a calculating way he swore was a tactic he'd used many times. He never minded a direct woman. It was always nice to know you were on the same page.

He waited for her to suggest they meet for dinner. He'd respectfully decline and still manage to be in the hotel restaurant the same time she was. He didn't want to appear too eager to spend time with her.

"So, Brady."

"So, Rae." He grinned, mimicking her tone.

Her voice was low and held a husky tone that flowed over him like warm water. "Do you surf?"

Chapter Two

"Not good, Rae. Not good at all," Raven muttered, as she stripped off her bikini and stepped into the shower that resembled a rock waterfall. "Why not bore the man into a coma? There were a million questions you could ask him other than if he surfed?" His answer surprised her when he admitted he did surf, but hadn't had the chance to go out for some time. Still feeling like an idiot with her question, she made her escape as soon as she could and came up to her room before she made any more mistakes. Who knew carrying on a conversation with a man could be so difficult?

She stood under the flowing water and looked at the bottles of body washes set on the shelf like a smorgasbord of scents. Shopping proved to be a feast for the senses as well as the eyes as she indulged in bright colored clothing with not a hint of black anywhere, along with cosmetics and bath and body products that would keep her smelling delicious for a lifetime. After settling on a bottle of body wash guaranteed to make her smell like buttercream frosting, she took her time with her shower. A lavish application of matching shimmer body lotion left her glowing all over.

"Brady Hayes." She rolled the name around in her mouth and liked the way it fit. She liked what she'd seen the moment she saw him. Rugged, muscular and above all else, hot. Now that was the kind of vacation souvenir that didn't show up in any of the gift shops.

A few bills slipped to one of the bellmen earlier gave her the information that Brady's suite was two doors down from hers. Not that she planned to visit him. She just liked having the knowledge. In her family, knowledge was the next best thing to gold.

It was a bit of knowledge she had picked up and used that allowed her to leave her half-brother's compound and spend some time at a gorgeous beach resort. Little did she know that Brady could turn into a nice bonus for her vacation.

As Raven left the bathroom, the sharp tang of something unpleasant struck her nostrils. She muttered a nasty curse used in her world and walked over to the writing desk. A many-petaled flower lay on the wood and she knew it hadn't been there when she went in to take her shower and it definitely wasn't something the hotel maid would have left. The purple petals were so dark they appeared black with sharp spines shooting out of the middle. The Astay flower was a rare species in her world and highly prized. She personally considered them ugly and smelly. And she knew this could only come from one individual.

She made a face and went to the closet, digging in the rear for a small leather case that was the only thing she'd brought from her world. With its covering of magic, it wouldn't be accidentally noticed. She sprinkled gray dust from one of the vials, and the flower immediately disappeared in a puff of disgusting oily smoke.

"Yuck." She coughed and waved the smoke away from her face. She stared at the burned mark on the desk's surface. She dug through the case and found a tube of a dull yellow colored salve that smelled just as bad as the flower, but she knew it was effective for what she needed it to do. A smear of the salve on the wood returned the surface to its usual highly polished sheen.

"It seems some don't understand what one month of not contacting Raven means," she murmured, returning the case to the closet then viewing the contents. The idea of wearing something that would catch Brady's eye was foremost in her mind. "You're not here for *that*, Raven, you're here for sun and surfing," she told herself. Her gaze settled on a white lace dress that didn't look the least bit old fashioned or virginal.

Just the ticket.

*****

Brady's jaw dropped to the floor when he watched Raven walked into the restaurant. She was every man's dream in a strapless white lace dress that barely skimmed her thighs. Blue stones at her ears matched the one that he'd seen in her navel that day. Not that she needed any jewelry to make her stand out. When she acknowledged him with a smile, he gestured for her to join him. One look at her and he knew he wasn't about to have her sitting by herself. Some guy would be hitting on her before she could sit down. He hadn't missed the lustful looks directed her way as she crossed the restaurant. It was amazing she still had her clothes on.

"Take pity on me. I'm not too keen on eating by myself," he explained when she took the seat across from him.

"I don't think anyone has ever pitied you," she teased, accepting a menu from the maitre'd.

As dinner progressed, Brady refused to believe that this woman who looked as if she was made to spend her days in the sun was Shar's half-sister. They were about as opposite as two creatures could be. He wondered if the mark had made a mistake because there was no way she wasn't human. Except while the mark didn't burn now each time he looked at her, there was a definite tingle there.

"So where are you from, Rae?" Yep, he was getting better at this small talk.

"The southern hemisphere," she said with a vague wave of the hand. "Pretty much all over. What about you?"

"My birth certificate says Seattle, but my old man was in the Army so I guess you'd have to say I'm from all over. We moved pretty much all over the world." He gazed at the creamy expanse of skin above the band of lace that caressed her tits. The swell of her breasts rose up just enough to catch a man's attention. He noticed he wasn't the only one.

You're here on bodyguard duty, bub. You're supposed to keep her safe from harm, remember? His brain reminded him. *I don't think Shar meant that you could ogle his half-sister even if she looks like every man's wet dream.*

You can't tell me you're not going to jump a sweet thing like her? His dick had other ideas.

Brady decided to let them fight it out while he listened to Raven's story. He had to admit she was good. She made herself sound as if she hatched from *The Brady Bunch.* Considering what he already knew about her he thought she obviously had no idea how scary that concept was. But then he'd never been a fan of *The Brady Bunch.* In his opinion, they practiced way too much togetherness.

But he did know one thing. He wanted to be alone with her and find out just what was under that wisp of lace called a dress. For now, he'd behave and concentrate on his mahi mahi and coconut ginger rice and try not to notice that Raven ate with a sensuality that was downright appealing to his own senses.

"Is that why you went into the military? Because of your dad?" she asked, picking up one of her coconut shrimp.

"They let me play with guns," he admitted, doubting the flippant comment would unsettle her the way it had other women. Judging from her grin, it didn't. He watched her bite into her shrimp and had a momentary vision of her biting into him that same way. He decided there was no way Shar could keep on an eye on what was happening here. Otherwise, he wouldn't have hired

Brady. He glanced out to the tiki torches dotting the pathway to the beach.

"How about a walk on the beach?" he suggested after taking care of the dinner check. He had never been this attracted to an assignment before, but then again, he'd never been with anyone like Raven before. If he wasn't mistaken, that attraction was very two-sided and he wanted to capitalize on it.

Her face lit up at his suggestion. "I'd love it."

She's a job, bub.

Brady muted the volume to that part of his conscience. Yeah, he planned on keeping her safe even if it appeared the one he needed to keep her safe from was him.

The moment they reached the beach, Raven slipped off her sandals and dropped them to the sand. Brady followed suit with his deck shoes. Soft giggles escaped her lips as they walked along the water's edge with the waves slowly foaming around their bare feet. Pretty soon they were far enough away from the hotel that only because of the evening breeze could they hear the band playing in the resort's bar. Raven hummed along to the faint music and executed a few dance steps that even in the sand looked graceful.

"You act like this is all new to you," Brady commented.

Her smile dimmed. "In a way, it is. I've never traveled much." She moved a step ahead of him and stopped, facing him. "I like you, Brady."

"Thanks. I like you, too." Finally, he could say something that wasn't a lie. He found lying to her burning through him like an ulcer. She was gorgeous, funny and sexy and he couldn't remember the last time enjoying time with a woman the way he did with her. It was more than the idea of taking her to bed. He enjoyed talking to her, too, and that was something Brady didn't always consider when he was with a woman.

Raven moved closer until her breasts brushed against his shirtfront. A rich scent of something that seemed familiar coupled with a hint of citrus teased his nostrils. Underlying it, he could inhale the even richer scent of an aroused woman. She was rapidly becoming an addiction to his blood. He wondered if Shar would insist on a slow and painful death if he knew Brady was having some pretty wild thoughts about his baby half-sister.

She fingered one of the buttons on his button down wild print shirt. He'd figured if he were going to a Pacific island he'd dress the part and picked up a variety of shirts worthy of Magnum.

He slipped an arm around her waist, bringing her even closer against him.

"You going to slap my face if I kiss you?" he whispered, feeling the need to find out just how sweet she tasted.

"Not as long as you kiss me now." She lifted her face. With the pearly rays of the moon playing over her delicate features, she looked like an ethereal goddess. He refused to believe she could be from the dark side.

Never one to turn down an invitation, Brady kept one arm around her waist and lifted the other so he could trace her face with his fingertips. He rubbed his thumb across her lower lip, feeling the soft plump skin give way under his touch. He followed it with the lightest of touches of his lips. As their lips met, the same shock they felt when they first touched hands was stronger this time. It was as if a soft voice in his head urged him to take it all when what he really wanted was to take it slow and easy. He wanted to savor this woman the way he enjoyed a glass of single malted Scotch. One sip at a time.

He nibbled his way across the slightly open seam of her lips then delved inside to find her taste headier than any Scotch. Her tongue danced with his, mimicking what his body wanted to do with her. He slid his mouth up to her ear, finding that sweet spot just behind her lobe. Her soft moan spurred him to nibble further while his hand at her waist moved upward to cover her breast. He felt her nipple push hard against his palm. He moved his hand in a slow circle, feeling the plump contours. Needing more contact, he edged his knee between her thighs. In response, she rotated her hips, rubbing against him.

"Brady," she moaned, moving her hand down to caress the bulge tenting his shorts. That electric shock fairly screamed through his body. Hell! If it happened just from her touch, what would happen when they got naked together?

"I want to look at all of you." This intense need was new for him and would probably get him in a shit load of trouble, but he had to know how close reality was to his imagination. "I want to dance naked with you in the moonlight."

Her smile sent a wave of heat through him as she leaned back at the waist and gave a sexy little wiggle. The top of her dress fell as if by magic. Hell, for all he knew, it *was* magic. Her skin gleamed like pure gold under the moon, her tits high and firm, the peaked nipples turned a deep pink color with arousal. His mouth fairly watered for a taste and he was never one to deny himself. He dipped his head and covered one breast with his mouth, his tongue curling around her nipple, feeling it harden even more against his tongue. Her throaty moan was music to his ears.

Then sanity reared its ugly head and while he was willing to ignore it, he knew he couldn't do anything that would embarrass Raven. He was past caring if anyone else was taking an evening walk on the beach, but why give them a show? He reluctantly dragged his mouth from her breast. Her sigh of disappointment told him she felt the same way he did.

"While the idea of dancing with you in the moonlight seems better all the time, I think we're kind of out in the open here," he said in a ragged voice. "No use giving anyone else a show."

Her face looked a little darker. Was it possible she was blushing?

"This isn't normally me."

He smiled at her soft-voiced admission. "Me, either." He looked around and noticed one of the beach cabanas a short distance away for those who wanted to enjoy the beach without the sun. Right now, it offered them the kind of privacy they required. "That's why I thought we could look for a nice retreat."

Catching the direction of his gaze, she smiled. "What a lovely idea." Pulling herself out of his arms, she spun around and ran toward the cabana. A flash of white momentarily covered her back as he realized she had shed her dress along the way.

Before Brady could blink, she was inside the beach shelter. "Fuck me," he muttered.

"Only if you get in here!" Her laughter easily carried to him.

He grinned as he realized he'd have to be careful around Raven with her acute hearing.

He didn't need to be told twice. By the time he ducked inside the covering flaps, a very naked Raven was stretched out on the chaise. He left one flap partially open to allow moonlight inside.

"You're very overdressed for this venture, Brady." She lay back on the cushion, stretching her arms over her head that thrust her breasts up into two pleasurable mounds. The blue stone in her navel winked in the darkness.

He didn't miss that the lady was a natural blonde. As he walked toward her, he pulled his shirt over his head then dropped his pants in one easy motion. He was grateful that it was too dark for her to see the mark on his butt. He had an idea it would be an instant mood killer.

Raven sat up, one leg extended, the other bent at the knee in a seductive manner. But it wasn't his rampant dick her attention centered on.

"Oh, Brady," she murmured, reaching forward to trace her fingertip along the scar on his leg. The newly healed area was usually sensitive to touch in a painful way but the pain he felt from Raven's touch was pure pleasure. It was as if she was healing him from the inside out. She leaned over closer and pressed her lips against the scar, sending that same electric shock throughout his system. "When I saw you this afternoon I wondered where the scar ended." Her fingers danced along his bare hip where the red and puckered skin gave way to smooth and tanned. She laved the wound with her tongue then looked up with mischief in her eyes. "It appears something else is requiring attention. My, you're a big man all over, aren't you?"

Before he could say a word, her lips covering the head of his dick and slowly slid down, her throat muscles relaxing as she took in all of him. Brady hissed a curse as he cradled the back of her head with his hands, steadying her as she slowly moved her head up and down, using her teeth to add a pleasurable friction to her action.

He closed his eyes and just allowed himself to feel the warm wet feel of her mouth on him. When she lifted her lips off, the tip of her tongue swiped across the slit at the top of his cock then started down again. He felt his balls tighten to the point of pain and he knew he didn't want the first time to be like this. He gently urged her away and pressed her back against the chaise, following her down.   He tasted himself on her lips as he delved beyond.

"I'd like nothing more than to return the favor, but I don't think I can wait.   I need to be inside you," he muttered, nudging her thighs apart.   He still tested her readiness, feeling her dampness before he settled between them.   With one thrust, he buried himself to the hilt.   Her vaginal muscles contracted tightly around him, moving in a countermotion to his thrusts.   He looked down at her face, watching her eyes glow with an unearthly blue light as she raised her hips to meet him.   He'd never been with a woman who was his equal in passion.

He bent his head and fastened his mouth over one nipple, grazing the tight pink bud with his teeth just as she'd done with his cock.   Raven arched upward and wrapped her legs around his hips.   As he felt her muscles tighten even more around him, he reached down and flicked his thumb against her clit.

Her eyes widened to saucer-size as the tremors raced through her body.   "Brady," she whispered in his ear just before she came apart in his arms.

He was positive the whole damn interior of the cabana glowed the same blue light he'd seen in her eyes.

Chapter Three

"I hope you don't think I'm normally that easy." Brady pulled on his shirt and shorts. There were times when it was a good idea to go commando. That way there was one less piece of clothing to find.

A naked Raven curled up on the chaise looking like a sleepy, contented cat. He swore she was even purring. He was tempted to pull off his clothes and have a repeat of the last couple hours. But if he wasn't mistaken, he heard members of the security staff walking along the beach probably making sure the guests weren't making use of the cabana the way he and Raven just did.

He looked down at the woman he likened to a work of art. He learned that her tan was all over and that some kind of small shock wave occurred when she stroked his dick. Not that he was complaining. The woman had magic hands and he wouldn't mind them on him all the time.

"While I'd like nothing better than for us to stay here and watch the sunrise together, I think the resort's security people are making their rounds," he murmured, glancing at his watch and surprised to find it was after three in the morning, which meant they'd been out here for about five hours. He walked out to the cabana's opening and picked up her dress.

Raven sighed softly and rose up onto her knees. The blue stones in her navel and in her ears seemed to wink at him.

"You are incredible," she said, slipping the dress over her head and smoothing it into place.

Brady's hands itched to do the smoothing for her, but he knew it would lead to a repeat of what had been going on for the past few hours.

While he hadn't been a sex hound since his early twenties, he hadn't been a monk, either. But he could truthfully say he'd never been with a woman like Raven.

He leaned over, trapping her between his arms, as he slowly and thoroughly kissed her. She smothered a low laugh as her tongue darted into his mouth, coaxing his out to play.

"Okay, minx." He playfully slapped her on the butt and hauled her off the chaise. "We gotta get out of here before we get busted by Security for having cabana sex."

"Won't happen." She looked smug, as she looped her arm through his.

"Why? You gonna smile and charm your way out of a lecture." He grinned since he so badly wanted to point out the sated sleepy look on her face would be more than enough proof they weren't out here stargazing. They slipped through the cabana's opening and stood outside, breathing in the night air sharp with the scent of the sea.

"Sometimes people don't notice me." Raven slid her hand down to curl her fingers through his.

"Baby, there is no way people wouldn't notice you." He allowed her to take the lead.

She lifted her head, listening as two male voices sounded closer. She looked back at the cabana with a faint hint of sorrow on her face as if she was mentally recording an important memory. "No, really, you'll see." She tugged on his hand.

As they retraced their steps at the water's edge where the gentle swells rolled up to cover their bare feet, they soon saw the faint outline of two men walking in their direction along the upper part of the beach.

"Just watch," she whispered.

Brady was ready for at least an inquiry if they were staying at the resort and a request for proof, but the two men didn't look their way. They continued talking in low voices and walked past them as if they didn't exist.

He knew he was good at slipping unnoticed in and out of dangerous situations, but there was no way he could have walked past someone the way they just had and not be acknowledged even if it was nothing more than a nod of the head. He and Raven might as well have been invisible for all the notice they were given.

"I get it. You've got super powers," he teased. Considering her family tree, he was positive she had way more than super powers, but since he wasn't supposed to know exactly who she was, he had to play it cool.

"If you don't want someone to notice you, they won't," she pointed out.

"As a soldier, aren't there times where you need to hide from the enemy?"

"I don't quite think of Security as the enemy, but yeah, there's been few times." *Give or take a few thousand.* "So what do you do when you hide from Security?" he whispered in her ear, punctuating the words with a quick flick of the tongue. She shivered under his caress.

"Take more than five items in a store dressing room, when I have more than ten items in my shopping cart at the grocery store. It's the little things." She bumped her shoulder against him.

"Cutting in front of someone in line?"

"Oh, no! That would be just rude!" She released the soft throaty giggle that shot a line of heat along his spine. He'd always thought giggling women were annoying. Raven was proving to be the exception. But then, Raven was proving the exception to a lot of things.

Guilt wormed its way through him. He didn't like that he had to lie to her when in many ways she'd been so open with him. He hadn't expected her to confess that her half-brother was a Dark Lord, but over dinner he still felt he got to know her pretty well. While she was sexy as hell, she didn't flaunt it and her conversation didn't center on her hair, nails, clothes or what she did that day. Considering he'd been on many dates with women like that, no wonder he'd rather go overseas for a good battle than have dinner with a woman.

Raven was proving to be the exception all the way around. So much so, he even considered returning Shar's very nice fee since Shar was already paying for his stay here. But he quickly banished that thought. A man had to make a living and if it involved spending time with a beautiful woman, who was he to turn it down?

They made their way past the reception area and to the elevator with smiles that refused to quit.

"What floor?" Brady asked as a matter of courtesy even thought he already knew exactly where her room was.

"Fourteen." She issued a small smile that held a few secrets.

"Same as me." He punched the button and leaned against the wall, watching her.

She couldn't help but notice his scrutiny. "What?"

"How can someone look as fresh and gorgeous at three o'clock in the morning as they did at two in the afternoon?"

She beamed at his compliment that was sincere, not something just to soothe any worries she might look weary.

"It's all magic." She held up her hands and wiggled her fingers.

"Magic, huh?" He grinned.

She leaned forward and whispered, "it's called concealer and highlighter that I lay on with a putty knife."

He reached out and gently rubbed his thumb across her cheek and down to the corner of her lips. He leaned over more and followed the same path with his lips. "I don't taste a speck of makeup on you. I didn't earlier, either." The elevator stopped and the door slowly slid open.

Raven pulled her room key card out of a hidden pocket in her dress and indicated which door was hers.

"I'm down that way." He cocked his thumb in that direction before taking the key card from her and inserting it in the slot until the light turned green.

"Thank you for a lovely evening," Raven said softly, the smile on her lips telling him just what she was thanking him for.

"Meet me for breakfast."

"I usually go surfing around five."

He grinned. "You're not going to make it easy for me, are you?"

Raven tapped her forefinger against her chin in thought. "Yes. And I'm not acting coy. I meant what I said earlier. This isn't normally like me."

Brady easily read the hidden words. "I didn't think you were, Rae. What I felt was an intense attraction that you also felt. We acted on it tonight. I'm asking for you to meet me for coffee, orange juice, eggs, bacon and toast or your choice of muffin," he gently teased. "Maybe take a drive around the island. I heard there's a waterfall on the other side of the island that's worth seeing. Check out the tennis court or play golf, although the last time I tried golf I broke more than my share of windows. I want to spend time with you even if we do nothing more than lay out on the beach," he said seriously, knowing he meant every word.

Her lashes swept down; hiding the eyes he enjoyed looking into. "I'll meet you at the lanai restaurant at eight. "

Brady brushed his lips across her forehead. "If I don't leave now, I won't leave at all," he whispered.

"Good night, beautiful Rae. I'll see you at eight. Don't forget to use the security lock."

"Good night, Brady," she whispered back and then slipped inside her room.

He waited until he heard the quick click of the security lock then moved down to his own room. Out of habit, he checked the traps he'd laid to make sure no one uninvited entered his room then stripped down for a quick shower. Just as he got ready to step into the shower, he inhaled the scent of Raven's perfume on his skin. He reached in, turned off the water and walked back into the bedroom. He decided he'd rather sleep with her scent surrounding him.

*****

Raven's smile as she crossed the room turned down as she wrinkled her nose against the pungent scent filling the room.

"Not again." She retrieved her case from the closet and pulled out her vial of gray dust to sprinkle over the Astay flower that laid on the desk in the same spot the first one had been. "If I'd known this was going to happen I would have brought more dissolving dust." Within moments, the ugly purple flower was gone but a purple envelope with her name written on the front appeared in its place. Without caring about the contents, she sprinkled dust over that too.

She opened the balcony door to let in the fresh sea air and let out the smell of burned flower and envelope.

She paused and walked out onto the balcony to view the ocean that looked a deep navy rimmed with white foam in the darkness. She leaned on the railing, enjoying the quiet of the night.

She had come up here to find a way to escape family duties. To find the kind of life she could never have

Below. The last thing she expected was to meet someone like Brady.

When she had dinner with him, she hadn't expected their evening to end the way it did. She thought they might have a few after dinner drinks; flirt some more and that would be it. But it felt so right. *He* felt so right. The pleasurable ache between her thighs was testimony of that. Brady was a large man all over and while he admitted he couldn't wait, he still made sure she could accommodate him without discomfort. After that first time, they couldn't get enough of each other. She could smell his musk on her skin, the taste of his cock around her lips and the feel of his heavy body against hers. Her breasts even tingled from the rasp of his beard when he nuzzled them. Males where she came from didn't have beards, so it was a new sensation for her. One she liked very much. Actually, everything about Brady she liked. And she knew Brady liked her and even if they hadn't known each other long, she knew it was more than just for sex.

Her smile disappeared. But what would Brady think if he knew the truth about her? Not that she looked like most of her family members. She was considered a rarity among her kind. One that came along only every ten thousand years, which was why Shar hoped she would go along with his plans for a family alliance with Pahso's clan.

"Not in this millennium," she murmured, pushing herself away from the railing and returning to her room.

She slid naked between the sheets and snuggled down among the pile of pillows she kept around her.

She had a month to make sure her half-brother understood she wouldn't return. A month to ensure that Pahso realized there was no way she would become his mate. She knew ignoring his flowers and notes wouldn't do the trick, but she needed some time to make sure she worded everything just right so there would be no discussion on the matter.

Meeting Brady insured that she was making the right decision. She didn't belong Below. She belonged right here.

She fell asleep with a smile on her lips and a mental note to wake up at seven.

*****

"You can leave the whole pot, darlin'," Brady told the waitress as she filled his cup. She grinned and promised to return with a filled coffee carafe along with a second cup.

He swore a shift in the air alerted him to Raven's presence. He looked toward the entrance to the patio-dining restaurant used for breakfast, lunch and weekend brunches. He was right.

Raven wore a bright pink vest-like top that bared her arms and flat belly and matching shorts with cargo pockets. She smiled and headed straight for him. He noticed a glint of gold on one toe. Damn, he always had a thing for a woman wearing a toe ring.

As he watched her make her way between tables, he noticed not one person, meaning male, looked up as she passed by. He refused to believe that not one man noticed someone looking that good. When he saw the glint in her eye he knew the reason.

"Good morning," she chirped, sliding into the chair across from him. "Ooh, coffee! Please, say you don't mind." She reached across the table and picked up his cup.

"I take it black and strong," he warned her. "And careful, that's hot. It was just made."

She lifted an eyebrow. "So do I." She sipped without a wince. "Just what I needed."

"Here, you go, hon." The waitress left a second cup and filled it with a smile at both of them. "You know what you want?" After taking their orders, she rushed off.

"You pretended to do that invisible thing again, didn't you? That's why not one guy drooled as you walked by." Brady tried to rescue his cup, but she refused to give it up.

"I like drinking out of a cup that tastes of you," she murmured, smiling over the rim of the cup.

Damn, if that didn't wake him up better than a gallon of high-octane caffeine injected directly into his veins!

"Not safe to tease a hungry man, darlin'."

She ignored his warning as she added more coffee to her cup. "I couldn't resist it."

"I'll remember that." He focused on her pink glossed lips on the rim of the cup. Lips he wouldn't mind seeing wrapped around his… He shook off the thought as the waitress appeared with their breakfast. "How about a drive around the island after breakfast? Take a look at that famous waterfall they talk about? I can sign out a Jeep from the front desk, have the restaurant make up a lunch."

"I can be ready any time."

That he didn't doubt. He left the table long enough to make arrangements.

He was looking forward to the chance of learning more about Raven.

An hour after they ate they were in a small open-air Jeep that hugged the narrow road leading up the mountain. A basket containing lunch was in the back. Brady's hand was sure on the wheel as he raced up the road. He was happy to see that the speed didn't frighten Raven; instead, she seemed to revel in it.

"The Concierge said it's about a half mile hike inland once we park," he told her, pulling into a small paved parking area. A small wooden sign by a nearby path indicated the direction for Woman of Secrets Falls. "Legend has it if you tell the woman in the falls your deepest dark secrets she will keep it safe for you."

"Sometimes it would be nice to have someone you can trust." She looked off into the distance.

"Yeah," he quietly agreed, pulling the basket out of the back of the Jeep with one hand and taking her hand in the other.

The climb was an easy one and they soon found their way to an outcropping of stone that overlooked a deep blue pool of fresh water and the falls that spilled into it.

"This is incredible," Raven stood at the railing, looking down into the water with its rainbow of colors." She bent further over the railing.

"Hey, I don't think you want to take an unexpected swim." He stood behind her, wrapping his arms around her waist, resting his chin on the top of her head. "You take that steep a dive and you could end up in some serious hurt. I'm not sure I'd want to carry you all the way up that hill, either."

She laughed. "I don't weigh all that much! Besides, I'd be fine. The water's deep enough for a dive even from up here." She looked over her shoulder with a glint of mischief in her eyes. "Wouldn't you like to check out the swimming conditions down there?"

"Even if there are *No Swimming* signs posted?"

Raven made a show of looking all around. They were the only ones there. "Come on, Brady, be bad with me." She moved her hand downward, caressing the front of his shorts. She found the zipper tab and slowly lowered it, delving inside. She circled his rapidly expanding dick with her fingers.

"You like breaking the rules and pushing limits, Brady," she murmured. "I see it in your eyes. In the way you carry yourself. This isn't all that big of a rule."

He moved his hips against the stroke of her fingers. "What makes me think you didn't wear a bathing suit under your clothing?"

"Good guess?" She gave his dick a soft pat and zipped him back up. "There wouldn't be such a well-worn path if it hasn't been used a lot." She moved out of the security of his arms and headed for the end of the curved railing. "Come on, Brady. Let's be bad together."

Before he could react, she had her clothes off, stood at the edge and with arms outstretched, executed a perfect swan dive.

"Raven!" He ran to the edge and looked over to see barely a splash of water when she landed. He was ready to follow her over when a blonde head appeared on the surface.

"It's wonderful, Brady! Come on!"

"I like my bones in one piece," he called back. "I'll take the path." He snatched up her clothes and the basket all the while muttering she could turn him old before his time.

"Are you coming in?" Raven rolled over and floated on her back in the middle of the pool.

"If a family with kids shows up you're going to give them an education." He toed off his deck shoes and pulled his t-shirt over his head. "After seeing you, no red-blooded boy will find anyone comparable."

"Setting high standards is always good." She floated lazily around the perimeter of the pool. "Come in and play Sink the Torpedo."

Brady closed his eyes. "Damn, you're killin' me." But he shucked the last of his clothing and made a shallow dive shooting straight for Raven who laughed and swam toward the waterfall going behind the sheet of water.

The two laughed and chased each other in the water until Brady dove under and swam up, grabbing Raven. She shrieked with laughter and tried to kick out of his hold with no success. But then she wasn't trying very hard. Paddling gently with her hands, she slipped her legs around his waist. Her mouth was cool and wet but quickly warmed by his kiss.

"You're a little crazy," he told her, inserting a finger, then two, into her pussy. He wasn't surprised to find her wet for him. She moaned softly and rotated her hips to his touch. He alternated between slow dips to quick flicks that quickened her breath. He kicked his legs to keep them afloat.

"And I bet you jumped out of an airplane with a parachute that for all you knew might not open. Who's the crazy one?" Her lips feathered over his face.

Brady held his dick and guided it inside Raven's pussy, thrusting upward in one smooth stroke.

Raven held on to his shoulders, pushing down as he thrust up. "See, you are crazy," she murmured against his lips.

Brady's euphoria was diverted when voices sounded from overhead; two of them suspiciously like kids. "Oh, hell," he muttered. With them in the middle of the pool there was no way they wouldn't be seen. "It can't be." Now he understood the meaning of the term 'the thrill is gone'.

Raven wiggled her hips to catch his attention. "It's all right," she whispered with a smile. "No one can see us."

"Rae, we're in the middle of the pool giving the kids an excellent view of outdoor sex." He gritted his teeth.

"And maybe Mom and Dad will get ideas," she joked. "Trust me, they won't see anything." She nipped his shoulder. "They only see water."

"Honey, did you get a good picture of the falls?" A woman's voice was heard.

"All of you stand there by the railing and I can get one of all of you along with the falls," a man directed.

"Dad, can we go swimming down there? It looks so cool!"

"No swimming allowed, sport."

Brady waited for kids to yell and parents threaten to call the authorities, but it didn't happen.

"Sweetheart, it's huge!" the woman said.

Raven's shoulders shook with silent laughter as she dropped her head to his shoulder. His hips moved upward, feeling the tight clench of her vaginal muscles

"This supposedly was a volcano. It probably won't blow again any time soon."

"Says you," Brady muttered, feeling the sensation build by the second. At the last moment, they slid down under water. He was positive the water up top looked as if sharks were thrashing about. When they finally surfaced, the family was making noises about leaving.

"Okay, you made your point," Brady said, as they swam back to the shore.

Raven squeezed the water out of her hair and shook herself free of excess water. "I'd heard that public sex adds to the experience." She shot him a mischievous grin. "They were right."

"Oh yeah, shoots the heart rate right out of the ball park." He pulled the blanket out of the picnic basket and spread it out.

"Brady?"

"Huh?"

"Do you have something you'd like to tell me?"

The hint of fury in her voice was his first clue that all was not right.

His second was when what felt like a firecracker zapped his ass.

"What the fuck!" He jumped and turned around to find Raven the Hellion. The air fairly crackled around her, instantly drying her hair and flying around her face. Even nude, she presented a formidable picture. Her eyes were glittering blue orbs that looked as if they could melt steel and right now, the one they wanted to melt was him. He started to ask her what the problem was when it finally hit him.

She'd seen the mark.

"Who are you?" Her voice throbbed with rage. "No one can hide their origin from me, yet you've managed to do just that. And no lies."

Brady didn't doubt that she wouldn't hesitate in turning him into a tiny spot if not worse. Who knew she had this kind of temper?

"It's not what you think. And I'm very much human," he said quickly, holding up his hands in what he hoped stood for surrender even in her world.

She swallowed several times. "Who sent you?"

"Shar asked me to keep an eye on you." He winced, aware how that was going to sound. By the look of hurt that crossed her face, it hurt even more than he feared.

"My…" she licked her lips. "My half-brother hired you to pick me up. To fuck me?"

"No," Brady hastened to assure her. "He just wanted me to make sure no one bothered you."

"So you fucked me so no one would bother me?"

He knew he was in deep shit and sinking fast.

"Raven, honey." He started toward her.

She held out her hands. "Do not call me honey and don't you dare try to touch me!" She blinked rapidly then frowned as she swiped something damp from her eyes.

Deciding he'd have better luck reasoning with her if he was dressed, he quickly pulled on his shorts and t-shirt while she picked up her clothing and put it on.

"Shar promised me this time was my own," she muttered. "He said he would leave me alone and now I find that he hired someone to…" She stopped and dropped to the ground. "He lied to me!" She looked up at him with angry damp eyes. "Get out."

"Raven, I can't leave you alone."

"Your job is done here. Don't worry, my half-brother will still pay you for your services," she said bitterly. "

He knew he had to take the chance even if she could turn him into a charcoal briquette.

"He was only thinking of you, I was only supposed to keep an eye on you from a distance, but then I saw you…"

"And thought I was a sure thing. I lived up to it, didn't I?"

"No, I never thought that. What I thought was that I was looking at a beautiful, funny woman who I wanted to see more of. Not as a job, but because there's something about you that makes me want more," he admitted. "I've never made love to any of my clients, Raven. What we had last night and just a few minutes ago, well, it was magic. It was something I never felt before. Maybe we haven't known each other that long, but I want to know more abut you. What makes you tick. Your likes and dislikes."

A slight softening of her features had him hoping he was getting through to her.

"You knew me because of Shar's mark."

He nodded. "Everything that's happened between us is just us, no one else. Hell, for all I know, Shar would probably have me boiled in oil for what we've done."

"Oh, no, that's only for minor offenses," she murmured, sniffing loudly. "So you knew all along about my family and it didn't disgust you?"

"If you saw my family on a Saturday night, you'd think mine was loads worse." He chanced moving closer to her but didn't dare trust her.

Raven refused to look at him. "I have to think about it."

As long as she didn't toast him, literally, he was willing to take it.

Chapter Four

Lunch wasn't as awkward as Brady thought it would be. Raven was unexpectedly quiet and he didn't coax her into conversation but let her take the lead.

"How do you know Shar?" she finally asked, nibbling on chunks of pineapple and papaya.

"He showed up about four years ago when I was in Afghanistan. Did me a favor and when I said I owed him, he told me he'd take me up on it when the time was right."

"Did you know then what he was?" She looked down, her loose hair spilling around her face.

Brady shook his head. "Not until later. "

"Many men would have run from him."

"Yeah, well, I've been called crazy in my time."

"What did he tell you about me?" She still concentrated on the sweet fruit.

"Not much. That you're his half-sister, can't see the family resemblance anywhere, by the way, and that you were basically taking a vacation before assuming some family duties." His stomach twisted as he uttered the last words. After twenty-four hours, he already knew he didn't want to give her up.

All he had to do was first persuade her not to hate him.

"Raven?"

She lifted her head. He was ready to shoot himself for the pain he saw on her face.

"You really hurt me," she murmured.

Shit.

Raven looked off into the distance then turned back to him. "Would you have ever told me the truth?"

"I'll be honest. I don't know. My work involves a lot of secrecy."

"But you weren't told to keep a low profile with me," she pointed out.

"No, but I shouldn't have…"

"Made love to me?" She finished the sentence for him.

He nodded.

"Do you regret it?"

There was no hesitation when he shook his head.

Raven put the container of fruit to one side and dropped to her hands and knees, crossing the blanket in feline grace that had him turning into sex hound and seeing the enjoyment of the position she was in.

"Mind out of the gutter, Brady," she murmured, lowering herself onto his lap. "I don't know what's happened, but it feels so intense…so incredible, that I want to see where we would go from here." She studied his face, searching for answers.

"Then we're in agreement."

She settled herself more firmly on his lap and felt his cock rising up seeking her pussy. She smiled. "I'd say we are."

*****

Raven entered her room and almost backed out again.

"Why can't anyone take a hint?" She pinched her nostrils with two fingers and walked into the room that was filled with the Astay flowers. She had just used the last of her Dissolving Dust when a small flame appeared on her desk.

"Raven, you have been gone too long." Pahso's ugly mug appeared in the flame.

"Not long enough."

"You must return to plan our nuptials. They must take place before the next meeting of Shar's family and my own," he ordered. "A portal will open not far from where you are." His black eyes slid over her with avaricious glee. "The sooner we mate, the sooner our offspring will appear."

Okay, that was it!

She stood in front of the desk so he wouldn't miss her words. "Get this straight, Pahso. I am not marrying you, ever. I told you that before I left and I'm telling you again. Don't tell me I'll change my mind, because it isn't going to happen. I'm staying up here and you'll just have to look for another mate." She waved her hand over the flame. It promptly disappeared and she used a spell to lock down a return visit.

"Raven?" A flame popped up.

"No!" While the spell locked out Pahso, she'd need a new one for Shar.

"I allowed you to go up there to find out that life isn't for you. Now you tell Pahso you won't accept him as your mate. You can't do that. Think of the family," he appealed.

"I'm not cut out for what you want of me, Shar. I don't want darkness. I want light. I want sun and the sea and beauty," she explained.

"It can't be."

"Yes, it can. As long as you give your approval and I beg you for that approval." She knew she needed to quit now and let her half-brother think it over. "And Shar." She paused a beat. "Remove the mark from Brady's butt. It wasn't nice to drag him into family matters. And I want your promise that you will never do anything to harm him."

Shar looked alarmed. "What has been going on up there?"

She smiled. "I'm still not entirely sure, but it's nice to figure out. Good-bye, Shar. Remember you promised that this time was my own." She did the same to make sure Shar didn't reappear.

She took a deep breath. She'd done it. She'd officially broken with her family. By informing Shar she wasn't returning Below, she was turning her back on her family and all family obligations.

She hummed a tune under her breath and danced around the room in sheer joy. She was free! Free to pursue anything she wished to. Her list was short and to the point. Everything had to do with Brady.

*****

Their steps moved in sync with each other as if they'd danced together for years. Raven met Brady's suggestion to try the club for dancing with enthusiasm. She was ready to get down and boogie.

But the best part was dancing in Brady's arms, moving slow their bodies brushing against each other, the build up to what they both know will happen later.

Raven had seen the sincerity in Brady's eyes at the falls and she felt as if she was falling in something. She knew about the word love, but she didn't feel she still understood it. If it had to do with what she felt for Brady, then she considered it the best thing in the world.

On the way back to the hotel, Brady had stopped so they could watch the sunset.

"When it appears as if the sun hits the water you'll see something that looks like green fire," he told her, keeping her in his arms as they watched the sun's descent.

"Magic," she said, smiling up at him.

"Magic," he agreed, kissing the tip of her nose.

Raven decided she had a month to find out just what was going on between Brady and her. She told herself if wasn't meant to continue she would manage and still make a new life for herself. There was still no guarantee that Brady wanted more than this month with her. But she didn't feel that he was lying to her or faking what he felt for her.

She had no idea a new life would throw her into the mainstream so quickly. Or that she would enjoy it so thoroughly.

"Tomorrow, we go surfing," she murmured against his throat, inhaling the musky scent of his skin coupled with the minty soap he used. She couldn't wait until she got him into a shower with her. Talk about showering a man with scents good enough to eat! She smiled and pressed a kiss against the hollow of his throat.

"Depends on what time we wake up." He nuzzled her ear then flicked his tongue inside the hollow. She shivered under his caress. "Did I ever tell you there's nothing better than make up sex?"

"Yes, you did and I agreed. Both times." The slow beat of the music vibrated throughout her body. She hazily thought what it would be like to dance with him naked in the moonlight. Or even revisiting the cabana where she learned what true magic was.

"Dancing is like fucking to music," Brady's words whispered against her cheek as he trailed his mouth across her cheek.

"You are such a romantic." She nudged her hand between their bodies, tucking her fingers in his shorts waistband then upward to rest her palm against the warm hair-roughened skin of his chest. "You know, we could hear the music just as well from my room."

"And here I was going to suggest the very same thing." He grabbed her hand and gently bur firmly led her off the dance floor.

Luckily, they didn't have to wait for an elevator and were in her room within five minutes. Raven breathed a sigh of relief there were no ugly and smelly

Astay flowers waiting for her. She opened the drapes, allowing the moonlight to spill into the room.

She tugged at his shirt. "I think I like you better naked."

"Funny thing, so do I, but it's *you* I like better naked." He made short work of her sheer top and flirty skirt. She had kicked off her high-heeled slides the moment they entered the room. "Woman, you're going to turn me old before my time." He slung her over his shoulder and headed for the bedroom.

"Brady!" Her squeal as she bounced onto the bed turned into a soft sigh when he followed her down.

"Now for some savoring." He kissed the top of each breast, and then moved down the center of her chest. He dipped his tongue into her navel swirling it around the stone, nestled there. He glanced up. "Holy shit, is this thing real?"

She nodded. "It's my birthstone."

"It matches your eyes." He lightly circled the stone with his fingertip then moved further downward to blonde curls. He watched them wrap around his fingers before trailing down to the pink slit that was already moist with arousal. He dipped a finger in then slowly stuck it into his mouth, licking her juices off the digit. "Why have a snack when I can feast." He nuzzled his way through the curls and lapped the moisture pooling at her labia.

"Brady!" Her gasp was abruptly cut off when he pressed his palms against her inner thighs further widening her to his gaze and enjoyment.

"You taste the way you look. Sweet and spicy." He blew gently against the ultra-sensitive skin bringing her up off the bed, but he wasn't finished. He grasped her hips to keep her still while he ran his tongue across the dark pink skin. When he nibbled gently on her clit, she about shot off the bed. But he wasn't about to let her go that easily. Each time she begged him to end it, he backed off just enough for her to catch her breath then he started in again with delicate licks, stabs of the tongue and nibbling until she was ready to fly apart. When she threatened to drive a fiery spike where it would hurt the most, he relented and moved in for the kill. The last nibble on her clit sent her over the edge. Before her internal earthquake subsided, he moved up and thrust deeply into her, driving as hard as he could, pushing her even further than before. His own orgasm erupted as she sunk her teeth into his shoulder. Brady poured himself into her until he felt he'd been wrung dry. To keep his weight off her body, he rolled to one side and brought her close against him.

"It just keeps on getting better."

"Not yet." Raven sat up and pushed at him until he rolled over onto his stomach. She straddled his hips, sitting on his ass. She leaned forward, pressing her hands on his back, trailing them down in a motion that was part massage but also sent a vibration clear through his bones and setting up a heat that was surrounding his cock.

"What is this?" he asked, half-soothed and half aroused. He thought the latter was gaining on the former.

"A massage." Her thumbs dug deeply into the indents by his ass but instead of the muscles relaxing, he felt that heated tingle again.

"This isn't like any massage I've had and I've had my share."

"I'm sure you have." She chuckled in his ear. "This is a special massage. Just relax and enjoy it."

He tried to shift to ease the pressure off his dick that was eager for more playtime. "The enjoying part is easy. Relaxing is going to take a lot more work."

The vibrating heat moved through his body again.

"Tell me, Brady, have you ever read the *Kama Sutra*?" She breathed in his ear.

"No, but I'd be only too happy to hear all about it."

"Why hear when we can try it. There was something I found very interesting." She leaned over, brushing her breasts across his back and whispered in his ear. The more she whispered the more Brady's cock got interested.

He rolled over and grabbed hold of her so she wouldn't tumble off the bed. "I've always believed in a careful study of good literature."

Chapter Five

There was no sound, nothing other than an odd shift in the air that brought Brady wide-awake. He laid there, eyes still closed but all senses on high alert as he tried to figure out what woke him up. But he didn't need to hear sirens, gunfire or rockets exploding to know something was wrong.

After assuring himself that whatever caused the unease in his blood wasn't in the room, he pushed the sheet aside and crept out of bed. He made his way to the balcony and looked down, scanning the pool and beach. The lack of moon didn't help, but luckily, he had excellent night vision.

There!

He carefully backed out of the balcony and swiftly made his way back to the bed.

"Raven." He shook her shoulder then covered her mouth with his hand. "You have to get up and get some clothes on." His whisper didn't travel any further than her ears.

She merely nodded and slid off the bed, blindly grabbing shorts and a t-shirt out of dresser drawers and putting them on. "What is it?" she whispered, watching him quickly pull on his discarded clothes and his deck shoes.

"We have to get out of here. Stay here until I get back. I'll only be a moment." He snatched up her key card and eased his way out of the room.

Raven started toward the balcony to see if anything was visible from there when she heard the click of her door. Brady slipped back in, carrying a backpack.

He grinned at her questioning look. "I'm like the Boy Scouts. Always prepared." He opened her mini bar and emptied it of bottled water and cans of energy drinks, adding them to the ones he'd taken from his mini bar.

"What is going on?" She caught his furtive glance at the balcony and she started toward it.

"Not now." He zipped up the backpack and grabbed her hand, pulling her to the door. He opened it a crack and peered out. After a long moment, he gestured for her to follow him. He pressed his fingers to his lips to indicate she remain quiet.

Raven remained on his heels as they crept down the hallway. Instead of heading for the elevator or the stairs, he chose a room that overlooked the back of the hotel. She watched him withdraw a small zippered case and use what looked like one of their key cards in the slot. He breathed a sigh of relief when it flashed green. He pulled her inside the room.

"There are people in here," she whispered.

"Which is why we need to be very careful and very quiet." But the lack of energy in the air bothered him and he moved whisper quiet toward the bed to check the couple lying there.

Raven held her breath until he returned to her and urged her toward the balcony.

"Are they — ?" She didn't want to think the worst.

"It looks like they were somehow drugged," he said grimly. "But it means we need to be out of here fast." He looked over the side of the balcony as he took a rope out of his backpack.

Raven felt a bit queasy. "We're on the fourteenth floor," she protested, remembering to keep her voice soft even if the room's occupants couldn't hear her.

His teeth flashed white in the night. "Then don't look down." He efficiently tied a length of the rope around her waist. "Just think of it as a rock climbing wall at the gym."

"I've never done that. I don't like heights."

Brady grinned and pressed a hard kiss on her lips. "You dove off that cliff."

"That was different! I was falling into nice soft water. Not onto a very hard pavement!"

"Then you'll just have to trust me, baby."

Raven barely managed to smother her scream, as Brady forced her over the side, although he was lowering himself and her at the same time. He remained even with her, silently ordering her to look at him and not up or down. Not that she could look down even if she wanted to. She hadn't lied to Brady. The idea she could fall onto the pavement had her nauseous and dizzy. It was only by focusing on Brady's face and the glint in his eye that she managed to make it to the ground without having a full-blown panic attack.

Once they reached the ground, he had the rope off her in quick order, back in his backpack. He led her around the perimeter of the hotel and toward one of the popular hiking trails leading up the mountain.

Guessing he wasn't doing this for some kinky reason, she remained quiet and close behind him, sometimes even touching his back for reassurance. Every so often Brady stopped and looked down at the resort. At one point, he took them off the trail and they moved upward at a fast and steady pace. He didn't stop until they were a good distance up the mountain and in a protected area that overlooked the resort.

Never so happy to stop, Raven dropped to the ground and just sat there.

"This will help." He bumped her arm with a bottle of water.

"If this is your idea of a pre-dawn hike, it so sucks," she grumbled, drinking half the bottle before slowing down to only take small sips. "What was really wrong with those people? And why is it so quiet down there?"

He dropped down beside her and rummaged through his backpack again, bringing out a couple of packets and a pair of high-powered binoculars. He dropped one packet in her lap. "Trail Mix. You'll need the energy."

"Sleep and then some coffee would have been better." She opened the packet and picked through the contents, eating the chocolate candies first then the cashews and peanuts.

Brady upended his packet and poured the contents into his mouth. "The raisins won't hurt you," he said, amused by the way she carefully picked around them.

She wrinkled her nose. "You can have them. I won't even tell you what they remind me of." She set the packet to one side. "Now are you going to tell me what this hike is about?" She glared at his back as with binoculars in hand he edged closer to the edge. "Brady!" She smacked his back.

He ignored her for about five minutes then looked over his shoulder. He gestured for her to join him then scooted back, settling her in front of him and handed her the binoculars.

"Look down there at about two o'clock," he murmured.

"Two what?"

"Think of a clock and look in that direction."

He kept his arms around her and guided the binoculars. When he heard her swift indrawn breath he asked, "What do you see?"

She handed him back the binoculars. "They shouldn't be here. It's not allowed."

Brady took another look, the binoculars bringing the images so close he felt as if he could reach out and touch them. Not that he cared to touch what he was looking at.

What appeared to be the leader might appear to be human, but the stiff way he walked and the way his head moved in an odd manner told him what he was looking at came from Shar's part of the Earth. The creatures behind the leader didn't bother with a human disguise. Their reptilian bodies reminded him of the creature from *Alien* times fifty as they slithered down the walkway. And he thought Shar's private guards were ugly.

What the hell did they do to the people down there and how were we spared? Or are we?

Then Raven's words kicked in. *They shouldn't be here.*

He turned around and faced her. "What the fuck are those things?" Brady's whisper may have been barely audible, but he may as well have shouted the words for the fury in his voice. He laid his binoculars to one side. He'd seen enough to last a lifetime.

Raven's shoulders rose and fell in a deep sigh. "The leader's name is Pahso and those are his private security guards."

"And you know this because?"

She looked down at her fingers lying in her lap. "My half-brother thinks I should marry him, but I told him I wouldn't. In our world, knowledge is power. I learned that Pahso means to use me to gain more political power and in the end he would destroy Shar to gain his power as well. I told Shar what I learned in exchange for my coming up here for a month. If Pahso is here, that means that Shar didn't find anything wrong with Pahso's dealings and even though I told them I will not take Pahso at my mate, they still consider the betrothal is on."

Brady felt the bile travel up his throat at the thought of the creature down there being linked to Raven. The idea it would actually touch her had him thinking murder.

Shar expected Raven to marry something like *that?*

"You're engaged to that hellish creature down there?" He made it a strict rule to never mess around with married women or even engaged ones. He might not have a lot of principles, but those were two rules he never went against. "Shar never said anything about you being engaged. He only talked about your duty to the family." He snorted. "But I guess that's part of your family duty, isn't it?"

"No!" Raven protested. At his glare, she lowered her voice. "It's not what you think."

"Then why don't you tell me what it means."

She winced at his sarcasm. Not that she could blame him. "Arranged matings are normal among the higher families. My half-brother arranged the one between Pahso and me. It's considered to be an excellent alliance between two powerful families who help rule our world. Shar sees it as a good political move that will further his own ambitions."

Brady felt sick to his stomach. "What you're saying is he's selling you for political favors?" Damn, why had he taken this job? Correction, Shar called in a favor and to be honest, Brady had no choice no matter how Shar made this assignment sound like your everyday bodyguard job.

She looked everywhere but him. "I told you. It's done all the time."

"So you're saying that thing down there is here to claim his bride whether you want him, or not?"

She blew out a breath and nodded jerkily.

He wondered why Shar hadn't clued him in on Raven's pre-marital status. "But you said you bargained for a month for your getaway."

This time she did look at him. "That's correct. But Shar didn't know that I have other plans. I had already intended on not going back. Not that I would tell Shar that at the time. I–ah–let him know when I talked to him that last night. I also talked to Pahso and told him that in no way would I ever be his mate." Her gaze flickered down toward the resort. "Considering that Pahso showed up here, I would say he didn't like my answer. He's not used to not having his way and he especially doesn't like being told no." A shiver worked its way over her body. Even in that short time, Brady knew every emotion that had gone through her. Seeing her experience fear was a new one.

"He wants you even if you don't want him?"

"He prefers it if someone objects." She looked away again then turned back to him. "You have to get out of here, Brady. Pahso, well, he could hurt you badly. Bad enough that you would pray for death."

Translation, he'd tear Brady apart until there was nothing left to mail home.

He held her shoulders, forcing her to look at him. "So what are you saying? That you've changed your mind and decided to marry tall, slimy and ugly after all?"

Her tongue appeared, dampening her upper lip. "He wouldn't be here if it wasn't allowed. It means that Shar allowed it since I was supposed to have had this time to myself. He will say that I'm just feeling pre-mating jitters and remind me it's my family duty."

Damn, she was gong to cry. He saw the moisture pooling in her eyes and he knew they'd overflow any moment now. If she cried, he was well and truly lost. He gripped her shoulders and pulled her roughly against him. His tongue thrust into her mouth, tasting the heady spice that was pure Raven even as he pulled her tank top up to her waist and shorts down her hips. Understanding his intent and wanting it just as badly, she unzipped his shorts and straddled his hips. As their mouths devoured each other, he held her hips and pushed her down even as his cock surged upward. Her pussy was wet and open, sucking him in until her damp curls nestled against his balls. When he opened his eyes, he found hers already open. This time they were an even deeper blue as if the color matched the intensity of her passion.

"Does he do this to you?" he asked roughly, thrusting upward and keeping her firmly in place. He needed this connection more than he had any other time. Needed the feel of her body surrounding his. "Can he make you scream his name?"

"No!" she sobbed. "I've never—" She pulled in a deep breath as she tried to gather her scattered thoughts. "I never would do such a thing with him! He doesn't believe in creating pleasure, only pain! He doesn't want his mate to enjoy but to suffer."

He felt fierce satisfaction to know she'd never had sex with that creature, but it didn't stop him from pushing her as far as he could. He rolled forward until she lay on the ground with him over her. His hips couldn't stop pumping as he sought the high only Raven could give him. He felt the blood flowing from his dick up to his brain and back again. Raven wrapped her arms and legs around him while her tears stained his shoulder. Her fingertips pressed against his spine, sending a flash of fire upward.

"I won't go back. I won't go back," she repeated over and over again.

Brady froze. That sick feeling was coming back. "Is that what this is about? You saw me as a way to stay here?" Sure, at first he'd lied to her about his motives. Could she have lied to him too? Was she that much of a manipulator? Anger simmered low in his belly.

Raven correctly read his thoughts. "No. I might do everything in my power to stay here, but I would never lie to you or use you." She framed his face with her hands and pressed her lips to his but he lifted his head from hers. Hurt flashed across her face, but she never veered her eyes from his face.

He felt his balls tightening and the sheer force of his orgasm ripped through him like a freight train. As soon as he could, he rolled off her and sat up, panting.

"I never lied to you," she whispered, reaching with shaking hands into the backpack for tissues. She froze when she saw his Glock tucked into one corner and a money clip securing an impressive amount of cash. She looked up and shot him a look meant to set him on fire. He was surprised that didn't happen. She pulled her shorts up over her hips and tank top down. She moved away a few paces and sat with her legs curved under her. For a moment, her eyes flashed that unearthly blue color, a hint of her heritage. "I'm not the one walking around with my half-brother's mark burned on my ass."

Brady relaxed at her show of temper. Here was the ball of fire he'd known from that first day. Then he saw the hint of vulnerability in the set of her shoulders as she retrieved her discarded packet of Trail Mix and picked through the rest of the contents and still leaving the raisins alone.

Damn, he always thought of her as someone who could handle anything thrown at her. So far, she'd given as good as she got. He never pushed a woman the way he'd just pushed her. Any further, he would have called her a demon whore. Something told him he would have deserved everything she did to him if he'd tried that kind of shit.

"I'm sorry," he murmured, reaching out for her. "And believe me, I've never said that to another woman."

She delivered a punch to his stomach that drove all the air out. He choked. "Okay, you're not ready to accept my apology just yet," he wheezed.

"I hate you." She pressed her forehead against his chest. "You are a brute. You lied to me. You fucked me as if you meant it. You made me eat raisins and I hate raisins." She sniffed. "And you smell really bad."

Brady wrapped his arms around her and rested his chin on the top of her head. He smiled as he listened to her whispered rants and curses she rained on his head. More than a few had him worrying about his masculinity. Once she ran out of steam, he planned to do just what she wanted-fuck her like he meant it.

She suddenly became silent. "And you are so not getting make-up sex."

Brady settled for raining kisses on her face. "Okay, we'll call it 'Raven's punishing Brady' sex."

She thought about it for a minute. "Okay."

Chapter Six

Rough appendages that were more claws than hands dragged Brady away from his protective curl around Raven's sleeping form. He lashed out at the evil-smelling bodies surrounding him and was struck in the face for his trouble. Raven woke up immediately and screamed as she was brutally pulled to her feet. Brady was only grateful they'd put their clothes back on after they fucked. He didn't consider it a good idea for the lizards to see them naked. He was furious enough with himself, as it was that he hadn't taken further precautions to make sure they weren't found this easily. Although he knew there weren't all that many places to hide on an island.

He fought their restraining hands until a blow to the head had him seeing stars. Through the haze, he saw Raven creating her share of damage with a few well-placed kicks and punches until one of the creatures grabbed her from behind and hauled her over its shoulder.

"Don't resist, Rae," he called out. "Don't give them a reason to hurt you." Fear built up like acid in his belly at the idea of what they might do to her.

"They don't dare harm me," she sneered. "I am sister to Shar, second-in-command and next to ascend. "If any of you try anything I will make sure you are turned inside out and left out for the maggots to feast on." Her shriek could have shattered glass as she continued raining curses on them.

One of the creatures roughly shoved its claws against Brady's shoulder blades forcing him forward. "Something tells me she was serious with that last threat," he muttered. "And I'm included with that do no harm bit." A ringing slam to the back of his head forced him to his knees. "Damn!" He ignored the cackling chuckles as he slowly got up then found himself the creamy filling in a creature sandwich as one walked on either side of him as he and Raven were herded down the trail.

As they grew closer to the resort, they saw Pahso ordering his demon gang around and feasting on the koi that had been swimming in the small pond by the reception desk.

Brady looked over at Raven. Her hair was tangled around her shoulders, a faint bruise marred her cheek–he'd get the asshole that did that to her–and she looked as if she'd been pulled backwards through a rabbit hole not to mention pissed as hell. She never looked more beautiful.

He cursed and fought the creatures that dragged him onto the patio dining area and received more than his share of punches to the abdomen and face for his trouble.

"Leave him alone!" Raven ordered, delivering a few kicks to her captors with little success. One delivered a stinging slap to her face that left her looking dazed. She quickly recovered and swore at them.

"If you hurt her, I will tear you apart with my teeth!" Brady yelled at the two creatures pulling Raven beside him.

Their dark chortles sounded like cackles as they pushed him down to the ground. Raven was pushed to one side. As she stumbled, a circle suddenly appeared on the ground and she was effectively trapped within its invisible confines.

"The females are used to pain. It is their lot. You took what was mine. I claim it back."

Brady lifted his head and faced the human-like figure, but he knew there was nothing human about the thing even if it was dressed like a typical thug in jeans, black t-shirt and shit kickers. Its shoulder-length hair hung down its back in a mass of oily black curls. A stench of sulpher permeated from its skin and stung Brady's nostrils.

"I smell your cum on the female," the creature hissed, swinging what Brady could only call a bad-ass sword guaranteed to slice him in half as easily as if he was soft butter. "The female is mine and you have desecrated her. She will be punished for that, and so will you."

"I am not yours, Pahso!" Raven shouted from the sidelines. "I told Shar. He will be angry if you dare harm me."

"Raven, shut the hell up," Brady ordered, not taking his eyes off what might look human but sure as hell didn't sound or smell human. Man, this thing stunk worse than a landfill. "Like the lady said, she doesn't belong to you."

A hint of a black forked tongue appeared past the creature's lips as it circled Brady, who turned in a tight circle so he wouldn't end up with a surprise attack.

"What did you do to all the guests and staff?" he asked.   He didn't want to think of the number of causalities involved if the creature had his way.

It smiled, if the stretching of what must be its lips could be called anything remotely like that.

It flicked its fingers as if they held no importance. "They are all asleep."

"He must have used a slumber spell. It would be an easy matter to use one that would affect everyone but us," Raven called out. "Since this is considered purely a family matter he would be barred from harming everyone here. They won't awaken until this is finished."

Brady did not want to think what finished meant. He had an idea it involved blood and pain. Namely, his.

Pahso's slitted eyes momentarily slid over her in a caress that was like black pitch. He turned his head and smirked at Brady.

Just seeing his action had Brady wishing for a long hot shower with plenty of soap. He hated to think what

Raven felt like. Judging by the look on her face, she wanted to tear the creature's head off.

"Shar spoiled you shamefully. He allowed you to run free when you should have been properly trained to stand by my side as my mate and perform your duties in a proper manner," it hissed. "It appears I will have to train you myself." The lust glittering in its eyes sent a wave of disgust through Brady's body. He didn't want to contemplate this thing touching Raven with even the tip of its finger.

"Shar doesn't control me! I told you before, Pahso, that there will be no mating ceremony. Believe me, since then I have not changed my mind!" Raven started to lunge for it, but the edge of the invisible circle bounced her back hard enough that she almost fell on her ass. She settled for pounding her fists against the invisible barrier and screaming threats at Pahso that curled Brady's hair and had him grateful she was on his side.

Shit! Brady had no idea what insanity he was caught up in, but it was definitely not good. If he wasn't careful, he had a bad feeling he could end up being dragged off to some dank hole populated by things that were pals of the psychopath facing him. Not to mention it was waving around a sword with the intent of cutting off his head and possibly his dick and not necessarily in that order. Brady was determined to not be dragged off to any hellish dungeon minus any body parts he considered important.

What kind of brother was Shar that he allowed this thing to come up here and just take Raven as if she was nothing more than chattel? Were politics that important to him that he would honestly want her to be with something this revolting?

He jumped backwards when the sword came too close for comfort. What he wouldn't give for his Glock right now, but one of his captors had crumpled it up like a toy made of tin. Maybe it wouldn't have killed the thing, but he figured he could do a lot of damage to it. All he knew right now was that he had to do whatever was necessary to keep it away from Raven.

The creature laughed as it lunged at Brady again, forcing him backwards. He windmilled his arms as he narrowly missed dropping backwards into the pool. He jumped to one side and moved until he didn't risk a dunking he knew he wouldn't survive.

Damn, he really hated being on the defensive! He was good at hand-to-hand combat, but this kind of fighting was new to him. Give him a crazed terrorist any day. Them he could handle. He yelped when a line of blood appeared across his chest.

"You son of a bitch, this is my favorite shirt!" he shouted.

Pahso smirked. "After I have cut you into tiny pieces and feed you to my pet, your shirt will not matter." A flick of the blade caught Brady's cheek leaving behind another stinging line of blood.

"Sword!" Raven shouted, throwing out both hands in Brady's direction.

He almost fell over when a flash of fiery light revealed a sword in his right hand. He shot her a quick mental thank you before grinning at Pahso.

"The female cannot do that!" the creature screamed, stamping its foot in fury. "This is our battle."

"If he is to fight for me, he will fight by our rules!" Raven argued. "I can provide him with comparable weapons. This will be a fair fight, Pahso!"

"I don't think shit for brains knows what a fair fight is." Brady threw a smirk at the creature.

Brady swung the sword in a wide arc, hearing a faint singing in the blade. There was no doubt there was a dark magic in the metal and the last time he hefted anything close to a sword was when he was eight and pretended to be a Jedi Knight with his light saber. But he'd been in trickier situations and gotten out of them in one piece. Of course, then it didn't have to do with his soul or a devilish creature. He felt Raven's eyes on him, sensed the fear and something warmer that he was afraid to put a name to. "Hey, shit for brains, you don't look so brave now that we're on even footing," he taunted.

Big mistake. This time when the creature lunged, he didn't stop. It was pure reflex that had Brady lift his heavy sword to use as a shield. The force of the blade striking his sent a vibration through his body. It was sheer force of will that kept his hands wrapped around the hilt and not dropping it. He pushed back, wielding the sword, managing to slice the creature's arm. Black blood streamed downward in a thick mass.

Rage shot through its gold eyes and it lunged again, swinging wildly but with the purpose of hacking Brady to bits. Brady ignored the aches and pains and fought to keep the deadly blade away from any part of his body.

*****

Raven fought the circle holding her, but Pahso knew what he was doing. As long as the circle was invoked, she couldn't move outside of it and was effectively in his power. She had hated him Below and up here she tipped into revulsion. All Pahso wanted was her family connections, so he could move up the ladder and eventually destroy Shar. That was the piece of knowledge she'd used to gain her vacation along with his promise he'd hold off any betrothal announcement between her and Pahso. Shar hadn't wanted to believe her, but he agreed to investigate the matter. She thought once she made it up here, she would have the chance to fully escape. Instead, it appeared all she did was endanger the lives of the people here, no matter that Pahso claimed they weren't harmed, but Brady was definitely in danger of losing his life. Because of the circle, she couldn't fight by his side, but she was able to provide him with a proper weapon. She felt dampness on her cheeks and lifted her fingers to touch the tears trickling from her eyes. It had happened before when she explained everything to him. Tears were unknown to her and now she had cried twice. If only Brady knew what a gift he'd given her.

She remained quiet because she feared words would distract Brady. She knew Pahso was lethal with a sword. She just hoped that Brady would survive, but if he didn't, she did know that she would do everything in her power to ensure Pahso was destroyed.

*****

Brady felt his strength slipping. A severe beating tended to do that. So far, he'd managed to protect himself from major damage although that last cut burned like a son of a bitch. He hated to think what might coat that blade.

As he backed up, looking for any kind of advantage, he caught a glance of Raven, trapped in some kind of hellish circle. She looked scared to death and not at all like someone who might see this kind of combat on a regular basis. But what did it were the tears tracking her cheeks.

No way he would allow that *thing* to touch her. He dug down deep for strength and somehow managed to find it. Cuts and bruises didn't seem to hurt as much as he lifted the sword higher and roared a form of battle cry as he surged forward. There was no hesitation as he swung the sword in an arc that connected with Pahso's neck, the sound like a knife slicing through a juicy melon. The creature's eyes momentarily widened then turned a flat black color before his head tipped to one side and his body to the other. Black blood bubbled out of his body in a steaming mass just before it burst into flames.

Brady looked at the other creatures. He hefted the blade, broadening his legs in a battle-ready stance as he waited for them to rush him and finish the job their boss had started. Instead, they disappeared in a puff of red smoke.

"Brady!" Freed from her circle, Raven toward him but before she could reach him, another creature appeared and kept its arms around her waist. "No!" She hit it with her fist.

"Get your paws off her!" Brady roared, advancing on it.

"Brady, don't."

He spun around, his sword ready. Shar, in another immaculate suit, faced him.

"He's one of mine," the Dark Lord assured him.

"Then tell it to let her go," Brady snarled, refusing to back down.

"Don't hurt him!" Raven yelled, struggling to get free but having no success.

Shar faced his half-sister. "You cannot stay here, Raven."

"Yes, I can!"

He shook his head. If Brady didn't know better, he'd even think regret was written on the creature's face, but what Dark Lord knows the meaning of regret? The kind of regret Brady sensed he was going to feel for a very long time if he couldn't find a way out of this for the both of them.

"I killed your choice of mate for her," he stated. "That makes her mine."

"In your world, perhaps, but not in ours. Raven comes from a very strong lineage," Shar explained. "One that doesn't include a human."

Raven pushed against her captor's arms. "I mean it, Shar, do not hurt him!"

"Silly female, I don't intend to harm, Brady. He kept watch over you while you were here and he has been suitably compensated for that task."

"Take the fucking money. I don't want it." Brady had a very sick feeling about this. That he just might lose this particular battle. He'd fought for his life many times, but he'd never fought for someone who mattered to him as much as Raven did. And now he would lose her because of a damn political battle. He cleared the emotion clogging his throat as he prepared to do something he'd never done before. Beg... "Please, leave her here with me. I will do anything. Give up anything."

Shar shook his head. "This isn't her world and while you have the heart of a warrior, you still wouldn't fit into ours. You have something we don't have, Brady. You have a conscience."

"I meant what I said. You can't take her," Brady growled, holding the blood-smeared sword away from his side. If he had to give up his life for Raven, he would do it without a second thought.

Rather than growling back or smirking like that damn Pahso had, Shar's expression still held regret as if he truly felt sorry for Brady.

"I had no idea this would happen, Brady, or I would have found someone else to look after Raven," Shar told him. "Emotion isn't understood in our world. What you two had was up here. If it will make it easier, I can wipe away memories of her."

"You do and you'll find your head in the same condition Pahso's was." He wasn't used to experiencing fear, but he sure felt it now. Then he looked at Raven, still help captive by the guard. No one's hands belonged on her but his.

Brady advanced on the creature, ignoring the guards' low murmuring that signified they wouldn't mind turning this into a bloodbath.

Shar looked at the guard holding Raven and snapped his fingers. At that same instant, Raven's eyes widened to saucer-size.

"*No!*" she screamed, realizing his intent.

In a heartbeat, Raven, Shar and his guards were gone. Even the corpses of the creatures Brady and Raven had killed were gone, not leaving even a hint of the death and destruction. The silver sword disappeared from Brady's hand and he stood there alone, the artificially slumbering guests and staff ignorant of the slaughter that had taken place on the serene island.

And Brady, the guy who never flinched from danger, who faced death with a big shit-eating grin, threw back his head and let loose the roar of an animal who'd lost his mate. When his throat could no longer work, he slid bonelessly to the ground with the stark realization he'd just lost what mattered to him most.

Epilogue

If misery had a name, it would be Brady Hayes.

It had been three months since he got back from the resort and not one day passed that Raven's name didn't enter his mind or her voice didn't haunt his dreams.

True to his word, Shar's payment was in Brady's bank account, but he hadn't touched a penny. If there were a way to return the money he would have done it along with a suggestion of where Shar could shove the money. He turned down jobs and spent his days at the beach. There he would watch the surfers and imagine one of them was Raven riding the waves.

And each night, he'd drunk himself into a stupor so he could sleep.

In a word, he was a fucking mess.

It hadn't made matters any easier when his pals decided to do their best to pull him out of his apathy after he returned from the resort.

After Raven was taken there was no reason for him to remain. What surprised him the most was all the guests and staff waking up without any idea a demon war had been waged there. The scary part was that there was no record of a Raven registered there. When he broke into her room, he found no hint of her ever staying there. It was as if she never existed except in his memories and his heart. Within an hour of Raven's disappearance, Brady felt a horrible burning on his ass and discovered the mark was gone. Damn thing hurt more coming off than going on. With nothing there to hold him, he boarded the next plane out.

When the doorbell pealed, he was tempted to ignore it, but past experience warned him the pounding on the wood would come next and he'd think about shooting his friends, no matter how good their intentions were. He pushed himself off the couch and stalked to the door, throwing it open with the intent of causing serious pain on whoever dared disturb him.

"Look, I have no desire to get drunk, get laid or..." he growled. He stopped short at the woman standing before him.

"Are you sure about that second item?" Raven asked in a low voice that he swore held a hint of uncertainty.

He didn't hesitate in hauling her into his arms and holding her so tight, she squeaked.

"Breathe! Brady, I have to breathe!"

He loosened his hold but not by much as he leaned back far enough to study her. Blonde hair, blue eyes, big smile and three months later she still had her tan. Her white knit top barely covered her flat belly and the scrap of denim disguised as a skirt showed off her long legs that he recalled wrapped beautifully around him when he made love to her.

"Why? How?" He shook his head. "Tell me this isn't a drunken man's dream."

"Then you don't mind I showed up here?"

"Hell, no!" Brady whooped loud and long, swinging her around in a tight circle. Her laughter was music to his ears. He kicked the door shut and swung her up into his arms, carrying her over to the couch. He settled her on his lap, his hands tightly holding hers. "I don't know and I don't care how you got away from there. You're not going back."

Her smile trembled at his fierce declaration. "Do you mean it? You really are happy to see me?"

"Hell, yes! You belong with me and this time he's not taking you from me. We'll find a place on the beach where you can surf all you want and we can dance naked in the moonlight. But I want you someplace safe, so they can't ever come after you again." He tracked every feature. For once, his memory hadn't faulted him. "I'll find someone who can help me with that. I promise there won't be any surprise visits from the family."

Raven placed her hand against his cheek. He swore her face fairly glowed. "I have something for you." She reached into her pocket and pulled out a black envelope, handing it to him.

He accepted it warily. His name was written in bold purple script across the front. "This isn't going to explode or melt me, is it?"

She shook her head.

He tore one edge off and watched a folded piece of black paper slide out. He unfolded it and stared at the neatly printed lines.

Brady,

You have given my half-sister a gift that she would never have found down here. It is something found among your kind, not ours. Therefore, if your feelings for her have not changed, which I have an idea they haven't, then she is yours.

If that is the case, naturally, some changes will have to be made, as Raven will not be allowed to return to her home. With the next dawn all memory of her past life will be erased with new memories of a human upbringing to take their place. Raven will be as human as you are. And by your accepting my half-sister as your mate, your memories of your meeting and all that happened at the resort will also be erased and new ones in their place.

If your feelings have changed, Raven will leave and you will never see her again and all memory of her will be gone. Don't consider this a threat. I'm only doing what would be best for you both. We don't use the L word down here. At least, not the L word you appear to feel for Raven. But I would say that is the L word Raven would use in regards to you and I sense that is the word you associate with her.

The decision is yours.
Shar,

Lord of the Dark

P.S. This letter will disintegrate the moment you finish reading it.

Brady yelped when the paper and envelope burst into flame and reduced to a fine ash.

He looked up at Raven. "Do you know the contents of this letter?" And received a barely perceptible nod. "Did you honestly think I wouldn't still want you? Hell, Raven, I haven't forgotten a word, a gesture, since that day we met." His throat felt suddenly raw with emotion. "I even went back to the portal, but it was closed."

She sucked in a deep breath at the realization he had tried to come after her. "It was just as well. Entering it without an invitation would have sliced you to ribbons."

"You won't miss your old life? Your relatives?"

She shook her head. "Shar finally came to realize that I no longer belonged there." She uttered a watery chuckle. "I think it was all the tears. They don't understand that kind of tears down there."

"And Shar's dreams of using you to further his political dynasty?"

"Did I tell you I have two thousand half-sisters? He can choose one of them." She leaned forward and buried her face against the curve of his neck. She inhaled the warm musky scent of his skin. "We don't dream, but down there I dreamed of you every night. I told Shar he would have to destroy me, because I would never do what he wished. If he thought Pahso's destruction was bad, he hadn't seen anything yet."

Brady's chuckled rumbled deep within his chest as he hugged her tightly again. "My bloodthirsty Hellion Barbie!"

"You fought Pahso for me. You risked your life when you didn't have to." She pressed butterfly kisses all over his face.

Her wiggling in his lap quickly had his dick standing at attention and ready for action. A less than subtle hint Brady wasn't about to ignore.

"You know what?" He stood up, easily hefting her up in his arms as he carried her to his bedroom. "Dawn will be here in roughly sixteen hours, twenty-two minutes." He stopped and looked down into her upturned face. One he intended to look at for the hundred or so years if he could have his way. "Remember that thing you did?"

One eyebrow arched upward. "Thing?"

"That tingly thing where you-ah—" he ducked his head and whispered in hear ear.

"Oh, that." She ran her fingertips across the back of his neck. A flash of red and black trailed down his back then moved around to his front.

"Whoa, Mama. Yeah, that." He carried her into the bedroom and dropped her unceremoniously on the bed then stretched out beside her. Within seconds, she was stripped of her clothing and his t-shirt and shorts lay on the floor. Raven's giggle soon morphed into a breathy sigh. "You don't think Shar could have let you keep that skill?"

"Brady!" She reached circled his dick with her fingers and gently squeezed.

He closed his eyes and just wallowed in the sensation of her hands on him. "Then, again, I'm sure we'll do just fine without it."

Other Titles by Dakota Cassidy

Sexylips66

Mac To the Future
By
Dakota Cassidy

Dedication

To the readers, please note that my portrayal of romantic cover models at large is a humorous poke at the lighter side of a pageant such as this and certainly in no way reflects the true character of the gentlemen that I've encountered at many a convention.

For Sean, RT 2005 cover model and contestant extraordinaire. Funny, smart, swoon worthy, but most importantly, a gentleman. Thanks for the inspiration for this particular character, but a deeper gratitude still, for showing us jaded women that men who truly love their wives *do* exist. And last, but never least, Maura, a bang up plotter and one of the nicest ladies I know!

Dakota ☺

Chapter One

"Jayyyyniiieeeee!"

If the face jock whined just one more time, Jaynie Renfro was going to puncture her own damn eardrums with the nearest sharp object. What a God awful bunch of man-girls. She cringed as cover model contestant and all 'round bloody pain in the ass, Douglas Athen's, voice tore through her overworked brain like a dentist's drill.

"Jaynie, I neeeeed hair gel. If I don't get hair gel my hair won't stand up properly and it would just be ugly. I'm telling you, that stupid Adam took it," Douglas whined at her as his chiseled, man-boy face collapsed and distorted into a pout.

Jaynie rolled her eyes.

For fuck's sake.

Hair gel?

Naturally, every metrosexual's worst nightmare was a day without sticky shit only girls should be allowed to purchase at the beauty supply store "You can use mine, Doug. How's that?" Jaynie was being magnanimous in her offer, but whatever it took to appease the pretty boy, she was on it

That was, after all, her job.

Douglas's boy next door, blue eyes grew wide. "Are you kidding?" He tugged upward on a piece of flaxen hair, highlighted for just this occasion, with two fingers and said, "You use *cheap* product, Jaynie. I wouldn't be caught dead using your stuff."

Jaynie's right eye twitched as it was wont to do more often than not since this week began. *Cheap beats the part where you're shit outta luck now don't it, man-girl?*

She was sick and freakin' tired of placating these men just because they were contestants in her mother's magazine pageant.   Working for her mother at *That's Amore* was a less than desirable gig come this time of year.

Because Jaynie was the sorry ass who got stuck with the *That's Amore* cover model contestants.

All of them wanted to win the coveted role of the *That's Amore* hottie 2006 along with the cash and a cover feature on a romance novel.

Jaynie didn't even *like* romance novels so how she was roped into this was beyond her. It was a bit more high profile than her real role as Editor in Chief of her mother's stupid magazine.

Douglas huffed at her with clear impatience.

Arghhh. These men—or maybe boys was a better term—were nothing short of divas and they grew worse as the years passed. Or maybe Jaynie was just growing weary of the long hours her job required and the demanding insistence of her mother the tyrant.   Well, maybe tyrant was harsh.   Driven probably better suited her and she'd turned *That's Amore* into a huge success as a result of that drive and her love of a good romance novel. Widowed now for ten years, her mother's passion was her magazine.

With a sigh, she caught Douglas giving her the eyeball.

He continued to give Jaynie the "look"

They were more trouble than toddlers, these models. Hell, at least toddlers couldn't *speak,* and if you gave them a Happy Meal they went away.

Jaynie shuffled her clipboard with the list of "needs" the contestants had and successfully dropped everything else she'd slung in her shoulder bag onto the floor.   She bent to gather the oodles of crap these men needed to survive a day.

Douglas stood staring down at her and tapping his toe.

Jaynie closed her eyes and clenched her teeth. Her head throbbed.

"M'lady, allow me to assist you in gathering your belongings," a smooth, accented voice called from above.

A ripple of a tingle slid up Jaynie's spine as Mac, one of the contestants for the annual *That's Amore* pageant, stooped to assist her in picking up her bag's contents. Jaynie looked up to protest, but she couldn't speak when Mac's deep green gaze met hers.

This must end, Jaynie Renfro.

No thinking about bagging the contestants.

Absolutely none.

Nada.

Stop those heinous, lust-filled thoughts that have plagued you since you met Robin Hood, this instant.

Oh, if only she could, but Jaynie spent far too much of her time daydreaming about Mac's hair and how her fingers twitched to touch the silken length of it. All the women, readers and writers alike, were atwitter over Mac's hair. It was simply the finishing touch on a man who was making her tongue stick to the roof of her mouth. His chestnut locks were long, well below his shoulders, and so shiny you could see your own reflection. Today, he wore it tethered back with what looked like a scrap of muslin.

Mac looked at her with questioning eyes and smiled that white grin any orthodontist would shed tears over. He cocked an eyebrow and waited for Jaynie to accept his offer of help. "M'lady?"

Mac's accent was fake, Jaynie reminded herself. It was all an act for the lust-crazed women at the conference. So she could just quit melting like so much butter in the frying pan of sexuality. As if Mac's accent being fake was any consolation for him being beyond smokin' hot and well on his way to a ten on the wet panties scale of sizzling.

He could fake *whatever* he wanted with Jaynie.

Center…focus…find your happy place or any place that doesn't involve hurling this sex God to the ground and rattling his bones. "Thanks, Mac. I appreciate it, but I can get it."

His long, tapered fingers shuffled her many papers around as he looked upward at Douglas. "'Tis a sorry day when a *man* cannot lend a damsel in distress his services," Mac scoffed with a deep growl.

Yeah, take that, face jock. Jaynie put her hand on Mac's strong forearm, rippled with muscle, and snatched it back. No touching the nice contestant. Touching led to naughty thoughts that had absolutely nothing to do with hair gel and far too much to do with slippery oils

Well, Jaynie was sure she could find a use for hair gel in her sexual fantasy about Mac, given proper time and just one freakin' moment alone.

Stopping now, Jaynie.

"Look, Sir Lancelot," Douglas sputtered indignantly, "I'm busy and I don't have all day to stand around. Quit showing off that fake, Renaissance fair, bullshit accent. Jaynie has stuff to do for *me*."

Mac rose with a slow, deliberate movement, towering over Douglas who was rather short in comparison. His wide chest heaved and his jaw, square and angular, clenched.

Jaynie could smell the menace in the air and she popped up between them in her haste to keep any controversy from occurring. "Douglas, you'll get your hair gel. Now, you both have things to do. Scurry off and do cover model things."

Oh, God, the smell of him was going to consume her loins and set them ablaze like an inferno when he leaned over her and stuck his face in Douglas's.

"Thou dost not wish to antagonize me, pretty one. I will slit your throat like that of a pig," he threatened with a clenched-jaw hiss

Hookay, no slaughtering of the pretty boys. Jaynie turned and placed her hand on Mac's chest and her fingers trembled.

Oh, oh, oh…it was *hard.*

Good adjective, Jaynie.

Hard.

That certainly was an adequate description for Mac's chest.

It was more than hard. It was—was… well, it was just fine and she refused to give any more thought to her head resting on it while lying upon fine Egyptian cotton sheets in a canopied bed, with a soft, tropical breeze blowing in a sheer curtained window, as she rubbed massage oil all over his big, hot, hunky body

So there.

Jaynie pulled her hand away from the only chest with hair in the entire contest. "Please, Mac, I'm fine, really. You need to get ready for the party tonight and I need to get Douglas some hair gel."

Douglas stuck his tongue out at Mac in a neener, neener kind of way, making Jaynie shake her finger at him in reprimand. Keeping ten men on their best behavior was like corralling greased cats. "Stop it, Douglas, now!" Jaynie scolded. "Shoo-shoo. Go wax your eyebrows or something."

Douglas skulked off with a sashay of his tightly packed butt.

"'Tis my belief that *Douglas,*" Mac said his name like he was the anti-Christ, "would far rather play with dolls than attend soirees filled with the likes of women."

Oh, alright, so Douglas was gay. Everyone knew it and there was nothing wrong with it. It sure hadn't kept the women attending the conference from shaking their groove thing with him at the nightly parties.

Jaynie groaned.

Mac picked up the rest of her things scattered about the floor and handed them to her. She pinched the bridge of her nose. Jesus, she had a headache.

"You are troubled by the pain in your head?" Mac's apparent concern laced his deep, honeyed tone.

I'm troubled with a pain in my ever lovin', cover model ass, is what I'm troubled with. "I'm fine. Nothing a little nap won't cure."

Mac grinned. His just-right lips curved into a smile that made the gleam in his brown eyes wicked.

Nap equals bed, Jaynie.

Had she just mentioned the notion that a bed might suit her purposes in front of the eye candy? The eye candy she'd been drooling privately — and okay — not so privately over for an entire week?

Sheeit.

It seemed no matter what she said, it had a sexual connotation she'd far rather keep to herself.

Oy.

She needed to get a grip and thwart all of this cover model lust. Not once in the several years she'd done this for her mother had she ever — not ever — not even once, lusted for the pretty boys and she couldn't afford to now.

The cover models were strictly forbidden, not only from the guests of the conference, but also from the staff.

Jaynie was the staff and her mother would have a chicken if she whiffed a hint of sexual harassment.

"Jaynie?" Mac cupped her elbow, looked down at her and brought her back to the present. "M'lady, are you well? Shall I escort you to your room?"

The heat of his hand, coupled with the mere scent of him, had Jaynie's head swimming. She cracked her neck.

Oh, no.

No.

No rooms.

No room going.

No darkened hallways alone with Mac on the way to the getting there either.

No darkened hallways with Mac pressed flush to a wall as she climbed him like Mt. Everest.

Nope.

Jaynie shook her head and moved as fast as she could on her damned high heels, away from the shelter of Mac's big body and out of the lobby of the hotel.

Shaky legs carried Jaynie to her suite of rooms, where she unlocked the door and collapsed on her bed.

Closing her eyes, she tried to block the image of Mac from her thoughts.

The rush of warmth that assaulted her loins when she thought of him wasn't easily assuaged.

Her loins were really becoming a problem.

*****

The heavy beat of dance music pounded in Jaynie's head as she encouraged the models to dance with the patrons of the convention. It was the first party of the weeklong festivities and always awkward for everyone involved. By week's end, it was Jaynie's experience, that libidos would surface, the word "inhibition" would become devoid in most of the guests' vocabulary and all this awkwardness would fade to a vague memory.

In other words, nearly every chick attending the convention would go cover model hog wild.

Yay for straining thighs and ripped abs.

Some were more restrained than others, but many exhibited behavior they would swear, by all that was holy, was so unlike them.

Shit, Jaynie would never forget that very lame excuse coming from the lips of a big-time author when she was caught in a more than compromising position with a cover model two years ago.

Jaynie had gotten the reaming of the millennium from her mother for that mess because she was responsible for the cover models.

It was a precarious balance of hormones and testosterone Jaynie dealt with on a yearly basis. So she kept an eagle eye on the men and the convention goers.

Her eagle eye spotted the men clustered together in a small pack, ignoring the guests.

For crap's sake. What was the matter with these men tonight? It was a dance not a round of "*Jeopardy*".

These women paid good money, not only to meet and mingle with their favorite romance novelists, but to ogle some good old fashioned hard bodies.

Sometimes, the hard bodies weren't quite sure how to handle that and it was Jaynie's job to help them. She ran a hand over her cocktail dress and slipped into the group with a confident stride.

Igor, the tall Slavic transplanted from Russia via Idaho, looked offended. "Ah, Jaynie. Did you see what zey do to me?" he asked, his accent more pronounced due to his distress.

Jaynie shook her head at his sharply angled face. "No, what did zey—er, I mean *they* do to you, Igor? For that matter, who are they?"

Igor's face grew hard and he lifted his chin with haughty disdain, crossing strong forearms over his chest. "Zey are heathens Zeeze women, zey squeezed my buttocks!"

Jaynie fought a giggle and covered her mouth with her hand. "I know, Igor, and what should you do when they do that? Do you remember?"

He gave a curt nod. "Dah, I remember. I tell them zey must not touch ze package."

Jaynie rolled her head on her neck. "Well, sort of. You can politely divert them to other things, like conversation. You just have to be quick, Igor. Now, please, go mingle and make nice. Those are your votes out there." Jaynie pointed to the sea of gyrating bodies costumed, perfumed and salivating for the men to join them.

"Yo, Jaynie?"

Jaynie turned to find Frank, dark and slick, the Italian Stallion from Brooklyn, behind her, also looking very unhappy. "Yo, Frank, whassup?" Jaynie mocked, because she really couldn't help it. Frank's New York accent was thick and his grey matter even thicker. He was the most buff of the crew this year. His abs sizzled like a steak in a frying pan and his thighs rippled even when he was standing still.

But Frank wasn't very bright...

Oh, alright, he wasn't at all bright and he tried way too hard to impress the women around him

Even Douglas made fun of Frank. If Douglas made fun of you — you had to know you had more issues than a *National Geographic* two-year subscription

Frank pushed through his fellow contestants. "Ya know, Jaynie. I been tryin' ta tell dese guys dat it's all about how ya deal wit da broads." Frank stood in front of her, his finely sculpted body literally glowing in the darkened ballroom. His "tan in a bottle" neared perfection, but for the streak on the collar of his white shirt.

Jaynie nodded and smiled absently. "I know you do, Frank. I appreciate it."

Frank used two fingers to point at his eyes, making a slow circle around his face with them, and said, "Dis is how I see it It's all about my *raaaawww sexuality*, ya know? Women can see it in my eyes. I ooze it and dey love me. I tried tellin' 'em dat, but who listens to me, ya know?" Frank shrugged the wide girth of his shoulders and rolled his dark brown eyes. Raw, sexual eyes, that is.

Ya know...

Ugh, Frank's *rawwww sexuality* was going to be the death of Jaynie. What Frank failed to comprehend was the entire convention thought he was an utter joke every single time he opened his mouth. He was very pretty to look at, in a Vinny Barbarino way, but dumb as a stump and his "wise guy/NY cabbie" accent wasn't helping him in the serious department.

Jaynie sighed. The week was only beginning and already her work was more than cut out for her. She turned to Frank and slapped a smile she'd give a toddler who needed appeasing on her face. "Okay, Frank, well, how about you show dese guys what it's all about, huh?" Jaynie mimicked Frank's finger gesture and circled her face with slow precision, centering on her eyes. "Go ooze, er, drip." Jaynie shook her head and started over. "Go whatever all of that raaaaawwwwww sexuality for me on the dance floor, k?"

Frank smiled his brilliantly toothy, white-capped grin and set out to show the others what a real ladies' man was. He strutted to the dance floor with exaggerated thrusts of his lean hips and did his best stripper imitation minus clothing removal.

No clothes parted the bodies of the buff and brawny. Jaynie made damn sure of it Her mother would have her head if a contestant messed with a reader at the convention.

Mac stepped forward, tall and dressed in leather pants and a black T-shirt, parting the crowd of the other models with ease and presence of strength.

Jaynie fought to maintain her now shallow breathing.

"'Tis done like this, lads," Mac said, pulling Jaynie to him, clasping her hips to his and whisking her off to the dance floor.

Oh-my-God.

If his body was any harder, he'd be the side of a mountain

Jaynie sucked in a breath of cleansing air. In with the good, out with the overactive libido.

"Dost thou fare well, M'lady?" Mac asked from above her.

She stared into his chest. "Thou dost just fine, thank you," she muttered, holding her neck stiffly erect in order to avoid resting her head on his chest. Finer than fine, in fact.

Mac pulled her hips to his and molded them with hands that splayed across her lower back. They fit together like two pieces of a jigsaw puzzle and this made for discomfiting thoughts.

Warm, okay, maybe they were hot, dirty thoughts Warm would imply her veins weren't sizzling.

"Tell me about Jaynie," he inquired against her ear, his breath warm and smelling of toothpaste, fanning her long hair

Jaynie has nothing to tell. If Jaynie were a smart girl, she'd shut up now. "What do you want to know?"

"What was it that brought you to this particular line of work?"

"My mother."

"Ahhhh, 'tis a difficult thing, working for one's relations," he said knowingly.

"'Tis, indeed," she joked, mocking his accent.

"I gather you are in the majority of those who believe my accent is false," he stated rather than asked.

"Well, isn't it? I mean, it's charming as all hell, but not even people from England say 'tis anymore. Not in this day and age, anyway. Though, I can tell you, the women are eating it up. So, if it helps you to be in character all the time, I'm cool with it," she said reassuringly. It was her job to pacify when necessary and if it made the trained seals perform, she was all for it. That just made her job easier.

"Excellent. 'Tis a fine day when the ladies are festive," he chuckled all smoky and resonant.

Oy.

Jaynie tried taking another deep breath, but it came out with a shuddering squeak. Her ribcage felt like a boa constrictor was wrapped around it, refusing to allow her to breathe easily when pressed up against Mac. "So, what made you decide to try out for the cover model pageant? The money?"

He threw his head back and laughed. "Shillings are not my motivation, I assure you, M'lady."

Since when wasn't twenty-five grand a good bit of shilling motivation? And what the hell *was* a shilling? "So, the money isn't your thing? What is? The attention?"

"'Tis a long tale, my arrival here. Let us just say this. I am here to claim what is *mine*." He said the word mine with such possessive ferocity, Jaynie felt that shiver wriggle up her spine again.

"Ahhh, you want to be on the cover of Lady Clarissa's next book, don't you?" Who didn't? To be picked for a cover on her book was to bask in the glow of romantic literature at its finest. Even if Lady Clarissa was a total biotch who wrote prose in shades of Barney purple.

His look was odd and the strange transformation happened rather suddenly, then was quickly replaced with a grin. "Indeed, 'tis a most coveted award, I would say. All the man-girls speak of it as though it were the fatted calf."

Yeah, the most coveted part was how Lady Clarissa would covet the model who won when the shoot for the cover was done. Lady Clarissa was, in a word, a real cover model 'ho. Okay, that was three words, but they fit Lady Clarissa to a T. She collected cover models like bunnies collected dust She was also mean and ornery and regretfully, one of her mother's best friends. But she couldn't tell Mac that. Her job wasn't to warn the pretty boys about their impending visit to boy-toydom. Tilting her head up, Jaynie caught him gazing at her and his hand caressed the swell of her hip with the slightest of movements while they swayed to the music. "What's your last name, Mac? All you put on your registration form was Mac. Is that like a gimmick? You know, like Fabio?"

"My full name is Cormac. Alas, Mac seems to have caught on."

"Cormac is your last name?"

"No. 'Tis my given name at birth."

"Er, then what's your last name?"

"I have none. I am simply Cormac of..." His sentence trailed off when the music turned from the slow tempo to an upbeat tune.

Realizing where she was and who she was with, Jaynie placed a hand on Mac's chest and let it rest for the briefest of moments before forcing herself to drop it to her side It was one thing to get the crowd moving, but quite another to linger and she was doing a helluva linger.

The crowd swelled around them and gyrating bodies replaced the swooning couples. Jaynie stuck out her hand and he took it, gallantly kissing the back of it. "Thanks, Mac with no last name I think we got the crowd moving. Let the games begin," she said with a giggle, before turning and with a brisk walk, heading to the outer edge of the ballroom.

Her hand tingled where Mac's lips had pressed against her heated skin and her heart crashed in an unfamiliar, erratic rhythm.

What the frig had gotten into her? She never dabbled with the cover models. Not in the eight years she'd been assigned this laborious task. They usually ended up boring her, or making her wish she'd babysat more as a teenager, so her herding skills weren't so sorely lacking now when she needed them most.

But Mac was different. He wasn't anything like the hundreds of contestants before him.

He didn't seem to care much about his chest hair not being waxed or doing two hundred lunges before the break of dawn so his thighs would be pumped up. He slept in, ate cheeseburgers like they were filet mignon and silently mocked the other men with a look of dry amusement on his face.

His disinterest baffled her. It intrigued her and again, she wondered why she found him so damned sexy. He might not be as pretty as the gelled, spray tanned hunks she was used too, but he was the talk of the convention with his chiseled good looks and his lean, sun weathered body.

He behaved as if the attention meant nothing to him, but every woman wanted a piece of Mac.

Jaynie wanted a piece of Mac, too.

A Big Mac, hold the pickles, hold the lettuce.

Just the Mac, thank you.

Oh, God. Had she just admitted that?

No pieces of Mac.

Ever.

Nocovermodelsnocovermodlesnocovermodels.

Chapter Two

"Where are ye, my good man? How would ye expect me to find ye if ye do not reveal your whereabouts?"

The sigh of exasperation in Mac's head was sharp, ping-ponging around his head.

"If I had eyes, surely by now, dost thou not think I would have told ye my location?"

Mac sighed too, letting his chest expand and deflate. 'Twas a most frustrating predicament to be in when one could not find the clues one needed to solve the mystery. Yet, that very mystery spoke in his head with the clarity of another body in the room. 'Twas frustrating, indeed. He was close. He could feel it in his warrior gut that he was close. "Aye, my good man," he acknowledged. "I followed your voice here in the hopes that I might find ye waiting for me Your tone is strongest when I round the corner of this hallway at the inn."

"'Tis a hotel, Cormac. Would thou please, please remember the language of our time?"

Mac paced the length of the cream-colored carpeting in the *hotel* room and ran a finger over his forehead, placing pressure on his right temple. "Forgive me, for I know not what I speak when I am skulking about another's hotel room, looking for you in dark corners," he all but shouted to no one. Sometimes, it became confusing when he had to remember the popular catch phrases of the time.

"Must ye bellow? Aye, Cormac. That temper is what always brings you to — to throw down!"

"To what?"

Again, the sigh of exasperation rang in Mac's head.

"'Tis an expression, lad. It means come to blows, Cormac. Your temper is what leads us to more trouble than we must involve ourselves in because you cannot shut yon trap!"

Mac laughed. "I do have what is called a short fuse, aye?"

"Aye," the voice in his head acknowledged.

A jiggle at the doorknob interrupted their banter. Mac hit the floor and rolled under the bed with the stealth of a cat chasing a tin foil ball. Egad! He did not need such interference when he was so close. It infuriated him to almost taste victory on the tip of his tongue yet, have it elude him once again. Balling his fists, he thanked the god's that the bed had room enough under it to fit his bulk.

Dainty feet with red tipped toes padded back and forth across the carpet and he heard the water run briefly before the occupant of the hotel room turned the lights off with a sigh and settled on the bed.

Her scent wafted to his keen nose. He knew that scent. The light fragrance of lilacs on an early spring day, mingled with the tart aroma of freshly peeled oranges.

Aye, he knew that scent.

It was the scent of a woman that was driving him mad with want and creating havoc with his nether parts. It was the scent of a woman that piqued his interest and made him smile like a daft schoolboy.

It was the scent of the lovely, overworked, underappreciated Jaynie.

His cock rose to salute her from his cramped quarters under the bed. Mac appreciated Jaynie, every womanly curve and luscious plane of her. He wanted to show that appreciation by wrapping her silken strands of chestnut brown hair around his fingers when he tugged her head back to nibble at the sweet skin of her neck as she arched into him, willing and pliant.

He wanted to appreciate every last ivory inch of her body.

However, he could not deviate from his course.

Her even breathing told him that she slept and with painstaking increments, he slid from under the bed.

Popping his head up over the edge, Mac eyed her sleeping form, supple, full, her breasts rising and falling with each small intake of breath. The stream of moonlight from the still open curtains illuminated her pale skin and the gleam of her dark locks against the white of the sheet on the bed

Gods forgive him, his cock burned with longing for her. His tongue itched to taste the sweet lips of her femininity.

"*My, man!*" the fierce whisper in his head echoed with insistence. "*Ye are only asking for trouble. Ye must not toy with this one, Cormac. She is not like the others. She is a* lady."

He shook his head. No, Jaynie was not like the other women. Women from many different times and many different places.

Jaynie was a rare delicacy of honesty and intelligence.

"*Do not play the games ye are noted for, my good man.*"

"Out of my head, damn ye! Give me a moment and I shall take my leave," he mumbled into the darkness. Mac felt the retreat of his oldest friend from the recesses of his brain and finally rose to stand over Jaynie.

She sighed into the darkness, raising an arm over her head, and the creamy swell of her breast lifted in her lace negligee.

Mac swallowed hard, staring down at her with the lust only the besotted knew.

"Mac…" she whispered, breathy and light.

His chest tightened when she spoke his name, making his innards shift. With a tentative finger, he trailed it over the plane of her cheek and Jaynie curled into it with another soft sigh. Again, his stomach twitched and his cock raged. His finger continued its voyage, along the length of her neck, between the valley of her breasts. Her skin was like the finest raw silk, lightly perfumed, and smooth.

Her breathing hitched when Mac circled beneath the curve under her breast and he found himself leaning into the arch her spine made.

Jaynie was a temptress, awake and in sleep, and Mac was finding it more and more difficult to keep his promise to leave.

Jaynie caught his hand with hers and surprised him by bringing it to her breast.

Surely, this was acquiescence he told himself. Or was that talking himself into believing what he chose to believe was acquiescence? Cormac of Anglesey never took what was not offered. He did not rape and pillage like his fellow warriors.

Jaynie rested her hand on top of his and squeezed it, forcing her breast into his palm.

Aye, this woman. She was not making reading her thoughts an easy go for him.

Jaynie tugged his forearm, pulling him to her, placing a hand on his chest, much the way she had when they had danced earlier this eve. It was warm, inviting, moving in a slow circle, creating friction that drew Mac to sit beside her.

She palmed his cheek, caressing his jaw when her eyes popped open and she smiled, slow and not a bit bewildered. "Oh, Mac," she whispered before closing them again and burrowing into the mattress, pulling Mac to lie across her chest.

Surely, that was acquiescence? Mac wasted no time molding her body to him, reveling in the way her full hips pressed to his.

Wrapping her arms around his neck, Jaynie fluttered another sigh against his ear and Mac was lost to the rhythmic press of her breasts against his chest. The fire in his loins swept over him and his manhood nestled between her thighs, throbbing for release from his constricting clothes He knew he must make her aware of his presence, for he was not the kind of man to take what was not offered.

"Jaynie," he murmured against the soft shell of her ear while she squirmed against him, wriggling her lower body against his. "Jaynie, 'tis I, Cormac. Do you wish to engage in the bed sport?"

"Oh, yesssssssss," she hissed back, pushing his T-shirt up and running her palms over his back, kneading Mac's flesh until he ground his teeth.

It was all the consent Mac needed. His hands moved with impatience over the satin of her negligee, pushing it off her shoulders and down past her hips. Smoothing a hand over the swell of her hip, Mac caressed the indentation of her waist, savoring her womanly curves while pushing her panties off and away. When he took her lips, he took them with gentle exploration, wanting to relish the full, pouty pillows he had spent far too much time wondering about. Yet, Jaynie opened her mouth fully to him, allowing his tongue to sweep over her teeth to meet hers in a duel of raspy silk.

Gods, her lips were indeed like pillows—just as he had imagined, soft, warm and tasting of fresh raspberries. Mac had to restrain himself from ravishing them, but Jaynie did not make the restraining easy. She lifted her upper body by clinging to his neck and swirled her tongue against his. The wet suction of their lips made Cormac forget everything else but the sweet sound of her mouth on his.

He could no longer resist cupping her breast, rolling a thumb over the rippled texture of her nipple until she moaned. Tearing his mouth from hers, Mac nipped at her neck, following a path of hot kisses until his tongue found her breast. He surrounded a nipple with his lips, enveloping it in the moist heat of his mouth, and his senses exploded. He fought to move with a slow pace, to relish the taste of her.

Jaynie arched into him with a jolt, threading urgent hands through Mac's hair.

He laved her nipple. Her whimper was desperate to his ears and invited him to explore further. His hands sought the smooth lips of her sex, tracing the crease where thigh and pelvis met, dipping between her flesh only to skim the hard nub of her clit.

Her cry echoed in the room and her breathing became sharp and ragged when her hands left his hair and clung to Mac's shoulders, gripping them, sinking her nails into the hard planes.

Mac spread her pussy with forefinger and thumb, flicking his middle finger along the wet lining of her sex while moving from her breast to kiss his way to her belly. He circled her navel, flicking his tongue over it and then resting his head at the top of her pelvis. With a deep inhale, Mac breathed Jaynie's scent while he moved lower to take his first sip of her. Rubbing a cheek against the soft flesh of her inner thigh, Mac continued to caress her.

Jaynie's hand reached down to find the outline of his mouth. She slipped a finger into it and Mac responded by suckling the digit. Bracketing his face, she guided his head to settle between her legs and Mac had his first glimpse of her sweet center. The moonlight cast a dim glow over the creamy wetness of her pussy and his tongue ached with the need to swipe at it. He wanted to watch as the pink entrance swallowed each inch of his cock. Bending his head, Mac inhaled again before flattening his tongue and taking a long taste of Jaynie.

Her gasp from above him was loud and punctuated the thick air as she lifted her hips and met his mouth.

Circling her clit, Mac teased it, slithering over it, swirling his tongue with rapid strokes. He could consume her flesh given the opportunity, drive into it with tongue and cock mindlessly forever, but alas, forever was not a gift he could offer. He must satisfy himself with the here and now, so Mac set about imprinting this memory—a remembrance to warm him on the nights when he could no longer be with Jaynie.

Her thighs came up to clamp around his neck and Mac dove deeper, stroking the juice of her pussy, placing his mouth flush to her and slipping a finger inside the tight recesses of her passage He felt her muscles tighten, flexing beneath his mouth and then heard the muffled scream of her climax. The ragged escape from her throat slipped into his ears, bringing with it the mingling of his satisfied groan

Her chest and belly heaved against his cheek and Mac tugged her to him, pulling upward until he enveloped her in his embrace. Jaynie buried her face in his neck, mumbling something he could not hear.

Mac stroked the long tresses of her hair until he realized her breathing was unusually slow. A quick glance at the beauty nestled in his arms told him she slept peacefully.

Was that not the luck that was his? A beautiful woman lay in his embrace and she slept the sleep of the dead.

It mattered not, he consoled his pulsing, burning cock. Jaynie was a treasure he would keep long after he was gone. He would pluck this moment out of his memory when he wished to savor the taste, sound and smell that was hers alone.

Mac's gut grew tight and his throat thick with regret.

Shaking his head, he slipped from the warmth of her lush body and attempted to shrug off the melancholy leaving Jaynie brought.

Leaving was what he did.

Leaving would be a task he would not cherish on his next leap in time.

Chapter Three

Jaynie woke with a startled grunt.

Naked.

The crisp sheets of the hotel bed rubbed against her skin.

Her *naked* skin.

Huh.

Had she been so tired she'd forgotten to throw on a nightgown?

God knew, those cover-boys could whip remembering to right out of her.

Running a hand over her tired eyes, her fingers sought her mouth. Her lips were a bit swollen and sensitive to her touch Probably came from biting them when Douglas whined about not having the proper hair product. Or maybe it was from fighting the urge to ravish Mac.

Jaynie's stomach clenched at the memory of his arms wrapped around her possessively, dancing to a tune she couldn't remember.

Oh, she was definitely slipping over the ledge of desperation. To long for a cover model was just this side of pathetic and something she'd never done in all her time as coordinator of the yearly pageant.

As she sat up, her nightgown, pale pink and rumpled, caught her eye. It lay at the end of her bed, reminding her that she had indeed at least thought to put it on. A frown creased her forehead and she stumbled out of bed to take a shower before beginning another long day filled with men who could out-whine a nursery school of small children.

Upon standing, Jaynie stretched, her limbs pleasantly sore and her ass panty-less.

Now this was odd. Where the hell was her underwear?

A momentary flash of hands, big and hard, clouded her vision, followed by the long silk of hair that she'd longed to touch, whispering along her thighs. She shrugged it off.

She'd been having naughty dreams and she knew exactly who the dreams were about...

Nice. That's very nice, Jaynie Renfro. You tart.

Grabbing the sheet, Jaynie wrapped it around her as though she could protect herself from the erotic thoughts she must have had before she fell asleep.

Today was the day she got a grip and quit thinking about Mac-O-licious. He was strictly off limits and all of this daydreaming, filled with girly sighs, would stop if it was the last thing she did.

Resolved to keep her promise to herself, Jaynie showered, dressed and stomped down to the hotel's workout room to find her wards.

Her gaze narrowed. Lady Clarissa had found her prey and she stalked it like a tiger pacing a cage with edgy restlessness.

Well, at least she had good taste.

She'd zeroed in on Mac and held him in her sights with the look of a rabid, fearless hunter.

Jaynie rolled her eyes when Mac's connected with hers, sorta desperate and cornered if you asked her, and looked away, turning her neck to the right and left to relieve the already mounting tension.

It was his own fault for being so — so — volcanically hot. It served him right if Lady Clarissa wanted him. He shouldn't wander around oozing bronzed muscles and reeking testosterone.

Sticking to her promise to herself, Jaynie made her way toward Igor whose attention was determinedly fixed on the weights he held in his hand. "Igor, you need to get ready for your private photo shoot. Gunther will be waiting and we all know how much he likes to wait," she prompted   Gunther   was   the   magazine's   official photographer

Igor dropped the heavy weights with a thunk and nodded. "Dah, I know of zis Gunther. He is, how do you say, fussee?"

Jaynie laughed her first genuine laugh of the day. "Yep, fussy would be the word. So, let's not let him get all riled up. Hurry up and shower and get moving."

Igor smiled back at her over his shoulder on his way out. "I sink you have other worries zan me, Jaynie," he reminded her with a chuckle and a nod in the direction of Lady Clarissa and Mac.

Wow, now that was fast. She had to give Lady Clarissa kudos for being able to stand so close to Mac without ripping her clothes off and hurling herself at him.

That was restraint honed to a fine point, if you asked Jaynie.

Lady Clarissa had Mac pressed tight in a corner, her round body dressed in a pair of trousers that were too tight and a shirt that left little to the imagination. She was giving him that predatory look Jaynie knew from vast experience.

Mac had a helpless look on his chiseled face when he crossed his arms protectively over his T-shirt clad chest. When he caught sight of Jaynie again, he mouthed, "Help me," to her and Jaynie knew if she didn't interfere, Lady Clarissa would make a fool of herself for the fifth year in a row. Her mother's magazine didn't need the bad press Lady Clarissa seemed so fond of evoking.

Taking another deep breath, Jaynie moved across the room and cleared her throat. "Lady Clarissa. How lovely to see you Can I interest you in a cup of coffee with me?" she asked, looping her arm through Lady Clarissa's and giving a gentle tug.

Clarissa's long red fingernails, attached to hands that were aging, pushed Jaynie's away. Her pinched face sent Jaynie a scathing look. "Not now, dear. Can't you see I'm busy?"

Mac slipped from her cloying grasp and backed away. "'Twas uh, eventful chatting with you, Lady Clarissa. I bid you good day." Mac made a gallant gesture with his hands and exited like the hounds of Hell nipped at his heels.

Jaynie bit her lip. "How 'bout that coffee, Clarissa?"

"I don't want coffee, Jaynie. I want *him*."

Yeah? And who here didn't? Jaynie tried one more time to appease her and her ginormous ego. "Well, Clarissa, I don't think that would be a good idea. You know the gossip mill and if the spotlight is on you, I know you'd want it to be in a favorable light." *Twit*.

Her perfectly painted lips curled into a sneer. "I've come to the point in my career where I care little about what others say. I do as I please and it would please me to *do* him." She crooked a finger to the corner of the workout room where Mac sat on the edge of the treadmill, obviously offended by Lady Clarissa's advances. "Now, scurry off and do Jaynie things like micro-manage those fags while I get a real man."

The nerve.

The absolute, pompous, arrogant nerve of her set Jaynie in motion. Her temper, for many years usually firmly in control, snapped like a thick rubber band She'd done this stupid competition for eight bloody years and she was tired of being treated like she was only the man-whore monger.

She did have a real job—a job that entailed skills far more complex than finding tanning gel and pacifying egomaniacal writers like Lady Libido here. Especially this writer who certainly wouldn't want the world to know her cousin Mildred in Passaic really wrote her books.

Oh, it was on now.

"Know what, Clarissa?"

Clarissa eyed her with disdain. Her icy blue eyes glinted irritation. "Haven't you gone to round up some hairspray yet?"

Between clenched teeth and a clamped jaw, Jaynie reiterated, "Know what, Clarissa?"

"What, Jaynie?" Clarissa fairly shouted in exasperation.

Jaynie leaned in with a whisper, keeping her voice to a murmur. "If I were you, I'd consider using the next advance you get for selling a book your cousin Mildred writes for you toward a boob job." Jaynie pointed at Clarissa's bountiful cleavage. "You're beginning to sag, Clarissa, and I'd doubt a man like Mac would be interested in saggy hardware. Oh, and while you're at it? I'd hit the drive thru at the botox clinic. You could use some eye work." Shove that up your not so tight ass, you Hemingway wannabe.

Clarissa's eyes narrowed to slits in her head and she gave Jaynie a tight smile. "Well, darling," she said slyly, her cat-like grin filled with malice. "At least I won't dry up and blow away from lack of male attention because I'm sucking up to my mother and chasing after her like some damned gopher!"

"Aye, M'lady. Jaynie is far from—what was it you said—drying up and blowing away? Indeed, she is quite the opposite," Mac said from behind the pair.

Jaynie whipped around to find him smiling a mischievous grin.

She shot him a look of confusion, followed by an angry glare. What the hell was he talking about and why the hell was he taking up for her?

"Really, Mac," Lady Clarissa preened, glowing with this new information. "How very interesting to hear that. Our little Jaynie isn't quite the innocent she'd like us all to believe, is what you're saying?" She turned to Jaynie and clucked her tongue. "Your mother will hear about this, Jaynie," she retorted before whisking away in a cloud of cloying perfume and hail damaged ass.

Jaynie watched Clarissa's retreating back and her temper, already stoked, flared. "Are you insane? Do you know what you just implied, Robin Hood? Lady Clarissa is, at this very moment, off spewing some bullshit to my mother about me and I'll have to sit and listen to at least an hour's worth of the good behavior speech."

Mac rocked back on his heels and looked down at her with those liquid, brown eyes teasingly "I spoke only the truth," he said with a solemn nod.

Fear of the unknown skittered along her forearms. "What?"

"I said there was no fear of you blowing up and drying away, M'lady."

"Drying up and blowing away," she corrected. "And what the hell are you talking about?"

"I speak of ye, Jaynie. You are most receptive to a man's embrace. I am witness to such. Lady Clarissa's implication was incorrect. Thou will not dry up, of this I assure thee."

Well, huh. She cocked her head and looked him straight in the eye. "What the frig are you talking about? How would you know anything about me and a man's embrace?"

For a moment, Mac seemed not to understand the question and then, a realization spread across his face. "Know ye not what I refer to, M'lady?"

"Um, no."

"How can this be?"

"How can what be?"

"That thou dost not remember."

"Remember what, for crap's sake?"

"Me, M'lady."

"You?"

"Indeed, me."

"You what?"

"Thou truly dost not remember?"

"Uh, no. Thou truly dost not. Thou thinks you're nuts."

"Nuts?"

"A big bowlful."

"I am not the man I thought."

"What man is that?"

"The man that leaves his lady with an impression."

"Of?"

"Of what?"

"What impression, Mac?"

"Why, a fulfilled one, M'lady."

"Fulfilled?"

"Indeed, glowing, in fact."

"Okay, let's stop this right now," Jaynie squawked, putting her hand up. "I have no clue what you mean by glowing or otherwise. What are you talking about? If you mean just being in your presence should make me glow, then you've got a bigger ego than even I can babysit."

"Hah! I do not mean my ego, Jaynie. I mean last night Do you not glow from our moments together?"

Ahhhh. He meant the dancing they'd done. Damn it, he was just like the rest of them. High on the cologne of *him*. His ego was as big as Douglas's or Frank's, he was just better at disguising it. One dance and he thought she was swooning and glowing over him. "Wow, I hate to burst your bubble, but one dance does not a glow make, King Arthur."

"Dance?"

"Yeah, *Lord of the Dance*. We danced last night. Or have you forgotten that in light of the fact that I'm sure you must have danced a thousand times more after I left?"

"I danced only with you, Jaynie." His eyes were warm when he spoke and his tone almost wistful.

"Then exactly what glow are we talking about here?"

"The glow of our bed sport."

Jaynie's hand flew to her lips, lips that she'd awoken to find swollen and chapped. "Explain bed sport, pal."

Taking her by the hand, Mac led her to the outside corner of the workout room where fewer people milled and Jaynie followed dumbly, apprehension pricking her awareness. "Last night we—well, we…how do you say it? We engaged in a *form* of bed sport."

Jaynie stretched a sore limb, dropping her clipboard to the ground. A limb that had been sore when she woke up and she'd attributed to stress. "Lemme get this straight. We engaged in this bed sport, as you call it. If we engaged in—in—whatever it was that we engaged in, how is it that I can't remember a thing?"

"Alas, I have no answer. I have never left a woman with such little impression," he mused, not entirely without that teasing grin of his. Leaning into her, Mac nudged her nose with a finger playfully. "Sadly, I took my leave before my true mark of manhood could be left. Thou were exhausted and slept like a newborn after a satisfying round at his mother's breast"

Jaynie's mouth fell open and Mac stuck a finger under it to help keep it closed. "You are *delusional*," she hissed from the compressed line of her lips

"Nay, M'lady. I am not," he whispered before he captured her lips, pressing his to hers and skimming them with his tongue.

A bolt of awareness, mixed with familiarity, shot to her loins in that instant and her heart sped up to lodge thickly in her throat A thread of remembrance flitted across her mind's eye and it made her push away from Mac with a frantic shove. "I want to know what's going on and I want to know now and while you're at it, get off of me. If we get caught like this, it could ruin your shot at the cover and my mother will have a hissy fit!"

"A hissy fit?"

"She'll be waaaay mad, okay? Now what is going on? I want an explanation and I want one now," she thundered, forgetting the hotel occupants in her fear.

Mac's face remained smiling, his eyes crinkling in the corners. Pulling her to him, he chuckled. "The explanation is simple. We made whoopee, as you call it here. Not complete whoopee. As I said, exhaustion played a role in thwarting my efforts."

Holy, fricken' cover model.

She'd done something bad and she couldn't even remember it?

And she'd done something bad with the man who made her panties wad up just glimpsing him?

It was insane. Yet, Jaynie knew it was true.

It explained her nightgown on the end of her bed and her sore body parts.

She'd slept with a cover model. Er, almost slept with one, according to Mac.

Her face grew hot and flushed.

Hoo boy, she was in deep kimchee.

Chapter Four

How did one tell another they were from the year 1450, on a quest for their magic sword? *Dost thou question my truths, Jaynie?*

She would have one of those hissy fits she spoke so fondly of should he reveal his intentions. Mac cared little who won the contest. Though, if it were based on brawn alone, surely he could best the wee man-girls.

He would love to see Douglas best him in anything that had to do with mead.

Mac could out-drink the man-boy with but one swill. That he was entertaining this foolery in such dire times was outrageous.

His business here in the year 2006 was critical and he must accomplish it and move on to his next leap in time.

He needed his sword back and he needed it back posthaste. One couldn't fight injustice if one was without weaponry

However, he would leave Jaynie with regret

Mac shook his head. She had fled his presence like a virgin maiden at a house of ill repute when he had revealed their encounter. He must apologize promptly.

Alas, thou hath found more trouble, Cormac of Anglesey. How many times must I warn ye, only trouble can be had from dabbling with the pretty maidens?

"She is different, my good friend, and had thou not been lost, I would not encounter the maidens. 'Tis you that led me here to this particular maiden," Mac accused in a whisper to the voice in his head as he rode the elevator to Jaynie's room. He hoped that was where she had gone.

"I do believe it was you who carelessly left me lying on a mahogany desktop while said dabbling occurred. 'Tis hardly my

fault I was confiscated by yon brat and sold on e-Bay. Ye are lucky I made my way here. I only called upon you for an eternity to come find me," the voice accused back.

His dabbling surely bested him every time, especially this time, when the fair Jaynie was the dabble-ee. His gut clenched in regret once again. She was by far the most interesting woman he had encountered in all his travels. He did not know why that was. Mayhap, it was the chemistry the people of the new millennium spoke so much of? Nevertheless, it existed between him and the beautiful Jaynie and he was loath to let it go.

"Have ye no clues as to my whereabouts yet, Cormac? I grow tired of lying immobile. I long for the blood sport."

"Had I a clue, oh Sharp One, surely thou know I would have come to your rescue. I do not cherish the situation I am in whilst I seek ye. I am being paraded about as though I were a mare at market. Oiled like a greased pig and chased after by many a maiden. Many a maiden, might I remind you, who are bound to another, yet seek my attentions anyway"

"Ahh, yes. The lonely, bored housewife of this new millennium. They are rampant, my friend. Some, not all, mind you, seek what they believe exists in these romance novels. Adventure, fantasies fulfilled. An alpha male, I believe they call it. I have heard much complaint about their willingness to discover and apparently destroy what they call hotties from this owner of mine"

"Have you not discovered who speaks this to you? A name of your new owner would be welcome at this point."

"What I hear is muffled, Cormac. I believe I suffer the indignity of lying in a closet."

Argh, 'twas frustrating. Mac vowed never to leave his sword lying about again. He could not leap in time to right wrongs if he did not have his sword. He had been stuck in this new millennium for over a year now and while he'd learned much, there were many battles to be fought that he was missing without his sword. He could not go into battle without his sword, handed down to him from his ancestors. Gad, he had been a simpleton to leave his sword carelessly lying on a desktop while he participated in the bed sport! It was priceless in this day and age and the boy who had stolen it had made a fine shilling on e-Bay, he was certain. "If only thou had eyes, my friend," he mumbled for the hundredth time.

"If I had eyes, I would have told you to leave yon maiden alone in the first place, Cormac! 'Tis my understanding that mead was what made you see her in a favorable light to begin with"

Cormac chuckled with a hearty bark. Indeed, the maiden in question had been less than favorable upon awakening. Mac had thus decided mead was a weakness he could no longer indulge. He had also learned that places for one with such a weakness were available to help him through his withdrawal.

Places like AA.

After reading the philosophies of the group and their twelve steps, Mac vowed never again to become so caught up in his mead that he might have to attend meetings where one earned chips for sobriety.

Or because one wanted to chew his arm off for waking up beside a less than desirable bed mate.

He'd found AA on the Internet. In fact, he'd found many things on the Internet whilst he searched for his beloved sword on this place called e-Bay. Mac had learned this new American slang and even wove it with his own native tongue upon occasion to try to fit in.

"Aye, I have sworn off the mead, friend. Now, I must go and make my apologies to Jaynie. Talk with me as I go, for you are loudest when I am in her room."

"That is not what is loudest when you are in her room, Cormac."

Cormac took the elevator to Jaynie's floor and listened with each step to his sword's calling. It must be in a room nearby and he was too distracted by the lush Jaynie to figure all the pieces to this puzzle. If his sword lay in a room, then Cormac must find the room and he must do so without skulking about like these serial killers he heard so much about. Surely, someone would wonder why he listened in at hotel doors like a lowly eavesdropper. If everyone would simply go away, he might have a chance.

There must be a master key to yon rooms, mustn't there? Cormac needed to find that key and it would probably entail wooing some scullery maid to do it.

But first, he must apologize to Jaynie and explain his presence here at this convention.

She would flip, as he'd heard people say.

She would not believe his tale. No one ever did until he was long gone.

Gone.

He did not like that word associated with Jaynie. For it meant he would not see her again.

He did not like that.

He did not like that at all.

*****

"Oh, no, you nut job! You go on back to your room and leave me alone. Do you hear me, Mac? I don't know what you did to me, but if you don't go away, I'm calling security!" Jaynie threatened through the crack in her hotel door, wiggling her finger at him. She hadn't been able to stop shaking since he'd alluded to the fact that they were intimate. Racing off to hide in her hotel room was all she was capable of right now. She'd been ignoring the repeated calls from her mother on her cell and anything that had to do with a cover model.

"I must speak with ye, Jaynie. Thou *must* listen to me."

"Thou ain't doin' anything of the sort, you—you—crazy Englishman!"

"Wales, I am from Wales," he corrected, winking at her with a velvety brown eye.

"Wales, London, fricken' Cornwall, it's all the same bloody accented place! I don't care where you're from. You're crazy and you'd better go away or I'm giving you up to my mother. They'll boot you out of this pageant so quick it'll make your head spin!" Jaynie shoved on the door, but Mac stuck a foot inside, preventing her from slamming it shut.

"Jaynie, I must ask that you listen to me. 'Tis important!"

"Listen to what? To you tell me that I've engaged in the—the—"

"Bed sport"

"Whatever sport with you!" she yelped. "No way, Robin Hood. No way can this be happening."

"But alas, Jaynie, thou know 'tis true…" he murmured, his eyes piercing hers.

Thou knew thou was in biggeth trouble, that's what thou knew. Lady Clarissa was off slitting her throat for her by telling her mother what Mac had said in the workout room Her mother would have a cow and she'd never hear the end of it. "I know nothing of the sort."

Mac slipped a finger between the crack in the door and ran it over her bottom lip. A tingle hit her smack dab in the nether regions and she jumped back. Oh, God, what had she done? Why was his touch familiar?

It would appear thou frolicked with the hottie, Jaynie—at least a degree of frolicking, anyway.

For whatever reason, Jaynie and her flicker of memory decided to let Mac in. He wasn't dangerous. At least she didn't think he was.

Were deranged men visibly deranged or did they look like your average, everyday citizen?

Well, that cinched it. Mac looked anything but average.

Grabbing her cell phone, she flipped it open in the event she might need to dial nine-one-one. She looked into the crack of the door and warned, "If I let you in, you'd better tell me what's going on, Mac. Do you hear me? I want an explanation and it better be good because I'm dead meat when my mother gets wind of this. Hell, I'm already dead meat. My cell phone's been ringing off the hook. Lady Clarissa has me nailed to the wall for something I seem to have missed." Her eyebrow rose in question.

"Aye, Jaynie, I regret my flippant response to Lady Clarissa. She angered me and thus, my anger made my lips loose." He nodded in confirmation of his own words. "Yes, loose."

Popping the chain lock off the door, Jaynie nodded back at him. "Yeah, loose is a good word. Do you know what Lady Clarissa will do to me? I can't believe you did that, Mac. Word will spread like wildfire and I'll be the talk of the convention."

"Truly, Jaynie, I regret my haste. Lady Clarissa needed to be taken down a peg. I acted irrationally. She is the most irritating wench I have encountered in all my leaps..." He stopped mid-sentence and moved closer to her, the heat of his body reaching out with invisible tentacles that drew her to him. "Won't you consider forgiving me?" he asked, giving her a mock look of apology

"I'll consider it when you tell me what happened."

Mac sighed and took her hand, leading her to the table by the window in her room and sat her down in a chair, finding the one opposite hers and sitting with her. "'Tis an odd mishap and 'twill be difficult to explain. I warn you, you will not believe my tale."

His face was so serious, his posture so stiff and unyielding that she found herself wanting to hear what he had to say, even if he made it up as he went.

"I am not from your time." He began with a slow statement of words.

"Huh?"

"I am not from the year 2006"

"What are you talking about?" It wasn't like he'd just told her he wasn't really from Peoria…

"I am a time traveler from the year of our Lord fourteen hundred and fifty." His face remained impassive, calm, as though he believed what he'd just said was something people said every day.

"You're a fucking nut!" she yelped, trying to pull her hand from his and pushing her chair back away from him, but Mac held her hand with a loose grip.

"Aye, Jaynie, 'tis a typical reaction."

"That's because it's typically nuts to tell someone you're a time traveler! Your application said you were from Kansas. It didn't say Kansas fourteen hundred and fifty, Robin Hood. So quit playin' with me and tell me what's going on because if you thought this wasn't going to freak me out, you'd be wrong. Not only are you claiming I indulged in some bed sport, but you're telling me I did it with a guy who believes he's a time traveler. I don't wanna sound judgmental, but you sound like a loon."

"I did have to do some finagling when I filled that out, 'tis true. I pass through this millennium often in my travels. I am aware of all the things it offers. Your new cyber highways, your language, your multitude of available quick fixes I should think you would be open to the theory of time traveling." His hand sought to soothe hers, stroking the back of it with a gentle, circular pattern.

"You-are-crazy," she said each word emphasized with succinctness. "Who let you out of the nut house? Are you on some kind of work release program? You know, the kind where they let the harmless guys work at

McDonalds because even though they believe they time travel, they can still flip a hellava burger?"

His chuckle, one she'd grown to enjoy during the past week, spilled from his throat with hearty resonance. "No, Jaynie. I have not heard of this release program and while I do enjoy a Big Mac at McDonalds, I have had no hand in creating one."

Jaynie relaxed a bit at his joking, but not enough to let go of her phone with nine-one-one available. "Okay, so you think you time travel. How about I humor you and you tell me how this time travel brought you to a cover model contest, of all things?"

"My sword," was the simple answer, followed by a grin. A grin so devastatingly handsome that, even though she doubted his brain cell reproduction, still made her legs weak.

"Your sword?" Slapping a hand to her forehead, she grimaced. "Of course, your sword. I mean, what good time traveler doesn't need his sword? I'm sure all people in the time traveling business need a sword," she said between tight lips and a tone that dripped derision.

Mac cupped her jaw, thumbing her cheek. "You do not hide your skepticism well, Jaynie."

"So, indulge me, would ya? What happened to your sword?"

"I lost it."

"Obviously. Where did you lose it?"

"In the year 2005. It was stolen from me and sold on e-Bay. Since then, I have been tracking it with a modicum of success."

"Uh-huh. I bet. Sold on e-Bay, eh? Who stole it and why?"

"A young boy with the lust for shillings."

"It's worth a lot of shi— er, money?"

"Indeed, 'tis worth many in your year."

"Explain tracking it. How can you track a sword and what's the big deal about this sword, anyway?"

"I tracked it via the sale on e-Bay and followed it here. 'Tis somewhere in this hotel, I have felt its presence."

He sounded like a man on a mission. A crazy one, no doubt, but he believed what he was saying. Jaynie didn't doubt that for a moment. "So what's so special about this sword?"

"It talks."

Well of course it did. Don't all time travelers have swords that talk? "It talks…" She said the words out loud and they didn't sound any less crazy than they had in her head.

"It does. The sword is what leads me to my next leap in time. It is my right hand man."

"And you leap around in time, why?" she asked incredulously.

"I am a warrior. I fight many battles in many different centuries. In my time, the year 1450, I am a well-respected warrior. The sword was given to me by my father upon his death bed. 'Twas my legacy so to speak and with it comes grave responsibility."

"Battles? So tell me, Quantum Leap man, what kind of battles are you fighting in this century? I mean, we have nuclear bombs and missiles. What can a sword do against terrorists?" She could not believe she was actually having this conversation. Yet, it didn't stop her from wanting to understand this world he'd created in his head.

"My sword has powers that have thwarted many a terrorist," he offered with mysterious evasion. "I leap to whatever destination is required of me and adapt as such to the year and its trends."

"And it talks to you?"

"Aye."

"Then why can't it tell you where the hell it is?"

"Hah! If only 'twere that simple. It cannot see, Jaynie, though we converse on a regular basis."

"Talk…you can hear it?"

"Indeed, in my head and it too can hear me. Yet, its location remains a mystery. My sword is almost like these radios you have. I must fine-tune the channel to get a good signal and the signal is strongest here in your room, Jaynie. Hence, I was here last night when you slept."

That alone should scare the bejesus out of her, but it intrigued her more than it frightened her. That Mac believed this craziness was indeed fascinating. "So, finish the story. You were in my room."

Mac's face lightened. "Yes, and upon your entry, I slipped beneath your bed. I did not wish to frighten you. In your sleep, you called my name…I always come when called," he grinned.

Jaynie's face flushed with guilt and embarrassment. She'd probably been dreaming about him. It sure wasn't the first dream she'd had in the week since she'd met him. "And you took advantage of me?" Just repeating that thought sounded wrong to her ears. Mac might be certifiable, but she just couldn't swallow the idea that he'd hurt anyone without cause. Warrior that he was and all.

"Nay, M'lady! I would never take what was not offered."

Oh, good.

Great, in fact.

She'd *offered* herself to him.

Jesus Christ in a mini skirt.

"You were sleeping, Jaynie. You are quite beautiful when you sleep and when my name escaped your lips, I answered," he said quietly, trying to hide his smile

The silence between them grew, cloaking them in a thick blanket. Jaynie avoided his eyes. Eyes that penetrated hers, searching for what she'd guess was some sign she believed his tall tale.

"You do not believe me, Jaynie?"

Well, duh. "Tell me something, Cormac? Would you believe you? If I told you I was a time traveler who'd snuck into your room because I could hear my sword *talking* to me and then, I—well, then, I— we— I—I. I don't know," she cried in exasperation.

"I can show you," Mac offered congenially, rising to stand by her hotel windows

"Show me?"

"Indeed."

"Show me what?"

"The leap into time."

"And how do you plan to do that?"

"I produce a portal."

"A portal…"

"Indeed, I conjure it in my mind."

"Do you have to squeeze really hard when you do that?"

His questioning glance made her laugh. "Um, hookay. You can show me this portal." If nothing else, watching him squeeze really hard to produce a figment of his imagination could be amusing

"Consider it done." Mac closed his eyes and either the room grew still, or Jaynie was spooked by all of this time trav ' talk. The lights flickered for a mere moment and a strange, heavy scent filled the air.

The whir of what sounded like Godzilla's old nemesis Mothra's wings to her ears permeated the room and Jaynie's eyes bulged.

Holy hole in the ozone.

Mac glanced at her from the opening of the shimmering, gaping black hole and smiled smugly.

Jaynie rose on legs that shook with each tiny step she took, but she made it to Mac's side and without thought for what might happen, thrust a hand into the portal.

It disappeared...

Jaynie yanked it back out and held it up to the light No damage, but it tingled with a thrum of electricity. It was an illusion. It had to be. Had she had the chicken salad with crystal meth in it for lunch?

"Wouldst thou care to watch the leap?"

Jaynie looked up at him smiling down at her so self-assured and her mouth dropped open. She nodded wordlessly because really, what else could she do but allow him to show her the most incredible thing her eyes had ever seen.

Mac squatted briefly using his knees and then hurled himself into the abyss of the hole, disappearing entirely and taking the hole with him.

Chapter Five

Rooted to the spot, Jaynie took lungfuls of air and began to pace the room without getting a freak on.

Oh, my God. Oh, my God. Oh, my God. Mac wasn't lying.

Either that or she was the crazy one in the room.

The sudden silence she'd experienced before Mac made the portal appear took the room over once again and then, the hole reappeared.

Mac slipped from the opening like he'd never left, jumping out with a whoosh of air and that peculiar whir of noise.

He bowed while she stood still, open mouthed and wide eyed. "Thou dost believe?"

"Thou dost think thou needs air, or Valium," she replied, dazed. Feeling behind her, she backed away from the portal's dimming glow and sat on the edge of the bed.

Mac came to sit beside her and put a soothing arm around her shoulders. "'Tis a lot to take in, I know. You have reacted rather well, I must say. Most women faint."

What a relief to know when presented with a time traveling warrior, who had a talking sword, she was a real champ. "Er, thanks. Okay, let me wrap my head around this. Forget the time travel thing. Why would you enter a contest like this while trying to find your sword?"

His chuckle was deep. "The shillings are quite appealing and the man who bought my sword from your e-Bay is a contestant in this contest."

"And you know this how?" she asked with a frown.

"My sword told me."

"So why enter the pageant? Why not just stay in the hotel and hunt him down?"

"Ah, well, I find it is a far better kill if you are close to your prey and I believe your pageant offers free room and board."

Indeed, it did. Maybe time traveling just wasn't paying what it used to. "Okay, so why can't your sword just tell you who has him? I mean, doesn't he have a clue as to who has possession of him?" Cheerist, she was talking about a *sword* like it was a living, breathing thing.

"He has been in a closet for some time now. The only clue he claims is that the owner 'talks funny' I dare say, they all 'talk funny' to my ears."

Jaynie laughed. "I guess they would. You talk funny, Robin Hood. You have a mix of old and new in your grammar."

"As I said, I am privy to the ways of many centuries, languages included, and try as I might to fit in, I manage to revert back to my native tongue, thus making some of my words a combination of old and new. My sword, and rightfully so, oft berates me for such."

Jaynie smiled at that. "Well, the women at the convention think it's charming. You just might win those shillings if you keep it up and all without trying."

Mac scowled. "I do not wish to win this contest, Jaynie. These men, oiled like greased pigs, and combed to within an inch of their lives, bemoaning caloric intake and muscle mass, are not men. I see the men on Lady Clarissa's book covers and I have yet to see a man from my time, with girl-hair like a Clairol model on television, wielding a sword so shiny one might see his reflection in it, whilst yon wench clings to his leg at high tide's crashing edge. The men in this pageant and on your romance novel covers are *not* like the men of my time," he said stubbornly, lifting his jaw.

Jaynie sputtered with a fit of giggles. "Well, funny you should say that, but we all think you look just like the guys on those covers. You're what those romance novels are all about."

He cocked one silky, brown eyebrow, turning to her to capture her in his embrace. "I demand that ye take that back, wench. I will not be compared to the likes of these *boys*," he said the word boys with disdain and then, he chuckled. "I venture to guess, the men in these novels appeal to you, Jaynie?" he asked, his lips dangerously close to hers.

"Those men don't exist," she whispered back, scoffing. "Those men are men we women make up with our vivid imaginations. A fantasy to buffer the reality of our real men — you know, men who scratch their balls and belch after a six-pack," she joked.

His hands threaded through her hair, lifting strands to run his fingers through them. "Do you have a real man, Jaynie?"

She snorted, avoiding the pressing stare he gave her. BOB was about as real as it got these days. "Nope. No man. I don't have time for men. My job is pretty demanding."

"Aye, the corralling of the man-boys, yes?" His eyes focused on her lips when he said the words.

She'd be offended if she thought Mac might have known she did have a real job "I'm also an editor for my mother's magazine. I do this once a year for the convention and believe me, it's more than enough."

"Jaynie?"

"Yeah?"

"I find that yon lips are making my blood boil and I can no longer resist them..." he said before capturing her "yon lips" and plunging his tongue between them, opening his mouth wide to encase hers in a kiss that left her panting

Jaynie's chest heaved against his, the swell of her breasts thrusting against the hard wall while she fought for breath. Lord, he had the tongue of a god, she thought briefly before she felt him tug her down to the bed, bringing her to lie on top of him.

The delicious press of his hard length seared the place between her legs and his arms went around her possessively, one hand splaying across her back, the other pushing at her shirt.

The heat Mac evoked when he touched her skin set her senses ablaze with flames of fire that shot to her pussy. His moan into her mouth was muffled by the tangle of their tongues, a slick, silken knot of flesh seeking flesh.

When Mac rolled her to her side and unhooked the clasp of her bra, Jaynie gasped as the cool air hit her nipples, tightening them to hard peaks. He gathered her breasts in his hand, tearing his lips from hers and kissing his way in a blazing trail of moisture to her nipples. With lips of sweet torture, Mac surrounded one, stroking it with his tongue, laving it with a swirling motion.

Jaynie's hips strained upward and he dragged her to him, molding the lower half of her body to his by cupping her ass with one hand and grinding into her. Her heart thrashed against her ribs and her pussy swelled, dripping with wet desire.

The deliciousness of his lips at her nipple was almost more than she could bear and she squirmed against the pressure of his mouth.

Mac tore at her shirt, shoving it up and over her head, almost never leaving her breast and then, drove a hand into her trousers.

She bucked against the contact, biting her lip and tunneling her hands into his long locks She heard the rasp of her zipper and electricity, sharp and blistering, settled in her belly. Shoving her pants down over her legs, Mac's hands roamed her naked flesh, urgent, insistent, forceful.

A shiver slipped up her spine when he lifted the corner of her panties and draped his fingers beneath the satin material. He cupped her pussy, letting the heel of his hand place pressure against the top of her pussy before spreading her inflamed lips and stroking a finger over her clit.

The simmer turned to a boil and Jaynie could think of nothing but feeling his skin on hers. She forgot that this was a man who claimed to have a talking sword. She forgot that she'd just seen a hole in the ozone of her hotel room the size of the Grand Canyon.

She couldn't keep track of what seemed like trivialities now when Mac's hands and lips were on her and especially not when he slipped along her belly with his mouth to rest his head on her thigh, shoving her panties to her knees.

"Ah, Jaynie, thy scent is maddening," he grumbled low before plunging his tongue between the lips of her pussy and capturing her clit.

Over and over he stroked the sensitive nub while Jaynie wrapped her legs around his shoulders, lifting her hips to feel every nuance of each wet pass. Her orgasm rose, sitting in the pit of her belly, and when Mac inserted a finger in her slick channel, she exploded, fucking his finger and arching into the rasp of his tongue.

Gasping for air, Jaynie threaded her fingers through Mac's hair and tugged him to her, tearing at his clothes, desperate for the heat of his skin pressed to hers. He rose above her to aid her in removing his clothing and she marveled at his sculpted beauty, straddling her. Her hands roamed over his chest, stroking the well-muscled wall, taunting a flat nipple with fingers that shook.

Lowering her eyes, Jaynie caught her first glimpse of his cock, long, hard, thick with desire and she reached between them to grasp it in a loose hold.

Mac's growled response echoed in the room, bouncing off the walls and settling with satisfaction in her ears

She grew bold, drawing out her strokes, thumbing the top of his shaft and using the small bead of pre-cum to lubricate her way.

Mac thrust into her hands and when she cupped his balls, tight against his body, kneading them with gentle fingers, he moaned long and low. The feral groan empowered her, encouraging her to grip him harder, but he yanked himself away with a sudden jerk

"Aye, Jaynie, you make me want to drive into you without care. I wish to take you with abandon. Yet, your pleasure is my goal. Open your legs to me, Jaynie. Open them, *now*."

Jaynie whimpered at his words, carnal and wicked, but she obeyed his command, spreading her legs and welcoming him.

Bracing his hands on her thighs, Mac poised at her entrance, the hard planes of his face tense, and with a slow stroke, he entered her.

She cried out as he filled her, stretching her with the silken steel of his cock.

His hips rolled with each plunge. The slick slap of flesh ringing in her ears, his hands firmly planted on each thigh. With each stroke, he pressed them open wider, sliding a hand along her thigh to find her clit again, caressing it until she burned with the need to come.

Jaynie wrapped her legs around his lean waist, pulling him to her until he fell forward on her and his head lay against her cheek.

They rocked together, their rhythm increasing, grinding in a dance, glued together by the sweat of their bodies.

Her pussy begged for relief and when the sharp claws of orgasm raked over her, Jaynie lost control, clutching at the hard globes of Mac's ass and thrusting upward with hard jolts.

Mac ground out her name in her ear, calling for her to come with him. The slow, measured thrust of his cock turned to a frantic drive of abandon and Mac too came, spilling his hot seed in her with a roar of satisfaction.

Their heaving chests crashed against each other's and Mac scooped her into his embrace, pulling her close and imprisoning her in his strong arms.

Jaynie burrowed against his chest and a tear stung her eye. Not for what they'd just done, but for what would most likely end when Mac found his sword. "So we have a sword to find?" she asked, her words muffled in his neck.

"Aye," his answer was somber. "We have a sword to find." Cradling her closer to him, Mac let his heavy weight melt into her and Jaynie stroked his back until his even breathing told her he slept.

Her eyes stung again with tears. The combination of what she'd witnessed, along with the most satisfying, gloriously fulfilling sex she'd ever had, made her realize how much she missed in life due to the pressure her mother placed on her and Jaynie decided she wanted this.

She didn't know what *this* was, but she wanted it and it was time to start getting it, even if it was just for a little while.

Mac was here for a reason. Dropped into her world because fate said it should be.

Now, Jaynie wanted to know why fate had involved her.

And as she let her eyes slide closed, she decided she was going to let fate, in all its odd happenings, have her.

*****

"Mac, wake up!" Jaynie squirmed beneath his sleep-heavy weight and gripped his shoulders.

"Aye," he mumbled, stirring and exhaling a long breath.

"Hey, do they have toothpaste where you come from?"

Mac's chuckle came from deep in his chest and it vibrated against hers. "Nay, but I know of this dental hygiene and I brush twice a day, rinsing with a plaque fighting mouthwash."

"Ahhh, then ye should get thee to the bathroom and practice some of those good habits," she teased. "Look, I figured something out and I think I know how we can find your sword."

Mac lifted above her, his strong arms holding him up. "Aye, Jaynie. Do not hold back. Tell me."

She smiled smugly up at him. "The costume ball tomorrow," she revealed with satisfaction. "You said that you can hear your sword best when you're in my room, right?"

Mac nodded above her, his dark hair curtaining them

"This entire floor is only the pageant contestants. Every room here is reserved for only them. So it has to be in one of these rooms and..." She paused, taking a deep breath. "The only reason I can figure a sword would be in one of the contestants' rooms is because of the costume ball tomorrow night! Someone must be coming with a costume that has a sword," she finished, smiling up at him.

"Aye, Jaynie, you are a genius!" Rolling off her, Mac's feet hit the floor and he paced the length at the end of her bed.

Sitting up, she smiled again. "Yeah, yeah. So how are we going to get it?"

"We must find the hotel's master key and search yon rooms, of course."

"Wouldn't it just be easier to wait until tomorrow and approach whoever has the sword? Let me look at each contestant's list of costumes? I mean, how many can be coming in a costume with a sword? We always have a variety of costumes—cowboys, firemen, pirates, policemen and at least *one* warrior," she said glibly.

"You would have made a fine warrior in my time, Jaynie. Your plan is solid," he acknowledged.

Her phone rang then and she scooped it up from the floor only to frown at the number displayed on the panel.

Her mother.

Well, she was in for a load of shit. She may as well get it over with now. "Hello, mother."

"Jaynie? Where have you been?" she yelped into the phone. "Lady Clarissa is threatening to pull her full page ads forever because of you."

Jaynie sighed, running a hand over her forehead and sliding to the edge of the bed. Mac wandered through, his mouth full of mouthwash, and he grinned at her. "Maybe you should let her do that, mom. I'd dare her to find another magazine as big as *That's Amore* who will put up with the grief she's given us over the years Not to mention the potential for bad press. She doesn't even write her own books, mother, and I'm sick and fricken' tired of appeasing her aging ass!"

A long silence came over the line and Jaynie held her breath for the roasting she was sure she was in for and then, her mother said, "You know what, darling? You're right. Lady Clarissa is a fake and it's high time she got a good dose of reality. I've grown terribly tired of her rants and diva-like behavior. I say we tell her to piss off."

Whoa. Hookay, piss off it is. Jaynie was flooded with relief for her mother's support and she gripped the edge of the bed to steady herself. "Mother?"

"Yes, dear?"

"I love you," was all she said.

"I love you too. Now come downstairs. There's a Douglas here—one of the contestants who seems to think he's the second coming and he claims you have his hair gel."

Jaynie couldn't help but laugh. "I'm on it, mom. Oh, and Mom?"

"Yes, dear?"

"Thank you."

"You're welcome. Bye, darling."

Jaynie flipped the phone closed and put it on her nightstand, the burden of her mother's wrath forgotten with the support she offered.

"'Twas your mother?" Mac asked, sitting on the edge of the bed with her.

"'Twas," she said with a wistful smile.

"And fear ye her wrath?"

"Nah, no wrath. She's okay and Lady Clarissa is in for some shit."

Mac pulled her to sit on his lap, his cock, hard once again, pressed against her ass. "I am glad, Jaynie 'Twould pain me to see you upset with your relations."

Jaynie wrapped her arms around his neck and squeezed him close. His hands covered her spine, stroking her flesh, and his breathing grew uneven. "We don't have time for that, Mac," she said regretfully. "I have to take care of a situation and monitor tonight's party."

"Aye and I must dress for yon party, yes?"

"Yes," she agreed, letting her head rest on his shoulder and clenching her eyes shut to fight off the incredible longing she felt to stay captured in his arms

"Jaynie?"

"Yes," she whispered, lips pressed to his skin.

"We must talk later."

Her gut clenched. Yeah, they had to talk about the see ya around sometime this millennium thing, didn't they? "No, Mac, it's okay. What happened here—stays here. I know you have to skip the light fantastic, Robin Hood. No pressure here. No explanations." She fought to control the regret and yearning in her voice. It kinda figured that she'd go and find a guy who was a time traveler. Luck surely wouldn't bring her a nice reliable breast implant salesman from Peoria.

"Nay, Jaynie. I cannot leave with this between us. Yet, I have an obligation to the world and to fate, but that is not the only thing that troubles me."

Pregnancy. He was worried about leaving his spawn in the year 2006. Did time travelers have to pay child support? Shaking her head, she lifted it to look in his eyes. "You don't have to worry, Mac. I'm on birth control. You won't have any residual effects from tonight."

He scowled. "Birth *what?* Nay, Jaynie. We must talk about my sword. Time is of the essence. I am called to battle and on the eve of the morrow, I must make the leap."

Time.

They had little left.

Jaynie's heart began to pound erratically, but she slipped from his embrace and focused on smiling, keeping things light. "Okay, Mac. I say we find your sword and get you back in business." Turning, she plodded off to the bathroom, closing the door and turning on the water so he wouldn't hear her tears. Her throat clogged with words she couldn't speak, thick like peanut butter.

Mac rapped on the door. "I'll see you downstairs later, Jaynie. But I remind you, we are not done. Not by one of your long shots," he insisted.

Jaynie splashed cold water on her face and took deep, wet gasps of air.

She would help Mac find his sword and then, she would set about nursing the broken heart she knew was coming.

Chapter Six

The costume party was in full swing when Jaynie entered dressed as a belly dancer. She and Mac had spent their last night together wrapped in a heated embrace. When he'd come to her door last night, she'd placed a quieting finger on his lips.

She didn't need words to soothe her. She didn't want regrets. She didn't need promises.

She just needed Mac.

One last time.

Mac of the infectious smile, skilled tongue and from another damned century.

Jaynie had made him promise not to speak if she let him in and he'd kept his word, wrapping his arms around her with the whispered word tomorrow, floating in her ear.

When he'd left in the early gray of dawn, their plan to find his sword in place, Jaynie lay on the side of the bed Mac had slept on, pulling his pillow close to her and sobbing into it. She reveled in the smell of it, the warmth he'd left behind on it.

There were no guarantees—even if Mac was from the here and now—that they could forge a relationship, but that didn't mean Jaynie didn't wish with all of her heart they could have had a shot.

She'd dressed for the party with a stomach that held no food and a heart that sat heavily in her chest.

There were three men who would most likely have swords tonight and Mac had said he would give her the signal when he knew which one of the contestants had it.

Her eyes scanned the burgeoning crowd for Frank, Gomez and of all people, Douglas. She'd laugh at Douglas for dressing like a warrior if her heart didn't hurt so much.

Mac was leaving.

His leaps in time were something he had no control over and he didn't know when he'd be back in her time again.

When he'd entered the ballroom, she'd caught her breath. He was dressed like Zorro. A low slung, black hat sat jauntily over one masked eye and his tight black leather pants hugged thighs that made her mouth water. His billowy shirt opened at his neck to reveal his chest, gleaming and bronzed.

His subtle nod in Frank's direction was her cue to make her way through the crowd and find a way to distract him and get the sword. It made sense. Mac has said his sword told him its new owner talked funny. Frank had that New York accent and it would undoubtedly sound funny to the ears of someone from 1450. Thankfully, Douglas wasn't the keeper of this sword of Mac's. She had little patience tonight for his whining.

Sure enough, Frank had on a kilt, no shirt and a sheath across his chest, holding Mac's sword in place. It gleamed in the low light of the ballroom, gold and silver. "Yo, yo, Jaynie. You look gooood." His eyes swept over her in appreciation and Jaynie fought back a round of hysterical giggles.

He had on work boots.

Mac would spend many a century berating his outfit.

She stood close to Frank and winked. "Yeah, you too. Niiiice sword ya got there. It almost looks real. Where'd ya get it?"

"e-Bay. I got it fer a steal too, but it was still a lotta moolah Da guy who sold it to me said it was real. Ya wanna touch it?"

Oh, how she'd lived for the day when she could touch Frank's sword. "Er, sure, Frank." Placing a hand on his arm, she ran a finger over the cool metal. From the corner of her eye, in the crowd, milling about the outer edges of the dance floor, she saw Mac shake his head furiously at her with an odd smile on his face.

Huh. She didn't know what he was trying to tell her, so she set about her task. "Can I hold it, Frank?"

"Hold it?"

"Yeah, ya know, like pretend I'm some samurai or something," she joked, hoping he'd take the bait.

"I ain't no samurai, Jaynie. I'm a warrior," he insisted, his perfectly chiseled face distorting into a frown.

With work boots. A warrior with work boots. "I know, but I want to pretend I'm a samurai. Oh," she said excitedly. "I know, let's take a picture. I'll get Gunther. How hot would you look with one of the female models, clinging to your chest? It'd be great press, Frank."

Ahhh, now there was the smile that could light a thousand darkened theaters. The word 'press' made Frank simply glow. "Yeah. Dat's a good idea, Jaynie. Where is Gunther, anyway?"

"He's off in the press room, silly. Come with me and I'll show you." Taking his hand, Jaynie led him out of the ballroom and down a long corridor, keeping her ears open for Mac's footsteps to follow.

"Jaynie!" The high-pitched call of her name made Jaynie swing around to see Lady Clarissa hot on her heels and Mac right behind her.

Glancing at her watch, she realized they had only a half an hour until Mac had to conjure up his portal and leave. God damn this woman! "What?"

Mac pulled up short and ducked into a hallway off the main strip of corridor. Jaynie's eyes caught his dark figure just as he peeked around the corner.

Lady Clarissa, costumed in an eighteenth century gown that shoved her boobs up under her chin, stopped in front of her and crossed her arms over her overflowing cleavage. "You're some little bitch, aren't you? You're jealous of me and you filled your mother's head with lies," she spat.

Jaynie sputtered beneath the veil that covered her lips, yanking it off and throwing it to the ground. "Are you crazy, you hack? I did not lie. If you weren't so busy chasing pageant contestants and you kept that libido where it belongs, there wouldn't be anything to tell my mother, now would there?"

Clarissa grabbed her arm with a hard tug and clung to it, sticking her claws into it hard enough to leave marks. "You listen to me, Jaynie. Rumors are circulating that I don't write my own books! You could ruin my reputation."

Jaynie twisted her arm out of her grasp and poked a finger under her nose. "I can't ruin something that's based on a lie, Clarissa. Your cousin writes those books and you know it. So scurry on back to pageant contestants that are young enough to be your grandchildren and back off before I start telling anyone who'll listen what a liar you are!" Jaynie yelled back into her face. Sheesh. Maybe Mac could hurl her ass into the century where women were bound and gagged?

The sharp crack of Lady Clarissa's hand across Jaynie's face stunned even the sputtering Frank into silence.

Okay, that was it.

It was on.

Girl fight!

Jaynie reacted quicker than she might have given herself credit for, shoving Lady Clarissa backward until she nearly fell over. "If I had the time, I'd kick your fat, lipo-suctioned ass, you two-bit hussy!"

Lady Clarissa's horrified gasp sent a thrill of satisfaction up her spine. The bitch. "I'll make your life hell, Jaynie Renfro!"

"Yeah? Like you haven't done that for the past five years every time I've had to wipe the drool from your botoxed lips when you're chasing after some cover model. Or cover up the latest Lady Clarissa indiscretion. Now, go back to that party, Clarissa, or I'm going to start calling plagiarism! Oh, and stuff your boobs back in that costume where they belong," she yelled, grabbing a surprised Frank's hand and dragging him behind her down the hallway, hoping Mac could clear his way to follow.

"Hey, dis isn't the way to da press room, Jaynie." Frank tugged back on her hand.

"Frank, if you give me any shit, I'm going to clock you. You got that, Vinny Barbarino?" she threatened.

"Hey, what da hell is goin' on?" He stopped mid-drag and wouldn't budge.

"Thou hath my sword, Frank"

Thank God, Mac was here. Jaynie breathed a sigh of relief.

"Huh?" Frank looked at Mac looming over him with a confused stare. "Dis is my sword, Mac. I bought it on e-Bay."

"Indeed and you bought it on e-Bay after 'twas stolen from me. I demand thou hand it over." Mac put his hand out to Frank and waited as if he expected Frank to just hand it over.

"Bullshit on dat," he yelled back, taking a defensive stance and shoving at Mac's chest.

"Boys!" Jaynie yelled. "Frank, that's Mac's sword. Now play nice and give it back"

"No!"

Mac hurled Frank up against the wall and towered over him, placing his hands on Frank's throat. "I asked nicely once, Frank. Give me my sword or I shall slit thy throat like that of a squealing pig, man-boy," Mac's voice thundered.

Jaynie grabbed his arm and pulled on it with an anxious yank. "Mac! Stop it. You can't just go threatening to kill people nowadays. This isn't 1450!"

Through clenched teeth, Mac said once again, "Give me my sword, Frank. Thou can do that willingly, or thou can put up a struggle." His eyes penetrated Frank's, gleaming with menace.

Frank gulped, looking from Jaynie to Mac.

"Unhand my sword, Frank," Mac said again.

"1450?" Frank squeaked, then, slumped against the wall.

"Jesus, Mac, did you have to be so fricken' harsh? You can't go around killing people in this day and age," she scolded.

Mac settled the passed out Frank on the floor and looked at Jaynie, an apology written all over his face. "Forgive me. I am fiercely protective and forget the year we are in and all of the silly rules that pertain."

"Forget it, let's hurry up before you miss this leap," she urged.

Mac grabbed his sword, running a loving hand over it, and the odd thrum of vibration that had accompanied the portal Mac jumped through was clearly in the air. He jammed his sword in his sheath and turned to Jaynie.

No sooner had she said that than her name was once again being yelled into the corridor. "Jayyyyynie! There she is, officer. That's the woman who assaulted me!"

Assaulted *her*? The God damned liar. She was going to kick her ass from here to the next century!

Jaynie's backward glance brought with it the vision of Clarissa and one of the hotel security guards running down the hall after her. Fuck! "Go, Mac. Hurry! I'll deal with Clarissa," she whispered fervently, pressing a kiss to his lips for what she thought would be the last time.

Mac grabbed her hand and began running, pulling her stumbling along behind him. "Ye are wanted by your law, Jaynie. I cannot leave ye alone. Let us hurry!"

Jaynie ran behind him as fast as she could in her pointy shoes, her chest heaving

Mac pressed the button on the elevator and it pinged open just when Clarissa and the hotel security rounded the corner. He jabbed the button hard again and thankfully, with a silent slide, the door shut

Mac gathered Jaynie in his arms and huffed out, "You were most brave against the evil wench, M'lady. A true warrior warring against a vicious viper"

"I should have slapped her teeth out of her head," she gasped back, letting her head fall to the strength of his chest to catch her breath. Biting her lip, she fought back the idea that these would be their last moments together.

Mac kept his sword at his side and mumbled something into her hair.

"What?"

He sighed. "My sword is rather fond of you, M'lady. He enjoyed your caress in the ballroom."

"Really? Well, tell him I think he's very shiny and I'm sorry we couldn't get to know one another better." Her voice hitched on the last words and she fought the sting of more tears.

Mac mumbled again and Jaynie's head rose to look up with a question, but the elevator door popped open, signaling their need to make haste.

"Never ye mind, Jaynie. Come, we must hurry."

Flying behind him, she glanced at her wristwatch and yelled, "We have eight minutes, Mac. You have to hurry and produce the portal!"

Mac swung around the corner, nearly losing his grip on her hand, and slammed up short against her hotel room door. "The key, Jaynie. Give me the key."

Jaynie pulled it from the low line of her harem pants and Mac slid it into the door.

Thrusting the door shut behind them, Mac bolted it, sheathing his sword and turning to face her, holding his arms open.

Jaynie flew into them and buried her face in his chest.

This was inevitably goodbye.

"How can I ever thank thee, Jaynie? Thou art a true treasure," Mac muttered into her hair.

"No thanks necessary," she whispered hoarsely. "Just take care, Mac, will you?"

His silence pounded in her ears. Tilting her chin upward, Mac gazed into her eyes. "We do not have to part, Jaynie. Come with me. Come with me and let us discover this thing between us."

Her mind raced with the possibilities, her heart torn over leaving behind her mother, demanding as she was. She couldn't just disappear without ever knowing when or if she could come back...

Her hesitance was evident and Mac must have taken it for her answer. Instead of replying his lips took hers in a kiss that held all the promise and possibilities for more of what they'd shared this week.

But they hardly knew each other... How could they have a future if she was in the future, or the past? What the hell would she do while he was off skipping through time? Make afghans? Learn to crotchet? What if he was some sort of time traveling gigolo and he said this kind of stuff to all of those yon maidens she was sure were left littered in stretches of time?

Jaynie let her lips melt against his in deference to her unspoken fears, reveling in her possible last moments in his arms. Wrapping her hands around his neck, she clung to him.

He tore his lips away from hers, his hands gripping her forearms as he whispered huskily, "Jaynie, I must produce the portal. The time draws nearer."

Nodding, she agreed, but didn't let go of his neck as he walked to the window of her hotel room, hanging onto him with her feet in mid air.

Mac closed his eyes and focused and when the whir of the portal's arrival grew to a heavy thud in her ears, Jaynie squeezed Mac to her.

"I do not wish to leave you, but I must go, Jaynie. I must," was his urgent whisper against her cheek.

God, how had she come to this? Clinging to a man for all she was worth. A man she'd known less than a week?

"I *must* go, Jaynie," he said again, regret evident in his tone, setting her firmly down and planting a kiss to her forehead.

Jaynie watched his back through a blur of tears, poised at the entrance of the portal. Turning, he gazed at her for one last lingering moment.

His dark chocolate eyes pierced hers, searching them, and when Jaynie stared back, she again saw his regret — flagrant, tangible, and rife with bittersweet remorse.

And then he grinned that grin that had first caught her heartstrings from the moment she'd laid eyes on him.

Without any more delay, Mac jumped through the portal and was gone.

Gone.

Mac was gone and he'd wanted her to go with him.

Gone.

The word reverberated through her head just as the banging on her hotel door began.

She heard Clarissa's screeching from behind the door, obviously looking for a piece of her hide.

If she never heard that woman's voice again… and then, it occurred to her.

She didn't have to.

Jaynie made a split-second decision in that crazy, heart pounding moment. Grabbing her cell phone from the nightstand, she flipped a silent bird to Clarissa then slammed her eyes shut and hurled herself into the fading portal.

*****

"I cannot believe you left yon beauty, Cormac! What kind of warrior takes no for an answer? For that matter, oh Fierce One, what kind of warrior does not hurl the fair maiden over thy shoulder and bring her with thee?"

"Hush, friend! I cannot force her to do what she wishes not. I do not wish to spoil our reunion with an argument," Mac said, defeated and unwilling to delve further into his deep disappointment over Jaynie's choice to stay.

"Hah! Thou art a chicken shit," his sword accused.

"A what?"

"Never thee mind. Thou has done something lame brained. I have no wish to dwell on what you could have changed, given the proper warrior attitude."

"'Tis good to have ye back, anyway, my friend."

"'Tis good to be held in the firm grip of a true warrior again, I dare say."

"Aye, together at last," he commented, finally focusing on his surroundings and sitting down on the edge of a cot that appeared to be in a jail cell. Well, wasn't that a fine turn of events? Leaving Jaynie wasn't difficult enough, but his next mission in time had left him imprisoned.

"Thou longest for thy lovely wench. 'Tis a pity your warrior heart doth not extend to the battlefield of love."

Mac grabbed his sword and sliced it through the air. "I said shut yon trap or I shall embed you in yon wall!" he thundered.

"I said take your filthy hands off of me! What the hell kind of place is this?"

A very familiar voice bounced off the stone walls of the prison. What in God's name?

"Argh, look what we found in the courtyard, prisoner." A greasy, long-haired jailer peered in at Mac, dragging behind him an incredibly feisty belly dancer with pointed shoes and long, dark hair, spilling down her back.

Slapping at the hands that held her, Jaynie placed hers on her hips and stuck her neck out. "Look, prison meat, knock it the hell off. If you put one more hand on me, I'm going to clock you senseless!"

"*Tell thy wench to clamp it, Cormac. Before she reveals us!*" his sword urged in his head.

"I see thou hast brought me company" Mac nodded at the jailer. "Send thy wench in, so that I might keep her lips from moving," he added, wiggling his eyebrows at the jailer.

The jailer cackled. "Aye, mate. She is a feisty wench," he agreed, unlocking the cell, shoving Jaynie into Mac's arms, and slamming the cell door shut behind her.

"What the hell is going on here, Mac?" Jaynie squeaked. "Where the frig am I and are we in *prison*? I can't believe I'm doing time! Who do I have to call to get the hell outta here? I brought my cell phone. Cheerist! All I did was take a harmless leap into a big ole hole because I met this guy who's awesome in bed and now look—"

Mac silenced Jaynie with a forceful kiss, keeping her from further ramblings and relishing the taste of her sweet mouth against his and when she molded to him, her body pliant and lush, he was grateful.

Jaynie had followed him.

For this chance with her, he would pay homage to the god's for a lifetime.

Epilogue

"How is your mother, my sweet," Mac asked while they basked in the sun that rarely popped out in England, it seemed.

"She's fine, honey. I'm just glad we were able to revisit 2006, so I could call her. Thank God, she never changed her cell number."

Mac's chuckle resonated in her ears. "I still am in disbelief that it held a charge for all of the leaping we do together."

Yeah, no shit. Jaynie couldn't believe it either, but when they'd revisited 2006, she'd bought a new charger, cleaned out her bank accounts and called her mother. It had felt like she'd been gone forever, but her mother claimed it was only a week. She'd also divulged that Douglas had won the *That's Amore* cover model pageant after much talk of where Jaynie and Mac had disappeared to on the night of the pageant. Jaynie's mother had shut Lady Clarissa up with the promise of a full page ad and paid off the security guard that had chased them the night they'd taken that leap.

Poor Douglas was now, undoubtedly basking in the glow of one horny Lady Clarissa. Mac had snorted at the very idea that Lady Clarissa might be able to wring anything out of Douglas other than a good fashion tip.

Jaynie shook her head again in disbelief. They'd only been gone a week… In a week's time, she and Mac had been to many a place.

Including jail

Jaynie shuddered. No more jail, thank you.

Mac had explained some scientific crap about this time thing and paradoxes and all sorts of things that made absolutely no sense to her. Science was never her thang. Nothing mattered but that she was with Mac.

It was the smartest thing she could have ever done. Their travels were exciting, their nights even more so.

"Dost thou regret leaving thy mother, Jaynie?"

"Nay, er, I mean no. I miss her a lot, but she wouldn't begrudge me the chance to see the real, live Alamo if she really knew where I was"

Mac pulled her up from the stone bench of the courtyard they were sitting in and Jaynie grunted. "Know what I do regret?" she asked him, smiling up at him.

"Certainly not this," he murmured against the fullness of her bottom lip, making her nipples press against her dress.

Her *Victorian* nightmare of a dress.

"I regret that we can't stay out of this damned century, Mac. I mean, really who the hell thought this up?" She pointed to her ribcage and made a face. "It's like the iron maiden and I'd bet the person that thought this was a good idea was a man."

"Ah, how my wench suffers for fashion. You do not like the corsets, I gather?"

"Mac, who could like this? I can't breathe and sitting through one more tea with that hoity-toity Duchess of Whatevertheplace is going to be the death of me. I swear, one day, I'm going to just rip my clothes off in front of them all"

Placing a hand on her waist, Mac smiled and pulled her to him until her head flopped back from the weight of her hair.

"And this hair. It's God awful, honey. Look at me! I look like I have two torpedoes on either side of my head."

Mac threw his head back and laughed. "I find you rather fetching."

Poking him in his non-corseted ribs, she narrowed her gaze at him. "Well, of course you do, because you aren't wearing it, Robin Hood."

Hauling her to his chest, he chuckled again. "I would prefer you weren't wearing it either." He wiggled his eyebrows at her in the way only Mac could, his intent clear.

"Oh, no, mister. There will be no slap and tickle because that means I have to fricken' fight my way out of this damned thing, only to put it back on again because I have to be at sunset tea or some such bullshit. They have a gozillion meals here, Mac, and then, they expect me to stuff myself into this torture chamber?"

"I will do that thing," he promised secretively, nibbling her neck.

"What thing?"

"The *thing*," he said again, low and rumbling.

"Ohhhh, *that* thing," she said with a catch in her throat.

"Indeed," he said against the top of her breast.

"Okay, but you have to lace me back up. I am not calling on that poor maid Gretchen to do it. She has other things to do Like tend to Duchess Whatserface."

"Abington," Mac provided, slipping a nipple from the top of her dress and laving it with the sweet rasp of his tongue.

Okay, so there was an advantage or two to this crazy get up. "Promise?" she prodded breathlessly.

"I do," Mac said. "Now, come, wench. My blood boils for thee."

"That's because you have yon tights on. It's bound to be constrictive," she pointed out with a grin.

Mac laughed again. "Have I told thee how happy it makes me that you followed me into the portal that eve?"

"Yeah, but you can tell me again."

"You make me very happy, Jaynie."

Jaynie's heart pumped in her chest every time he said those words. "Yeah? Well, you make me happy too, even in this God forsaken century.   I could really use a Starbucks low fat, mocha latte."

"Have I told ye of our next leap in time," he asked, tugging her to the courtyard door and pulling her hastily along the stoned corridor to their chambers.

God, she sure hoped it involved a century with at least a cup of coffee. "Where to next?"

He smiled knowingly. "1952"

Well, shit.   There was no Starbucks back then. "How come we always seem to land in a time where women are supposed to serve their men like slaves and wear heels while they do it?" she asked suspiciously.

"I go where I am summoned."

"You listen to me, Cormac of Anglesey I am not wearing heels and a stupid dress.   Got that?" she threatened.

"Naked on you is lovely," he assured her with a wink.

Jaynie giggled. "C'mon, warrior, let's make some nookie before I bust a gut." Taking his hand, she pulled him to the bed in their chamber and threw him down on it. Straddling him, she said, "Promise me the moment we get to 1952 you'll find me some coffee?"

"Anything for you, M'lady." He sealed his promise with a kiss and Jaynie forgot all about Starbucks and microwaves and cell phones and Internet access and…and…

The End

Time Thieves
By
Brit Blaise

Dedications

For Tina Gerow; I give thanks for the evening you walked into the Valley of the Sun writer's meeting...and the journey began.

Chapter One

Daken landed stark naked in a spiral of light, grateful to be covered by a thick cloud of energy. His team immediately followed, all four appearing one after another in rapid succession, the stink of sulfur strong in the air surrounding them. Light and glowing energy particles cocooned each warrior, all naked and shivering from the trauma of their journey across time.

As he fought back the pain, Daken made certain four pairs of blue-black eyes stared back at him before he turned his attention to the pure titanium cylinder to his right. Vapor rose like a dense mist from the glistening exterior beaded with moisture. It would be several minutes before he dared touch it.

Peck managed to stand first. Daken's ego pressed him where his muscles failed and he pulled to his feet seconds later.

"Shit, Daken. When'd you get the scar on your ass? The ladies are going to be all over that."

Daken shrugged and leaned over the cylinder. Traveling through time always made him weak, each successive occurrence growing worse. "I got it the same place I got this." He lifted his left arm to show a scar which cut an angry jagged line through the dark hair on his pit and snaked along the inside of his arm down to his elbow.

Once he pushed to his feet, Kaze moved nearer to see. "That looks like a sonic sword wound. Did one of the newbies at base camp cut loose when you rode them too hard?"

"I got this when I came here a little over two months ago on recon for this mission. When you were briefed, I told you the Korin have taken to hiring bodyguards. I didn't tell you they'd armed one of the idiots with a sonic sword. Hopefully, it was one time only, but be prepared for the worst."

"You mean the best." Peck gave him the thumbs up. "You've got the best scars of any of us. When you finally retire, you'll have your pick of the choicest women."

Daken didn't want to retire, nor had he seen a woman among his genetically engineered peers, choice or otherwise, who interested him. For some unknown reason, the most beautiful women were attracted to the imperfections of the Time Warriors. "Save the chatter. We need to get our pants on before we're arrested for indecent exposure."

"In twenty-first century Las Vegas? Indecent exposure is part of the ambience," Houston said, not the least bit timid to show his naked physique as he gave a languid stretch. The starless night sky hid them, but not from each other. Their vision, keen even on the blackest of nights, made it easy to see.

When the noxious gases surrounding the cylinder dissipated, Daken pressed the tip of his callused index finger onto the panel. After his print registered, the lid opened with a lengthy hiss. Inside, five long containers held their clothes and swords.

Chiron grabbed his container before Daken gave the order. "You don't have to ask me twice. I hate coming across naked." He opened it and pulled out the leathers engineered to fit him alone.

Professional grade simulated leather, good enough to fool anyone. Daken stepped into his pants and reached into the front pocket before he zipped. "You have to admit, this makes it worth coming." He held up the key to the storage unit on the opposite side of the barbed security fence and across the blacktop from where they'd landed in a barren desert lot.

"Choppers." Peck moved faster. "It's too bad bikes are illegal in the twenty-ninth century. Then again, I still have two-hundred and four more crossings. Maybe I'll get it out of my system before the council retires me."

Daken didn't like to be reminded it was his final crossing. "Put the empty boxes back in the cylinder. Peck, you and Houston carry it to the storage unit." Daken finished dressing and stowed his deactivated sword in the specially made compartment inside his boot. "Let's get moving."

When Daken inserted the key into the lock, he knew right away someone had tampered with it. A closer look showed scratches. "Swords!" he barked. The hum of their swords activating helped him to concentrate on what he was doing.

The cheap lock could've been purchased anywhere since an expensive one would only attract the wrong kind of attention. Daken opened it with a click and lifted. The racket the door made would've awakened the dead. Inside, a second door had an activator pad much like the time cylinder. A quick scan of the silver exterior showed no sign anyone had gotten this far, no fingerprints or scratches to mar the smooth surface. He drew his sword and rested his finger lightly on the surface until the pressure inside released and the doors automatically folded back with a swift snap.

"Hold it right there. Get your hands in the air. Raise them above your heads."

A flashlight in his eyes momentarily blinded him. The feminine voice didn't worry him, but the muzzle of a gun in his face did. He didn't have time for this nonsense. And where had she come from? How had she come upon them unawares? Had the noise made by the archaic exterior door allowed her to approach without any of them noticing?

Daken focused on her pupils, dilated from the darkness and fought the irritating distraction of the butterscotch color surrounding them. Damn, but he loved butterscotch.

"Give me the gun," he told her and sent her a telepathic message to obey him. She gave a butterscotch blink and released her tight hold on the gun, allowing it to dangle from her trigger finger where he could reach up and remove it with ease.

That was easy enough. He delivered another telepathic order for Peck to turn off her flashlight. Peck was a master at telekinesis. "Stand still, we need to find out who you are and what you're doing here. You want to make it easy on us and just tell us?"

She blinked again, but didn't open her mouth to speak.

"Colonel?"

The sound of Chiron's voice reminded Daken he'd been staring at her plump lips instead of concentrating on the job. Damn! "I guess we have to do this the hard way. Kaze, you search her for ID. Houston, make sure she's not hiding any more weapons."

Both Kaze and Houston moved nearer. "She's dressed like a security guard. What the hell would a woman be doing out here all alone? This is a bad neighborhood."

Daken took a moment to look around. "Maybe she's not alone."

Chiron gave a salute. "I'll see if I can find anyone else."

"Stay in the shadows."

"Always."

The woman groaned. "There are *five* of you? Oh, shit. I only saw two. My brother is right. I have no business messing with guns. They make me stupid."

At the sound of her voice, Daken turned back to see

Kaze struggling to get his large hand into her back pocket. "Hell, Colonel. I think maybe you need to do this. I'm overdosing here."

Daken hesitated. If Kaze was overdosing, it would be ten times worse for him. As the Borka aged, they became more sensitive to the female species and Daken had at least a hundred years on Kaze. He turned to Peck who shrugged.

"Sorry, Colonel. It's a command responsibility."

Peck called it straight, Daken didn't have a choice. As the man in charge, he couldn't ask his men to do anything that could potentially end their careers. Any of them would die for him or each other, but none would risk all for a twenty-first century woman. The last thing he needed was to start their mission with a reaction to female pheromones. Traveling back in time had its drawbacks, and this was a big one. To make matters worse if she was affecting Kaze, she'd probably have Daken on his knees with his face buried in her crotch. "Someone better be ready to kill me. I'd rather be dead than be disgraced by a woman."

"Wimp," Kaze huffed. "She's already disgraced us all. We let her get the drop on our commander. None of us saw her."

It reassured Daken to know he'd not been the only one to miss her stealthy approach.

"That makes me feel better," the woman said. "I still don't have a clue what you did to make me give up my gun without an argument. Truthfully, I'd argue for *way* less. Ask anyone who knows me. Was it some kind of drug you sprayed in the air? It smells like rotten eggs. Really gross!"

"She gets the drop on us and then tells us we stink."

Daken glared at Kaze. "I don't find this amusing."

"What's it matter? This is your last mission, isn't

it? You get to go back to a hero's welcome and have your wounds licked by the most beautiful women in existence. Submissives, just like you like them."

"Submissive," Daken said, more curse than word and listened to his men chuckle. He wondered if he was already looking at the most beautiful woman in existence. Butterscotch eyes, sumptuous lips, and freckles across her cheeks and over the bridge of a button nose. Then to cap it all, she had two *very* distinct bulges under the pockets on her shirt. His fingers itched to test their weight. And she was tall, almost six feet. If not for the ugly ball cap, she'd be a knockout by anyone's standards.

Decades of selective breeding and genetic engineering had made the current population of twenty-ninth century women too petite, too polite and much too alike. Somewhere over the past centuries the powers-that-be, *think-tanks*, decided shorter, submissive women were preferable. But they'd gone too far when they took away their ability to procreate in the traditional way, leaving shells of what women used to be. Damn them! Idiots.

Their stupidity created the Korin, who traveled across time to get what they couldn't get in their own time. Rich white men in a thousand years would still be ruling and making stupid decisions, while dumb asses, like Daken and his crew, cleaned up their messes and tried to understand their place in life. Some things never change.

*****

Am I scared stiff? Jenny's brain was sending messages, but her feet had tuned her out. The flash light she still clutched in her hand stopped working, but she hadn't turned it off. She'd had it on long enough to get a good look at the scariest biker dude she'd ever seen in her life. The mental image burned in her brain. The guy had muscles on top of muscles on his bare arms, covered with dark hair and an assortment of really ugly scars.

He had a thick, black, lightning bolt tattoo encircling his muscled neck like a dog collar and pointing down. She knew that well because she first aimed the light where she assumed his face would be. The guy had to be almost seven feet tall. No wonder it took awhile to find his face. A jagged scar cut across the end of his eyebrow and down his cheek and stopped him from being the most handsome man she'd ever seen. But maybe that part had been her imagination.

"Why can't I move?" she asked. "How'd you do that?" The previous two nights, she'd almost caught the intruders, but these weren't the same guys. She was after a couple of kids, not five bikers on human growth injections with steroid chasers. The kids hadn't worried her. These guys, at least the two she'd seen, had her ready to pee her pants like a little girl.

Just when she thought it couldn't get any worse, the handsome devil stuck his hand in her back pocket and cupped her ass.

"What's taking you so long?" another voice said. Jenny thought she'd seen two men trying to break into the storage unit, certainly not five. She wasn't *that* stupid.

"It took me a second to…just shut the hell up. I have my hand in her pants now."

"You look scared shitless," came a third rumbling voice.

Five against one, she was in deep shit, no gun, nothing to use as a weapon other than her flashlight. "I'm the security guard here and I've already called for back up. You hurt me and you'll only make it worse for yourselves."

"Your name?"

What would it hurt? If she told them her name, she'd be less impersonal to them. "Jenny Bender."

"Check her out."

"Sure thing, Colonel," one of them said right away.

"Colonel, huh? As in title or name?" she asked.

He didn't answer her question. "Widen your stance. We need to make certain you're not carrying another weapon."

She didn't want to give in to his command. Her body, however, had a mind of its own in a very strange otherworldly sort of way. She leaned forward placing her hands on the wall and spread her legs wide. This guy was dangerous!

He didn't touch her, but he was wheezing like he'd just run a marathon. What the hell was that about? "She's clean. No weapons. Here's the scanner."

Jenny had a feeling she'd entered an alternative realm. "What kind of criminal *scans* for weapons? Who are you guys? And how the hell can you see what you're doing? I can't see my own hand in front of my face."

"I'm not finding anything, Colonel. Can you hold her while I get her fingerprint?" another voice to her left said.

Suddenly the earth moved under her feet, and he grabbed her as she stumbled, almost tumbling head first into the blackness. What was happening? He could make the earth move, too?

"A tremor...a shadow quake." With his arms still around her waist, he pulled at her hand and held it over a smooth surface, causing it to glow at her touch.

Earthquake? Jenny had never experienced an earthquake.

"This isn't good. Our job to catch the time thieves just got a whole lot tougher. Not only do we need to find the Korin and stop them, we need to see what they've done now to change the course of history."

Jenny smiled inside. Relief washed over her. "I get it. My brother is playing a trick on me, isn't he? He's trying to get even for my getting us both suspended. You tell him, he can pay my share of the rent if I lose this job, too."

The colonel held the small glowing device out to one of the other men. It gave off enough light to allow her see her captor's shadows, their features still eluded her. "Take a look. Jennifer Bender died tonight. She was stabbed by a couple of juvenile delinquents vandalizing storage units. It isn't the Korin who've changed history. *We* have."

"What're we going to do with her?" another of them asked.

The one in charge groaned. "This isn't in the plan. I need time to think. We're sure as hell not going to kill her to make history come true."

This had to be her brother's idea of a joke. He had a wicked and twisted sense of humor. "I know my brother is behind this."

"When did you see us? Did you see us on the security cameras? How long before you put the gun to my head?"

What would it hurt to tell them? "I didn't see you at all. This was the third night in a row that two stupid-ass kids were going from unit to unit, busting the locks and making me look bad. They were so dumb, they were going in order. I figured they'd hit this unit tonight. My brother told me not to try to handle it alone. He sent you guys, didn't he? He's trying to teach me a lesson."

"We must've scared off her killers," a shadow to her right said.

"We came here to stop the Korin, and stumbled into a nightmare. Let's erase her memory and figure out what we need to do to make this right."

"You guys are *good*," she laughed. "Go ahead. Erase my memory and make me forget the creep who took my virginity in his parent's bed when I was seventeen. No wait. Make me forget Bobby. I almost married the jerk and never knew he was a drunk and a cheat. I wasted two years of my life."

The next instant, a blinding pain cut into her skull. "Are you doing this, too? Knock it off."

"Why is she still talking?"

"Hell if I know, Colonel." With so many voices, she couldn't begin to keep them straight, hard as she tried. If she had to identify these guys in a lineup, she'd make a fool of herself.

"Zap her harder. Standard operating procedure."

Another pain hit her, but it didn't hurt nearly as badly as the first. "I have no idea what's going on, but you guys are real jerks. Whatever it is you're doing, stop it. I'm sure my brother didn't tell you to give me a headache. He does that just fine on his own."

Chapter Two

Jenny awakened with the most dreadful headache she'd ever experienced. She didn't have time to worry about pain, not while lying on a bed surrounded by four giant bikers from the deepest bowels of hell. They stood towering over her like they'd pounce if she moved a muscle. In the dark, she'd only guessed how big they were. Here, wherever *here* was, she couldn't believe the lies her eyes told her.

"Are you guys planning to make my head hurt worse? Or something else?" And why in the hell didn't the *something else* part scare her more. In fact, despite their size and the bizarre circumstances, they didn't scare her much at all. She needed her brain examined. Had they somehow disabled her fear?

They all looked as if they'd been cut from the same cloth. It was almost eerie how similar they were, dark angles, bulging muscles, more scars than she could begin to count and all of them debasingly handsome. All had midnight blue eyes framed by dark lashed. Each wore their dark hair too long. Long enough to be mistaken for rockers.

"Are you guys related?"

The one standing at the end of the bed shook his head harder than the rest. "I'm Kaze." Then he turned to the one in charge, the one with the lightning bolt on his neck and shrugged his huge shoulders. "I didn't think it mattered. Until we get this figured out, we may as well be polite."

"I'm polite," another one said. "Chiron."

What kind of names were Kaze and Chiron?

"Me, too," said a third, right before he dropkicked the second guy, who landed half on her bed, and half on the floor. She bounced into the air and scrambled to get away from him, clawing at the bedspread, because her legs still didn't want to work correctly.

"You two take it outside. Kaze, make sure they don't draw attention. And keep an eye out for Peck. He should be here by now." The colonel turned back to Jenny. "My name is Daken. I'm in charge here."

"Where is *here*? Do you know the penalty for kidnapping?"

"Lady, we saved your life. You should be grateful." He stopped talking and tilted his handsome face to watch his men leave. The color of his eyes seemed to change as he spoke. They lightened from very dark blue to a blazing sapphire. Of course, in the muted light of a sleazy motel room, it could be in her head. It would seem her imagination was getting a workout.

"Don't get too bloody and don't let anyone see you," he told them as they shut the door.

"They're really going to fight?"

"My men would rather fight than breathe. It's what we live for."

Okay. The man was a kook. But the most handsome kook she'd ever seen. Just like in the storage unit, she didn't seem to be able to budge. It came in waves, as if her movements, or lack of, depended on his concentration. "Why can't I move freely? Don't tell me a hundred and twenty pound woman worries you."

"One-hundred and *twenty*?"

"Excuse me?" Damn him. Yes, it was a very good thing nothing worked. After she popped him in the nose, she'd only embarrass herself. She'd more than likely be drooling, panting and maybe even begging. It'd been a very, *very* long time since anyone had caught her attention. Probably too long, because she actually considered inviting him to crawl onto the bed with her.

"Thank the Gods for small favors," he continued.

"At least we have that much control over you. Nothing else seems to work."

He wore leather pants so tight they appeared painted on. His matching leather vest hung open to expose a wide chest covered with dark hair. The six-pack on his perfect abs had a scar cutting across his tanned skin before it dipped into his pants, as if pointing to the immense bulge of his package. Was that part of him scarred, too?

Where did that come from? Jenny didn't normally think about a man's privates once she'd held a gun to his face.

*****

A shadow tremor passed over them again and the course of human history changed with each passing second. Daken scratched his head. What the hell was he going to do with her? They were already short on time. "Was it *us* again or the Korin?" He said the words to himself, knowing she didn't have the answers.

"What's with all the earthquakes? I lived my whole life without an earthquake and now two in a short time."

"It wasn't an earthquake. We call them shadow tremors or quakes, sonic vibrations traveling across time and space when someone changes the course of history."

Daken watched her face darken. In her place, how would he handle this? She opened her mouth and then shut it before opening it a second time. "You expect me to believe this shit? Pretend I believe a word you say and tell me who you are."

What would it hurt to tell her? The more she knew of the truth, the crazier anyone would believe her to be if she repeated what he was about to tell her. "I'm Colonel Daken Parker, head of Shadow Team Ten. This is my last mission before Peck takes my place as team leader. I'm scheduled for mandatory retirement."

"You guys are some kind of team? Shadow Team Ten. What a name." She chuckled, but her face remained closed and tight. "And two of your men had to go outside to fight each other because it's part of their mission?"

"My men live to fight. A day without a fight is not a good one, even if we have to fight each other. It's how we survive. The Korin are ruthless, and they outnumber us ten to one. Only the Korin and the Borka can travel across time and live, but the Korin do it with minimal damage to their bodies. The Borka can only travel a limited number of times, or risk losing their lives. The council has given us an exact number they will not allow us to exceed. This is my last crossing."

Her amber eyes followed him as he moved while he spoke. Other than that, she didn't stir from the center of the bed because of his control over her limbs. "You're so full of shit. What year in the future do you come from?"

Daken didn't expect her to believe him. "More than eight hundred years in the future." He completely released his mental hold on her and she rolled up to sit cross-legged in the middle of the bed. He took a step back as he caught her scent. She had as much power over him, maybe more, only she didn't know it. She'd almost killed both of them, when he had to hold her on his lap and drive his chopper to the hotel. Then again, he might've been hurt badly, but not killed unless the fall beheaded him.

She huffed. "This ought to be good. What's life like in the future?"

Daken didn't like to talk about it. For a select few, earth had never been better, but the majority of earth's inhabitants weren't so lucky. "The world is overpopulated and thanks to the people of the twenty-first century, we have limited natural resources. When the Korin travel back to the past, nothing good comes of it. They come to use the earth as their own personal pleasure palace. They're debauched and immoral with no conscience to speak of. And they kill without a second thought, in the most cowardly ways conceivable."

"Why doesn't the law in the twenty-ninth century stop them?"

"The Korin isn't only a race. It's a secret society of time thieves. All its members are from the ruling class, sons of the richest and most powerful men history has ever known. One percent of society in the future lives well, ninety-nine percent of Earth's inhabitants don't. They live to serve the one percent or die. The Borka are the exception to every rule ever made. We're heroes to the common people, the exact opposite of the ruling class. But the ruling class welcomes us with open arms because we are willing to die to save the future of the Earth...the world they believe belongs only to them. Without *us*, their future could be in question. They hate living with us, but can't live without us."

"You've given a lot of thought to this ridiculous story."

The door slammed open. Kaze rushed in with Chiron and Houston on either side of him as he helped them into the room. They had one sonic med-stabilizer to share among the five of them. If anything happened to it, they'd have to curtail their fighting and save themselves for the real wars. He removed the stabilizer, no bigger than a common-era credit card from the hidden pouch in his belt and gave it to Kaze.

"Watch Kaze. Maybe seeing will convince you."

"Why do you care if I'm convinced?"

Peck came in as she asked the question. "I'd like to hear the answer to that. We've been making bets on what Daken intends to do with you. I thought perhaps he'd take you back across with him since he thinks women are too tame in the future."

She reached up to the ridiculous ball cap covering her head. He'd begun to wonder if she was bald under the cap and the bandana she wore under it. When she removed both at once, his heart stopped and then pounded double time. Her short curly mop of hair was like waving a red flag in front of a raging bull. Behind him, Peck huffed.

"Is that real?" Kaze asked.

"Are *you* for real? Do you think I'd go around looking like a carrot top if I had a choice? I'm allergic to dyes or it would be dark, maybe even black." She looked away from Kaze and fixed a cold stare on Daken with her butterscotch eyes. "I'd like to hear what you have planned for me too."

"First...watch Kaze use the stabilizer. Move to where you can get a good look at what he does."

The woman, Jenny, got up from the bed and walked to stand next to Kaze, who appeared ready to bolt only a second later. "How did you ride on the bike with her? I can't stand this close to her with wanting to fu..."

"The stabilizer!"

Kaze rolled his eyes, but shut his mouth and began to run the device over Houston and Chiron's bloody faces. The results were immediate. The only thing it wouldn't do was remove scars. It fused skin to skin, repaired broken bones, removed swelling and did what their bodies would take days even weeks to do left on their own to heal naturally.

Jenny's eyes widened. "How are you doing that? Is this like stunt double movie magic?"

"We can eventually die of old age, but the average age is approaching one thousand years. There's no physical damage that will kill us, except decapitation. We've found cures for every known disease."

Jenny...he didn't like thinking of her by her first name...Jenny turned back to look at Daken like he'd lost his mind, shaking her beautiful mop of curls. He knew a sure fire way to convince her. "You want Kaze to cut his finger off and fuse it back to show you?"

Kaze stopped his administrations to Chiron and Houston. "You cut your own damned finger off. Just because it heals fast, doesn't make it hurt any less."

"Let's say I believed your crazy story. You still haven't said what happens to me."

"The key lies in the answers you give me. We've learned you are a policewoman, on suspension for not following your superior officer's direct order. Your brother spoke up in your defense and also was suspended."

"My brother got a week without pay. I got three. That's why I took the job as a security guard. I pretty much live from week to week on the pittance I make. My brother and I have a mother with Alzheimer's to support. She was only fifty at the onset and our father died while we were still in our teens. Or did you already know all of that?"

Daken knew. "And you're worried you'll follow your mother's footsteps."

She blinked her beautiful eyes. Daken moved closer to her. "About three months ago you started having a rash of rapes on your beat. Both men and women, all of them raped by the same guys. They're brutal and they take perverse pleasure in degrading the men, tourists coming to town to a have good time, getting more than they bargained for."

"How could you know that? I got suspended because I threatened to go to the press. It's bad for a town whose main trade is tourism to have this become public knowledge. I thought people had a right to know, so they could protect themselves."

Daken agreed. "There were three of them that you know of. All of them are blonde, good looking and seemingly respectable business types, who spend money like water. But all your information comes from the sidelines, none of the victims remember anything. Then a few weeks ago, they went too far. They raped and murdered two underage girls, who'd skipped school and were looking for a good time."

"These rapists are the Korin? They're the men you're after?"

"We've tracked almost a dozen of the Korin this time, more at once than ever before. Those three have broken from the rest of the pack and are on their own. They are in their comfort zone here. The others are smart and not drawing attention to themselves by targeting people who'll be missed right away."

"This is all about sex? These men travel across time just to get *laid*?"

"I shouldn't have to tell you rape isn't about sex, it's about power and control. Not every member of the Korin can have their lust for power sated in our society. The positions of authority do not pass hands easily and we've yet to discover for certain how long we can live. Some of the elders have been alive since this century.

"Your police force could be the best in the world, but they won't be able to stop them. Backed into a corner, they'll kill anyone and everyone. They aren't permitted to take lives in our time. Not even the elders will purposely take a human life. They can only satisfy their blood lust here and only *we* can stop the carnage."

"You said I had questions to answer?"

"How badly do you want to stop them? Enough to risk working with us? Well, maybe working *with* us wasn't the right words. Could you stay out of our way and keep your mouth shut until we finish our job?" Daken could see from her tight expression she didn't like his proposal. Maybe he could tempt her with something more personal. "If I could give you back your mother, would you never speak of us as long as you continue to live?"

"I wouldn't even tell my brother, but if I agree then

that means I'm also agreeing I should already be dead."

"The elders say nothing happens by chance or without purpose. The fates may have put you there for our paths to cross."

"And how do I know you guys aren't like the Korin. I mean, how can I be sure you won't...you know...use me?"

Daken couldn't help it. He had to laugh, even when her furrowed eyebrows showed she didn't appreciate it. "Among the five of us, four are virgins. We've taken vows of celibacy, not for religious or moral reasons, but because sex weakens us to the point we're unable to fulfill our missions. If I've been able to resist women for three hundred and fifty years, what makes you think you could tempt me?"

"You've just told me *why* you guys need to fight every day."

Another shadow tremor shook the room, this time much harder. "We need an answer from you and we need it fast. The longer we're here the more likely we put our world in jeopardy."

"This is bad. We've had three tremors in less the two hours. I'd be willing to bet they've killed again," Peck said.

"She rides with you," both Kaze and Chiron said at the same time.

She looked at Daken and frowned. "What's their problem?"

"The same as mine...*you*. Let's move."

To anyone looking as they roared and rumbled down the Vegas strip, they came across as bad-assed bikers. No one would mess with them, except maybe the local law, but even that was unlikely. Jenny wasn't sure what she wanted. If anyone in her squad pulled them over, she'd be free. But she wasn't sure she wanted to be...not yet. Not if there was a chance he'd told her the truth and her mother could be cured...get her life back.

"Do you have to do that?" Daken yelled over the noise of the engine.

"Do I have to hold on to you? What's your problem? You act like it bothers you to have me touch you."

He growled. Jenny had to admit, learning this bad boy biker could be a virgin made her curious...too curious. Could she tempt him? Women in the twenty-ninth century must be totally different. No way would hunks like these be virgins. Today's women would eat them alive.

They cruised into the parking lot of one of the ritziest joints on the strip. Jenny could only imagine the warm welcome they'd receive.

"Are we overdressed?" Daken asked after he parked, like he'd read her mind.

"Be prepared. People are going to stare."

"Yeah, but not a single one will look us straight in the eye for longer than two seconds."

Jenny had to agree. "Do we know where to find them...the Korin?"

"We? Yes, *we* know their room number, but they may not be in their room. *You* will stay out of our way, won't you? One thing you should know, the only way to kill one of the Korin is to behead them. Death is our last resort, but it could happen. We prefer to send them back to stand trial. The first three we are after are not highly placed, nor as rich as they need to escape long punishment. If they are sent back, they'll get life in suspended animation. In all likelihood, they'd prefer death."

Behead? For a twenty-six year old, Jenny believed she'd seen her fair share of bad guys, but not once had she used her gun. In this case it wouldn't matter anyway, a gun shot or even several would only slow them down.

If...they were to be believed. Did she really? After everything she'd seen so far, she leaned more toward believing than not. But *beheading*? "I'll stay out of the way."

"Does this show you I'm speaking the truth?" He took her hand and ran her fingers along the side of his neck. The tattoo had kept her from noticing the brutal scar, but she could feel it. Someone had evidently tried to behead *him*. "If this goes well, we'll visit the nursing home where your mother lives in the morning. I can't give her a complete cure right away. It would draw too much attention. But I can give her enough help to allow her to leave the nursing home at least."

Jenny eyes burned and throat closed. Never in her widest dreams, did Jenny think she'd get her mother back. If they could give her mother a meaningful life again, Jenny would do anything they wanted, within reason. "I'll stay out of your way. I promise."

Chapter Three

Jenny didn't like the dark, never had. Daken, on the other hand, didn't even slow down as they moved through the completely black corridor. Somehow, one of them had managed to cut the power to the hotel. She didn't think that was possible. More proof they weren't from this world. When he stopped short she collided into his back.

He gave a breathy groan.

"Wait here. Chiron and Peck are coming down the hallway from the opposite direction. Houston is staying below to watch our backs. I'm putting this in your pocket."

Jenny didn't have a clue what *this* was.

"It's a communicator. You only have to hold your hand over your pocket and apply pressure, it doesn't take much. I'll get to you as fast as I can if you need me. Now, stay right here. I don't want you anywhere near these perverted idiots."

Jenny wanted to argue, but she'd promised. Besides, the blackness surrounding her kept her prisoner. "You can see in the dark?"

"Yes, we can see. So can the time thieves, only not as good."

"You got to give her credit, Colonel," Kaze said. "There's not a woman in *our* world who'd come with us to confront the Korin."

"Be careful, you're starting to sound like me. You don't want to end up three-hundred and fifty years old without a woman you love more than fighting."

This was surreal. Had he just complimented her in an offhanded way? Jenny had the urge to grab him and plant a kiss on his full firm lips, one he never forget for the rest of his hundreds of years back in his world where no woman had his love. Instead, she bit her lip and listened to them moving down the hallway without her. There was no sense kissing him, it'd only spoil *her* remaining time alive. Or would it?

The sounds of freighted people opening the doors to their hotel rooms and calling out soon filled the hallway.

"Don't worry," she said. "City wide blackout. Nothing to fret about, it's almost dawn. Just stay where you are."

"She's right. There's no lights outside," someone yelled.

Jenny had only been trying to console those scared in the dark, she had no idea they'd somehow caused the lights to go out in the city. Wouldn't *that* change history? What about accidents because of it? No, they could heal anyone who shouldn't be hurt. She reasoned they couldn't control anyone who happened to see what they were doing and then later spoke about it.

"A city wide blackout?" an unfamiliar voice rumbled beside her and caused the tiny hairs on the back of her neck to tingle. "Funny, I don't remember that happening on this day in history."

A chill followed the tingle. She grabbed for her pocket, but a hand caught hers, pinning her to the wall behind her with a thud. This guy meant business and he smelled of sex, lots of whiskey and *vanilla*. One of *them*…the Korin? She didn't dare take a chance. She used her other hand to gouge where she hoped she'd find his eyes. She connected with his Adam's apple instead, so he was either a basketball player or Korin. He started choking and gasping for air, releasing his strong hold on her hand.

She kneed him in the dark, hoping to connect where it would hurt the most. If he was anything like his otherworldly counterparts, his package made a sizeable target. At the same time, she reached for her pocket to compress the small lump. Not waiting for it to work, she pummeled the groaning, gasping form in the darkness.

"I told you to call if you *needed* me."

Daken. Relief washed over her.

"Maybe you should stop beating him, before you actually make me feel sorry for him. He has to go back to stand trial knowing everyone will mock him for getting his ass kicked by a woman."

Jenny stilled, the adrenaline pumping through her so hard, it made her half-giddy. "It's dark. I wasn't sure."

"Trust me. You got your man." Daken nudged between her and the man she'd beaten. "Time for you to go back where you belong. And time is what you will be spending for the rest of your miserable life. I hope it was worth it. Jenny, stay right where you are. I'm sending him back."

Jenny wished she could see. In the next instant a hand grabbed her arm, jerking her forward. The floor under Jenny's feet gave way and she began to freefall. A second large hand caught hers and she clung to it. She could feel the large silver ring Daken wore, grateful it was him. Caught in a whirlwind, Jenny held on with all her might. A second later, the lights came back on as Daken pulled her into his arms against the firm wall of his chest. She looked down to see the floor right where it belonged.

"I was falling."

"We have an audience. Maybe we should find our room," he said and then touched his lips to hers. His gasp matched her own as he surprised her. The tensile stretch of his mouth on hers as he touched her in the most pleasing way possible, made her mind jump ahead to what else he could do better than anyone before. How could her mind go from a mere touch to wanting everything he had to give in one fell swoop?

More otherworldly magic? It had to be. When his mouth became more demanding, her heart soared. She wrapped her arms around his neck and kissed him back. Nothing had ever been as important as communicating what his kiss did for her. It showed her all the possibilities life had to offer. It gave her hope and more. His mouth on hers was the gateway to completing her, of revealing her place in life.

This was crazy.

Insane!

Nobody would believe her. She didn't believe it herself. Was she falling in love, truly in love for the first time in her life, but with a warrior from over nine hundred years in the future? If so, did she have a chance of getting him to love her back? Did she...have a chance when she couldn't even think?

*****

Daken didn't know what to do. This warrior woman had him by the balls. He wanted her right then more than he wanted anything. Living a long life had its drawbacks. Nothing surprised him in more years than he could remember. The feel of her lips against his did more than just surprise him, it stupefied him. It had to be the pheromones thick in the air around them, nothing more.

Didn't it?

"I want you." Had those words really come out of *his* mouth?

She pulled back and slowly opened her butterscotch eyes. "What if you're the best thing to ever happen to me? How do I live without you when you're gone, never to return?"

"Colonel, you are not going to believe this."

Those were words Daken definitely didn't want to hear coming from Peck's mouth. Not now. Especially, not now. Peck wasn't easily shaken. Daken reluctantly released Jenny, and allowing her to stand off to his side.

"What?"

Peck stopped next to Jenny and slowly waved his hand toward everyone still outside their rooms. All of them stopped whatever they were doing and went back inside immediately. "Houston took off after the third Korin on his own. I was too busy to stop him." Peck glared at Jenny, still close enough to Daken for him to be affected by the heat pouring off her.

Daken cleared his throat. "Jenny caught one of them. She was beating him to a pulp when I got here."

Peck stopped scowling and gave a curt nod. "He was probably sending her telepathic messages and didn't have a clue she wouldn't get them. We need to find Houston."

"I think he was drunk. He smelled like he bathed in whiskey and vanilla," Jenny said. "Maybe Houston's man is drunk too?"

Daken didn't like the thought of one of his men out there on his own. "Which way did he go?"

Peck took off. "This way."

"Stay close." Daken didn't wait to see if she listened. Houston should've known better. Between Kaze and Houston, the two newest additions to Shadow Team Ten, Daken didn't know if he'd survive his final mission. Their status as the leading team was in jeopardy. Team Twelve had been breathing down their necks for some time and this could be the final screw up allowing them to take the lead.

They entered the stairwell and saw Chiron running up to the landing ahead of them. "Up," he said and kept moving.

The whine and clash of a sonic sword connecting with a metal surface would've told them where Houston was, even if Chiron hadn't. Daken wanted to look back to Jenny, but didn't dare. His comrades needed his undivided attention.

"Incoming!"

Houston's shout from above would've ordinarily had them diving for cover, but there wasn't anything to duck behind in the stairwell. The door leading to the eleventh floor was only feet away. His men would know what to do, but would she? He reached back as he dived for the door Chiron opened. When his hand connected with hers, he couldn't believe it. All four of them made it through the door before the explosion.

A sonic bomb, the size of a marble would do serious damage, maybe even kill them, but the percussion from this one hardly registered. Seconds after it detonated, they were moving again.

The smell of sulfur was thick when they ran back into the stairwell.

"Fuck!" Peck said.

Daken pushed ahead, knowing what he'd find. The blood trail dripping down the stairs found him first. Houston's mangled body lay flat on the floor in a pool of blood on the twelfth floor landing. But he still had his head, so there was hope. With a handheld device it would require far more time than Houston could spare. The smell told Daken, his teammate had tried to return to the future for help, but didn't have the power to do it on his own.

"Peck, notify base to await Houston's return. I'm sending you back, buddy."

Houston stirred and opened a single eye. The other side of his face was covered with blood, loose skin and tissue. "I got him, but he threw the bomb right as I sent him across. I knew you guys were coming with no cover. I had to throw myself on it."

"Don't worry about anything. Just think of all the scars you'll get from this." Together Daken and Peck sent him across.

Daken keyed his communicator. "We need a

cleanup team. We have sonic bomb damage."

He turned to Peck. "This is my fault. I should've watched him more closely. I knew he had it in him to go off on his own."

"It's a lesson most of us had to learn at one time or another. We'll deal with the fallout after we finish our mission."

Peck was right. Now wasn't the time to hash it out. If Houston didn't have a chance, they'd already know by now. It only took seconds with a high-tech whole-body stabilizer. "Let's get back to base and see about finding the remaining Korin. Three down and eight more to go."

Peck twitched, a nervous gesture Daken recognized as trouble. "What else?"

"They had a phone book open in their room with a name underlined. John H. White."

Daken worked through the possibilities. "This is the year John and Amy White gave birth to a baby boy in Vegas. Why would the Korin be seeking one of their own?"

"Elder White is a conservative and some even think he champions the plight of the commoners, but there are rumors his son is one of the most debauched of all the secret society and a close friend of Lawzard."

Daken agreed with Peck. "But they can't be trying to kill Elder White because then the son would never be born. Not to mention how Lawzard would respond to one of his closest companions being eliminated. No one, Borka or Korin wants to cross Lawzard. He's our biggest foe. We've never come close to catching him in nearly fifty tries, nor have any of the other Borka teams. Unless this is a new plan to control some of the more perverted Korin, before they do irreparable damage, none of it makes sense. Since this will soon be your team to command, I'll leave it to you to contact Elder White with this news. Do it on the ride back to our hotel. Let's get moving before housekeeping gets here and complains about the mess we left them."

His men didn't need to be asked twice. The cleanup team was comprised of Borka who for one reason or another weren't chosen to become a shadow team warrior. They had a choice of joining the rest of the common population or remain with the Borka in a less prestigious position. Most remained and their attitudes showed their discontent.

Daken didn't relish the ride back. Normally riding a chopper was right up there with fresh air and steak, but riding with Jenny changed the equation. She slid onto the bike after him, snuggled up to his back, and wrapped her arms around his waist. As much as it bothered him physically, her actions reassured him. He gave high marks for how she conducted herself. She hadn't spoken again since the action in the stairwell, but holding him like this spoke volumes.

Back at their room, Peck picked up the phone to order Chinese while Kaze and Chiron went into the adjoining room probably to talk about *him*. Daken didn't need to be told what happened to Houston had been his responsibility.

Jenny perched on the end of one of the beds.

"You did good tonight," he told her.

Peck got off the phone and nodded. "I didn't know a woman could witness something like that and keep her mouth shut. Not once have you complained. Maybe you should come across with us and teach our women a thing or two."

"He'll live through that? There was so much blood."

"He'll live or we already would've heard. We might've even been replaced by Shadow Team Twelve by now, but Houston evidently convinced them it was his fault and it won't happen again." Daken turned his attention to Peck. "Were you able to reach Elder White?"

"Negative. Nor did I leave a message just in case it's intercepted. Mind if I step next door and try again where I can concentrate. Maybe you'd like to tell Jenny about what's happening. I'm sure she has questions."

What's happening? Since when do you trust a woman with warrior business? Peck ignored Daken's mental question and continued into the next room.

"I do have questions. Do the Korin use bombs all the time?"

"Not bombs like you're accustomed to."

She huffed. "I'm not personally accustomed to bombs. Bombs 101 wasn't offered where I went to school."

"The Korin don't like close contact where there's a possibility they can be beheaded. They use *sonic* bombs, no bigger than the end of my thumb, but deadly. They are on a time delay. It takes a few seconds for them to fully charge after they're released. When Houston threw himself on it so quickly, he stopped it from gaining strength. The Korin prefer using anything that will hurt us from afar. I'm impressed by the way you handled yourself." Daken had intended to say more, but his communicator vibrated. He placed it next to his temple to receive the telepathic message.

"You are in violation of your orders. You and your team need to return immediately to stand charge for treason."

Daken jerked the communicator back and disabled it before anyone realized he'd heard the order. "Fucking hell. Get in here!"

Peck came running with Kaze and Chiron trailing behind. "Is there a problem?"

"A problem? Disaster is more like it. Did you contact Elder White?"

"Negative."

"We've been ordered back immediately to stand trial for treason."

Peck winced. "We always knew this could happen one day. Fucking Korin."

Daken didn't know it could happen or at least he'd managed to convince himself otherwise. "I don't want to burn off my last entry to be placed in suspended animation for doing my job. At this point, it's each man's decision. All of us know the Korin suspends first and then asks questions, *maybe* later. A charge is as good as a conviction."

"Why the hell did they tip their hand. Why didn't they let us return after our mission and then charge us?"

Peck was right.

"Maybe they think we're too stupid to understand what they intend to do with us. Kaze, when you requisitioned the med-stabilizer, didn't you mention you had a problem at the supply depot?"

A worried look came over Kaze's face. "I had to fight to get it. I thought the jerk was having a bad day, so I slipped it into my pocket when he turned his back. Do you think we're in deep shit just because I copped a stabilizer?"

Daken wanted to knock himself in the head. "This has nothing to do with what you did. Why didn't I see it? Peck, try to reach our men. See if the rest of our team is safe."

Peck held his communicator to his temple. "I got someone, but I don't know who. What the hell is happening?"

"Stop!" Daken commanded. "Don't try again. They'll get a fix on us. Let's move. Now. We're *all* fucked."

"Houston," Peck murmured.

Daken didn't want to consider what might've happened to Houston. "They could've let him die. But if it's any consolation, by sending him back they'll believe we're completely unprotected here. They don't know we have the med-stabilizer. We have that at least."

"I never did trust the Korin," Kaze said.

Peck nodded. "Me, either. And I risked court martial for just this eventuality. I have a secret stash of equipment and plenty of cash."

Daken wasn't surprised or angry by what could be perceived as treason. "I'm thankful I was the only one with my head up my ass."

Chapter Four

They found a sleazy motel on the outskirts of the strip and took inventory of all the equipment available to them.

"I stored three million in cash, and almost a half ton of gold bars."

And Daken believed he *knew* Peck. They'd been friends and partners for over a century. "Half a ton of gold? What did you know that I didn't?"

Peck walked to the window and slit the curtain a fraction to look out. "I didn't *know* anything. It's more an extreme lack of trust. My mother was bound by law to never speak of my father, but that didn't stop her from talking to me in secret. She never believed his death was an accident. She raised me not to trust the Korin for a second. And the fact I can't reach her either, speaks volumes. I've never been out of communication with her. She's gone underground. "

Daken remembered Peck's father. They'd never spoke of him...ever. "Do you suspect a revolution then?" Daken had heard murmurings, but the common people always spoke of freedom from oppression. Peck's father's voice had been one of the loudest. It was one of the few things that hadn't changed on earth. "Your *mother*? You listen to the revolutionary ramblings of a woman?"

Peck shrugged. "I know you and most of the Korin don't believe women are capable of much aside from serving men, but you're wrong." His gaze wandered to Jenny, still perched on the end of bed. "Old friend, I have the distinct feeling you're going to discover exactly how wrong you are."

Daken sat down next to Jenny. "You've been silent through this."

She chewed her fingernail and didn't look at him.

"Did you tell anyone about me? Did you tell the Korin in charge you interrupted my death?"

Daken at first felt sheepish and then relieved because he hadn't. "I didn't get a chance to say anything. I intended to, but I didn't want my ass reamed."

Jenny's tight expression eased. "I'm glad you didn't. I don't think you should trust anyone outside this room right now. And I don't want to get my brother involved in this mess either. Or my mother. For the time being, maybe we shouldn't do anything to draw attention to her. I mean, if you have the ability to heal her, we don't need to think about it while the heat is on."

An unselfish woman? This was new to Daken. "You surprise me."

She tilted her beautiful face up to Peck and winked before she turned back to Daken. "And I was wondering. Even if you didn't tell them, do the Korin have a way to find out about me?"

Curious how her mind worked, Daken weighed the possibilities. "Unless someone had reason to look for you specifically, no, I don't think so. You don't need to worry they'll send someone to finish you off."

Jenny gazed back to Peck, still at the window. Why did she keep looking at *him*?

"And they'd never suspect you'd allow me to get involved in this?"

Daken almost laughed. "Never. I'd never suspect it myself. Besides, you're not really involved. We just haven't figured out what to do with you."

She smiled at Peck, who beamed at her. Daken didn't like it. Not at all. He'd never seen her smile and the effect nearly made him weak in the knees. Her face became magic, lifting him from the chains of their dire situation, showing him a hint of a brighter future. *That was bull shit!*

When she turned away from Peck, her smile faded.

So did Daken's hope. "If I'm really careful...you know like maybe quitting the force and taking a personal assistant job for an out of town business man and his company, maybe I could stay alive and not come to the Korin's attention?"

Daken didn't like the direction of her logic. "That's possible. I suppose we're your new employers?"

"Yes. My brother wants me to quit the force anyway. I'd actually be making him happy. I know I'm new to this, but the way I see it, this is bigger than me. This is about helping the future of mankind."

"You'd do that? You're willing to help us?" Peck was right. Daken had underestimated her.

Jenny nodded, then shrugged and next shook her head, all in rapid succession. "Yes. No. I don't know. I had my life planned out. It didn't involve getting involved with Shadow Team Ten, or anything remotely resembling what you guys are here for. Then again, I didn't plan what most women do. I didn't want to get married, nor have children. I was always too afraid I'd end up with Alzheimer's, like Mom. If you can save me from that and give my life more purpose than I ever imagined, wouldn't I be a fool not to jump at it? Or would I be a fool to believe all of this?"

"Did you forget what happened in the stairwell? This is a dangerous proposition. Now we'll be fighting all of the Korin and maybe even some of the Borka, so it could be deadly for all of us. You're sure you can do this?"

She ran both hands through her mop of glistening red curls. "I'm already supposed to be dead. Am I right about this? You guys may never be able to return to the future until this is settled? And everything you're about is keeping the earth's inhabitants safe now and in the future?"

Daken couldn't comprehend the fight ahead or even how to put it to words. How could he make her understand? "Something *like* that, in a simplistic way I suppose."

"This is the opportunity of a lifetime. Even for a woman…especially for a woman. I've decided. Say the word and I'm yours to command."

Peck huffed and jerked back to the window where Daken couldn't see his face.

"You're enjoying this, aren't you?" he said to the back of Peck's head.

"Immensely. I'd always hoped to see the day your mind was opened."

Daken didn't care for Peck's reference to being closed-minded. They'd found one in a million in Jenny Bender. Daken didn't doubt it for a second, but he wasn't certain it was a good thing.

Jenny tilted her face up, her amber eyes crinkling at the corners. "This is all a dream, isn't it? Or a nightmare? I'm going to wake up soon."

Daken checked his sword, and stared at Peck. "Nothing is turning out as we planned. Maybe you should share this with Chiron and Kaze."

Peck paused at the doorway. "I think you need to be completely honest with Jenny and do it fast. We could all be gone or dead in the blink of an eye."

Daken turned to her, suddenly unsure. "Peck had the forethought to be prepared for this eventuality. He should be commanding the team instead of me. If not for him, who knows what would've happened to us."

"If he was in charge, with all his advance preparation, the men would wonder if he somehow caused this. It'd be hard for them to trust him."

He turned around and a beam of light filtering through the window spotlighted the prominence in the front of his tight leather pants. "I don't…what are you looking at?"

*****

Jenny jumped. He'd caught her staring *there* again? Try as hard as she could, it was impossible to ignore the protrusion. "Sorry."

"I can't seem to stop from getting hard whenever I'm near you."

Jenny didn't want to get too excited by his admission. "But it isn't really just about *me,* is it? I mean, couldn't any woman do that to you?"

"I have to admit I try to stay away from your kind." He gave a kind of laugh, but his eyes were dark, almost pained.

"But yet you've agreed to keep me close…very close."

"Are you suggesting we make the most of it?" He started to pace.

Had she suggested that? No. But, did she dare? Why the hell not?

He'd probably regret it once they finished, but Jenny decided she could live with that. She stood and started to undress.

Daken looked a little lost. She patted the bed to let him know exactly what she had in mind. "And this is just a thought, but if you could use telepathic control you have, use it on my clit."

A fraction of a second later, her clit grew hard and throbbed. He gave a shy smile.

Uh, oh. She'd been teasing. However… "I wish I would've showered first. I didn't plan on seducing you."

His eyes narrowed. "I appreciate that. I haven't thought of much else from the second I laid eyes on you. And my poor performance on this mission shows it."

"Maybe you need a quick fuck to get it out of your system." She began unbuttoning her very unflattering, unisex shirt, thankful she'd chosen a sexy bra.

Halfway down the shirt, he took a step back.

Damn.

For a second she hesitated, and then moved faster. She'd seen him staring at her chest often, so she knew he wanted to see what was under her shirt. "Why exactly do the Borka pledge to celibacy?"

"It isn't so much a pledge as our way to hold onto our way of life. The alternative is to become part of the general population. We're treated as heroes." He stopped talking to suck air when she peeled the shirt off.

"And how is it you know sex will spoil everything for you?"

"The Korin are our examples. Look what giving into the desire for sensual pleasures has done to them. They are weak in mind and body. Besides, Peck's had sex and he says it isn't worth the risk."

"I wondered which one of you was no longer a virgin." As she lowered the straps on her bra, she got a sudden dose of vulnerability and hesitated. "We don't have to—"

"Don't stop," he rasped. "I'll lock the door.

"If you're worried, we don't have to go all the way. There are all kinds of things we can do to give pleasure to one another."

"Like this" he said as he walked back toward her and delivered another telepathic clench to her clit.

"How do you do that?" He'd nearly made her come and he hadn't even touched her…physically. "Try using your finger instead of your mind. You might enjoy it. Actually, why not use your telepathic gift and your finger at the same time." She sat on the edge of the bed to untie her ugly work boots and toed out of them. "This is just great. I'm trying to get romantic while wearing the ugliest clothes a woman could wear. If you accept, it's proof positive any woman would probably do."

"And again, I'll remind you I've proven any woman won't do. This is my last mission and I may never return to my life in the twenty-ninth century. I think it's long past time, unless you need a commitment…"

"I've never thought of myself as easy, but I'm not a prude either and it's been too long since I've been interested in the *possibilities*." While she spoke, she pulled off her thick socks and unfastened her cotton slacks. When she stood to unzip them and allowed them to drop to the floor, he rewarded her with a lopsided grin. A scar she hadn't noticed on his lip became visible with his smile. Still, until he touched her, she held herself in reserve.

When her fingers started toward her panties on their own volition, she gasped. "How do you do that? And, why do you do it? Don't people in the twenty-ninth century touch anymore?"

"I'm thinking of kissing you. I've thought of it continually. The earliest of civilizations believed to kiss is to exchange souls." He closed the space between them so fast, she jumped again. He didn't give her time to react, just pulled her against his hard body and lowered his head across hers.

Jenny had been kissed and kissed *well*, but from the moment their lips touched she recognized trouble.

This kiss changed the rules.

All of her senses became inflamed in a single blazing instant. His scent came to her a fraction of an instant before the firm pressure of his lips. He smelled earthy and clean and the touch of his mouth on hers made her tingle everywhere. How could a man who'd never made love, kiss like this?

Or was it his words…a kiss couldn't exchange souls?

Could it?

He took her breath away. There was so much to discover about him. She locked her finger behind his neck and he lifted her, giving her the opportunity to wrap her legs around him. His leather clad sex pushed against her heat.

Something was different with him, not that she had a lot of experience...but this was so different, it worried her. She didn't want to worry. She wanted to let go and enjoy. What did she really have at risk? Another heartache?

She wanted the kiss to continue.

She wanted it to end.

She didn't know what she wanted, so she reluctantly pulled her face away. "We really should get you out of those pants."

One of his hands swept down to pull her panties down and run his hand over the curve of her ass cheeks. "I can see, taste and touch you all at the same time. The colors," he pulled at her red satin panties until she wondered if he intended to rip them.

"You need to let me down to get them off. And don't you even think about ripping them. Remember, I'm poor."

He lowered her and then bent to remove her panties. "The textures, satin and skin, but especially the aroma..." He seemed to want to linger down there.

"My vote would be for tasting first, and save your sight."

He sat her on the bed in front of him. "I imagined you'd taste like butterscotch."

"I suggest you start here then." She pointed to the juncture between her legs. "And use your imagination."

His deep baritone chuckle rumbled inside her belly and moved lower. He shrugged out of his leather vest and the lightning bolt tattoo on his neck seemed to get lost with the bare expanse of his chest to be ogled. The man's pecks were covered with a sprinkling of dark hair and...she pulled him down to capture a nipple in her mouth.

He groaned and then roared with laughter, nearly shaking free of her mouth. "I didn't know a man's breast could find fascination for a woman. And to think I didn't want to shock you by doing this same thing to you."

Jenny ignored him and alternately sucked and ran her teeth over the hard nub. And she was only getting started. She linked her fingers inside his leather pants. She didn't know a man could go commando wearing leather, but anything that made this faster was okay with her.

When she inched her hand down, he caught her hand in his. "Have mercy on me. If you touch me, I'll explode. My brain is hardwired to avoid this at all costs and right now my body wants you like I've never wanted anything or anyone."

Jenny tried not to allow his words to excite her too much. Searching for her heart's desire had never gotten her anything but pain and heartache. "I risk having my heart broken, what do you risk?"

"I risk creating a moment of time that will snare me. A moment so perfect, I'll never want to leave. I risk letting my men down again by the distraction of a beautiful redhead. I risk an entire civilization depending on me."

"Well, if you put it like that."

*****

He was going to make love. It made him so anxious even his palms were sweating. It was time. And she was *the* woman. If he didn't make his move, Peck would beat him to it. He'd seen the way they looked at each other.

Daken's cock ached more than any wound ever had. His balls were so tight, he could hardly move. No way did he dare let her touch him. Her invitation to feast might redeem him from total humiliation. Placing a hand on both her knees, he pulled her legs farther apart, and the sweet aroma of her urged him forward. The foam of red curls at the juncture of her legs invited him to nuzzle his face before he gave attention to the hard little nub peeking out at him. He buried his face in her soft curls inhaling deeply.

He needed to taste and ran his tongue along the length of her slit, lingering at the opening of her channel. Licking her juices only satisfied him for a moment, as he searched for the spot inside that would make her writhe even more.

One inch.

Two.

He found her sweet spot and she lifted from the table, screaming her pleasure. He tongued the spot while she came. Her fingers dug into his hair and she pulled. "Butterscotch," he said once she finally stilled.

His aching balls made him focus on *his* needs. He unzipped his pants and freed his cock.

"No way is that thing going to fit. I don't want to sound ungrateful, especially after you just gave me the best orgasm of my life, but no way."

I promise you, the best is yet to come…literally. I won't hurt you. I'll know if I start to hurt you."

She continued to glare at his cock, but leaned back on her elbows and opened her legs wider. He moved to positioned himself at her core. He took it slow while they both watched the union. He communicated with the part of her brain controlling her pleasure and in the next moment she began to shimmer around the head of his cock. Her breath came in short, hard pants, accented by an occasional squeak.

"More," she panted.

Daken thrust deep inside her tight heat.

Chapter Five

"Peck has found more of the Korin. Three, maybe four of them. We have to go."

There was so much more Jenny wanted to do with Daken, to him. They'd only just begun. But she couldn't argue with the future of all mankind, present and future at stake. She jumped from the bed and dressed as fast as she could. "Where are they? What happens now?"

Daken held his hand to his temple, which she understood, meant he was communicating silently with Peck. "They're playing poker in one of the casinos on the strip. Peck's already there. They haven't spotted him, nor will they. Peck won't wait for me if he can get them alone. Damn. We need to hurry."

Jenny moved faster, leaving her bra and panties behind. They only pulled out of the parking lot when two choppers roared out of a side street to join them. Kaze and Chiron. A chill ran down her spine. She'd assumed they'd be at one of the newer hotels at the other end of the strip like before. They must be close. The tension poured off Daken's body.

Once they all parked, she stood back while the men gathered and Peck walked out of the hotel to join them. Peck nodded to her and then frowned. Was he unhappy about Jenny and Daken? When Daken locked the door, Peck had to know what they were doing inside the room alone. What did he think about it?

"They're at a table known for big rollers. On our best day, none of us could look the part," Peck said. "We need to bide our time until they grow bored and move on."

"How long have they been in there?" Daken asked.

Peck shrugged. "Maybe two hours. Long enough to take everyone's money, unless they met someone rich and stubborn. Or maybe they'll allow new blood to join in. Someone who might be able to lure them to a more private place. What about Jenny?"

Daken turned to Jenny and she tried to appear calm. "I could do it. Buy me some sexy clothes in one of the casino shops. I know I could lure at least one of them out...you know. Come on to him."

Daken shook his head. "I don't think so."

"Why not, Colonel? It's worth a try and we won't give them a chance to hurt her."

Jenny agreed with Kaze. If Daken wanted an argument, she'd give him one. "Can they do the communicating thing you guys do?"

"Their powers are weak, almost useless from years of debauched living. Their telepathic powers are no more than parlor tricks when compared to someone like Peck."

"Give me a chance. I'll only go for one. How many are there?"

"At first, we believed four," Peck told her. "But I can only read three."

There's not a single Korin Peck can't detect at close range. There must only be three." Daken reached his arm toward her and then dropped it limp against his side. "Let's get you into some sexy clothes."

When he heaved a sigh, Peck laughed. "You thought you'd have more control over her once you had sex?"

Kaze and Chiron gave each other a high five. Jenny didn't know what was worse. Having three of Daken's friends know she'd had sex with their colonel or having Daken believe he could control her with sex. "What gives you the right to want to control me?"

Daken shot a glare to Peck. "Now isn't the time for this. Let's get you dressed."

Oh, she'd get dressed all right, but Daken wouldn't like it. She could almost guarantee it. She took the lead, walking twice as fast as normal. Even as she approached one of the shops, a beaded number in the window caught her eye.

Red. She remembered how Daken's eyes sparked when he saw her red undies.

Buying clothes quickly became *shopping with the Neanderthals* as Kaze and Peck offered so many suggestions, she agreed with them just to get out of there.

"Take the tags off the garments. She's wearing them." Peck said to the clerk.

"What size shoes did she say?" Kaze asked Peck. "These are better."

She already had a cute pair of strappy sandals with a just a hint of a heel. Jenny looked at the shoe Kaze held in the air. "I don't think so. I'm not good in heels and those will give me a nose bleed."

Peck shoved them toward the clerk. "We'll take these, too."

Jenny shrugged. "I'll wear them, but be prepared to heal me when I bust my ass."

Jenny teetered out of the shop on her too-tall shoes, dressed in a skin tight, red, beaded, strapless dress. It reached mid thigh and if she lengthened her stride, she could see the black lace garters holding her expensive stockings up. She'd brushed the devil out of her curls in the dressing room and applied some of the make-up, Kaze had purchased at a nearby shop. The whole process had taken much too long.

The scowl on Daken's handsome face as they walked could rival a thundercloud.

"What the hell were the Korin thinking when they decided short women were better? Get a look at those legs. Holy shit."

Chiron's words startled Jenny. Not the content, but

because he so rarely spoke at all.

Peck placed a restraining hand on Chiron. "You have a lot to learn. It's okay to admire a woman's legs, but not this woman. Not any more. Not since—"

"That's enough," Daken thundered.

"He has to know or he'll just be thinking it and get you riled. What if he gets a flash of that sexy garter and gets a hard on? What if she—" Peck shut his mouth when Daken's fist was inside it.

What had she done? She'd created a monster. No, she'd created four monsters.

Peck rubbed his mouth and smiled. "See? Now you guys know what will happen if you so much as have an innocent thought about her. Keep control or poor Daken will have to beat the shit out of you."

Kaze got serious and stepped in front of Daken. "Is it true? Are we all going to end up like you? Having feelings for a *woman*?"

Daken glared at Kaze like he'd lost his mind, but then turned toward Jenny with eyes dark and hungry. She shivered.

"Hell, if I know, Kaze. Peck lied to us when he said sex wasn't great. It's the best thing that's ever happened to me. Only I haven't figured out if it's sex with Jenny that made it so incredible or sex in general."

"Idiot." Peck hissed. "How did you get to be three-hundred and fifty without learning the first thing about women?"

Jenny wanted to slap Daken or better yet, kick him where it'd hurt most. "And I haven't figured out if sex with you is good or if sex with any *Borka* would be just as good. Do you have an answer for *that*, Peck?"

Daken growled. "Enough of this. We have a job to do." He walked ahead into the casino.

As they went, Peck moved nearer. "Remember to keep an open mind. Don't resist and we will be able to communicate with you."

In the area designated for poker, Jenny realized the guys had disappeared. And, she immediately understood why. In the corner, on a dais raised a foot above the other tables the Korin were playing poker. It was early in the evening, so not too many of the tables were occupied. That table had eight chairs, and six played. Four of them were Korin. The four were big, blonde and beautiful in every sense of the word, clean, stylishly dressed and impeccably groomed.

She made her way toward them aware of all the stares. Peck had given her a small beaded purse, and said she had enough money inside it to play. She hoped he was right, because she was a novice at best. She worked too hard for her money. No way would she gamble it away.

All four Korin stopped playing to watch her approach. She didn't make eye contact, knowing she might prick their vanity.

"May I join you?" she asked when she reached a chair, still not looking at any of the time thieves. When one of them huffed, she opened her purse and tried not to show her surprise to find *five* wrapped stacks of bills. She pulled them out and placed them on the table."

The dealer looked up. "Have a seat. Do you want it all in chips?"

Jenny didn't know how much it *all* was, but the dealer didn't appear overly surprised as he handled the money.

"For starters," she said.

When the dealer finished sorting her chips, she had the biggest pile on the table by far.

"Now maybe I won't be the only one losing my shirt," one of the two twenty-first century players said.

None of the Korin even spoke to her. She wasn't sure what to do next.

Don't look or speak to them. They're used to having

women throw themselves at them. How is it you women say? Play hard to get.

The only problem with having a man in her brain, well maybe not the only problem...she didn't know which one was speaking. Daken or Peck?

All of them are interested, but they want you to show your interest first. The one on the far left is the alpha. He expects you to choose him. If I were you, I'd go for either of the next two. But whatever you do, stay the hell away from the one sitting next to you. None of us can get a reading on him. I didn't see him earlier. And we know him. It's Lawzard. He's the worst of the depraved monsters.

As if he knew the words in her head, the one sitting next to her pushed his chips toward the rest. "I have a date with three beautiful blondes."

Jenny wondered if any of Shadow Team would follow him.

No, it could be a trick to weaken us, a ploy to pull us away from protecting you. We'll get him later. You just concentrate on getting their attention. Three is a good number.

Did he mean all three? Did he mean sex with three men? At once? This had to Peck in her mind. No way would Daken make that suggestion.

I've heard some women are curious to know if they can handle three men. I think you would find them interested in the idea. But first, win a few hands of poker so they aren't suspicious of you.

He expected her to win? As if! Jenny had only hoped not to lose too quickly. However, with Peck's help, an hour later the pile in front of her had grown significantly. The Korin didn't appear any too happy.

You're bored with poker.

"I'm bored with poker."

Ask the three of them to fuck you.

Just like that? Why did she trust Peck knew what he was doing? Women didn't go around asking three guys to fuck her just like that. Did they?

She turned to the one in the middle. "Do you know any other interesting games? Maybe something the three of you could play with me...alone?"

The alpha laughed. "First you make us pay, then you want to play. We have a room in the tower."

Jenny pushed her chips toward the dealer, who began to count.

"One hundred and eighteen thousand," he said after he'd finished.

Once they'd all finished cashing their chips, Jenny really started getting nervous. For some reason Peck had gotten quiet...to quiet. The dealer made several suggestions about caution, making it clear he thought it inappropriate for Jenny to go to a room with three strange men while she had a boatload of money.

As they walked toward the tower section of the hotel, the alpha moved to take her arm. It was hard not to flinch. Thankfully, other people were in the elevator or she might've bolted. One of them moved closer and rubbed up against her ass. Were they picking their positions?

As soon as the four of them stepped out onto the fourth floor together, a second moved to stand in front of her. Yes, that was what they were doing. When the one in front started to kiss her, she pulled back, colliding with the one still in the rear.

"I'll use my mouth, but not for kissing."

"I'll use her mouth." The alpha stated his position and no one seemed to care she didn't want to kiss.

"What room?" she asked.

"At the end of the hall."

Jenny looked down to see a fire exit sign. Were her rescuers just on the other side of the door? How far did they want her to take this charade? She heard a distinct growl in her head.

Daken.

She pushed ahead, walking fast as if she was anxious for the fun to begin.

"The last door," one of them said and she move faster. Behind her they laughed.

She was a good five feet in front of the nearest Korin, but they were big and tall and she resembled the leaning Tower of Pisa in her heels.

The exit. Come fast. Stay to your left.

Jenny dived for the exit just as the door slammed open. Daken and Peck flashed by her with such speed she barely had time to recognize them. Once in the stairwell, she turned as the door was closing to see a head roll in her direction. Her first thought was gratitude it wasn't Daken.

In the next instant, a blinding pain hit her between the eyes while a large hand closed over her mouth. "Tell Daken, Lawzard wishes to speak with him. Tell him I could have easily killed you, but I spared your life as a token of good will. If he doesn't agree, next time I won't be so generous. And there will be a next time, be assured. I snared you easily and I can do so again. Any time I wish."

When he removed his hand, Jenny tried to scream and found she couldn't. Lawzard smiled at her, as if he knew. "Daken has chosen well." He drew her against him and kissed her hard...not so much a sexual kiss, as a b— of dominance.

"Make sure he hears my words."

He let go of her and fled down the was out of sight, the pain in her head s sank to the floor in a heap. What just was happening on the other side of the

When the door slammed ope wasn't too close to it. The residual p she could handle at the moment. door in the ass too.

"Jenny! What happened

answer?"   Not only was Daken covered with blood from head to foot, he was pissed with *her*.

"You jerk! Why are you angry with me?"

Peck moved around Daken's shoulder.   "You worried him.   We couldn't hear you thinking a single thought.   Not like the last time, when you were silently screaming,"

"I was screaming again. Where were you?"

"What?"   Daken demanded.   "Did something happen?"

"No, I'm sitting on the dirty floor in a fancy beaded dress, because I wanted to look for spare change.   Of course, something happened.   My head is killing me." Jenny struggled to stand and a pair of strong arms lifted her to her feet.

"I thought you said the Korin didn't do the headache thing as well as the Borka.   Trust me, I hurt every bit a bad as when you guys tried it."

"Lawzard," Peck said.   "He left you alive."

"He had a message for Daken."   Jenny touched her fingertips to her swollen lips.

"He kissed you?"

"Daken get your priorities straight."   Peck gave him a nudge.   "What message?"

"He wants to talk to Daken."

Peck rolled his eyes.   "Impossible."

"He kissed you?"

"What else did he say?"   Peck shot a glare to ken.   "Get a grip."

Jenny really wished her headache would ease. wasn't helping.   "Let me see if I can do this word d.   He said, 'Tell Daken, Lawzard wishes to speak Tell him I could have easily killed you, but I r life.   If he doesn't agree, next time I won't be And there will be a next time, be assured I I caught you easily enough this time and I can do it again.   Any time I want.'   Yes, that's what he said."

"We've got a problem."

"No shit. So what are we going to do about it?"

Chapter Six

A shadow quake washed over them in strong waves. "I didn't get their position," Peck said. Jenny finally understood what they hadn't told her. Peck could tune into their position when a quake happened.

This time Jenny wanted to watch while they sent the time thieves away. She didn't look away even when Kaze picked up the severed head she'd seen earlier and shoved it into one of the remaining Korin's hands.

"We need to finish here first. Pick up his body," Daken told the other Korin. Neither of them argued. Daken waved his hand with the silver ring in an arc and the floor seemed to disappear under their feet. This had been what Jenny had experienced in the dark on her first encounter.

While the men disappeared in a mist of light and sparkling particles, another two magically appeared in their place. Jenny hadn't expected it and from the look on Daken's face he wasn't any too happy about it. He activated his sword, but Peck laid his hand on Daken's arm.

"They're from Shadow Team Twelve, sent here to apprehend us, but I sense no hostility," Peck said. "Besides, I know Jargon, well."

The tallest one saluted Daken first and then Peck. "Sir, we're not here to take you back. Orion and I have come to join you in the fight against the Korin."

Peck turned away from the newcomers and searched Daken's face. "Jargon speaks the truth."

Daken deactivated his sword and reached for Jenny's hand. "We need to get out of here. If *they* can find us here, so can others."

"Take Jenny, I'll set off the sprinklers to clean this blood."

Daken gave a curt nod to Peck. "We'll meet at the hotel where we can find out just how compromised our world has become. Hurry."

The short ride back to their hotel proved more difficult than she'd imagined. Sitting on the bike with her dress hiked to show everything...gave them an audience.

The attention they drew had Daken growling the entire trip. "If this is how it feels...I don't know if it's worth the aggravation."

"Keep the commentary to yourself. First, you say haven't figured out if sex with me was incredible or sex if it was sex in general. Now you're saying you don't know if having sex is worth the trouble. Just keep it yourself, jerk."

Inside the small hotel room, Jenny didn't feel quite so feisty. Only moments later, Daken's men arrived. Having to share space with six immense warriors intimidated her. Plus, the two additional warriors both seemed shocked to see a woman in the same room with them.

"Were you hoping I'd disappear?" One of them looked away, but the other laughed.

Daken moved to stand where everyone could see him and stared at the laughing warrior until he stopped. "What do we need to know to stay alive?"

He stepped forward and gave a salute to Daken. "Sir, I'm here because the Korin have placed more than half of the Shadow Team warriors in life-suspension. They say it's to protect the warriors, but it's no coincidence those remaining are weak minded and easily managed.

The second one saluted, and looked at Jenny with suspicion before he spoke. "It all happened so fast, most didn't have time to escape. If not for Jargon here, I would've been suspended with the rest. He and Peck always believed this could happen."

Daken bowed to Peck. It was a sarcastic gesture. Jenny experienced a twinge of empathy for the man who now dominated her life after only a short period of time. This had to be difficult for him to hear. He'd trusted Peck with his life.

"You shared your distrust of the Korin with Jargon?" Daken's voice didn't reveal his pain, but Jenny knew he had to be suffering.

Peck shook his dark head. "I know how bad this looks, but I didn't dare reveal my suspicions to you. Or any of you, for that matter. Putting a voice to my thoughts would've been treasonous. Jargon and I have a commonality allowing me to talk freely to him. Jargon's mother and mine are half-sisters. Both are leaders of the resistance."

The tension in the room made Jenny shiver.

"Neither Jargon nor I promoted the values our mother's raised us to believe as long as the safety of mankind as a whole wasn't in question. We were to content to follow the Korin's directives. However, both of us prepared for the eventuality our mothers might be correct."

"I prepared a little more than Peck," Jargon said. "I have safe-houses, equipment and supplies stored for our use. We may not have the freedom to return to the future, but we won't suffer for lack of material goods in the here and now. And I believe as Peck does, this is where they will attack, cowards that they are.

"We need a plan," Jargon continued. "Peck's second in charge of Shadow Team Ten, just as I was for Team Twelve, but neither of us wants any leadership responsibility here. I realize you might be tempted to second-guess your position, Colonel. But we need you to continue in control."

Jenny watched Daken react. She could see the

conflict written in his pained expression.

"Control? I've never felt more out of control in my life. The only thing I know for certain, I wasn't ready to retire as team leader before this mission." Daken ran his fingers through his long black hair. "I'll take responsibility, but I need to know everything you two have kept to yourselves. Everything. We have to find a way to keep the Korin from changing history and keep our freedom."

"I brought this." Jargon dug into his pocket and pulled out a silver tube, not much bigger than a lipstick. "There are fourteen units inside, enough for all of us and more if any of our brethren find a way to escape suspended animation."

Daken took the tube into the palm of his large hand and Jenny moved closer. The lid snapped open with a tiny hiss. "Implants. What do they do?"

"These will prevent our own from reading our thoughts. Peck is skilled enough to implant them."

"Damn!"

Jenny watched the exchange, curious if it would work on her, too. Daken caught her eye. "I don't know why you have a natural resistance to some of our most powerful suggestions, but this wouldn't work for you. Your body would more than likely reject it."

Jargon laughed. "Daken, you surprise me. I thought it'd take longer than a day for you to accept a woman among us. Now Peck on the other hand...I thought he'd have a harem by now."

"It only took a few minutes," Daken said with a huff. "You need to know she's the best thing that could have happened to us."

Daken managed to surprise her. "I wouldn't say the *best*, although I like hearing it. And getting threatened by Lawzard isn't exactly a shinning moment."

"Lawzard?" Jargon questioned. "He's the most

evil of all the Korin. He beheaded two of Team Twelve."

Just what Jenny wanted to hear! "Great. What did I do to piss him off?"

Daken placed his large warm hand on her arm. "Lawzard does nothing half-way. There's a purpose to his madness. We'll discover it and protect you."

A shadow quake hit, throwing Jenny off balance in her heels. Daken caught her and held her close until it subsided.

Peck turned to Jargon. "Did you get anything?"

Jargon shook his head and looked sheepish. "I wasn't prepared. Next time I'll be ready."

"They're close...very close. Lawzard?" Peck started to pace with his hands to his temples.

Daken went to the window, reached for the curtain and then stopped. "Lawzard is more powerful than any of us imagined. We'll use Formation A-2. Now."

Jenny didn't have a clue what Formation A-2 meant, but all the warriors gave Daken a salute and then left the room in a rush.

Peck was the last to leave. "Watch over her. Lawzard is crafty. I think he may have powers we're not aware of."

"She's not leaving my sight."

Jenny liked the sound of that, but she was still angry with him.

Once everyone left the room, he reached for her and she went willing into his embrace. His warm breath on her face excited her.

"I'm glad you're here. Otherwise, I don't how sane I'd be. Watching how you unflinchingly accept the madness makes me stronger. I pledge my life to keeping you safe."

"You already have. You saved me at the storage units and then again with the Korin. Now it's my turn to repay the debt."

Daken pulled her against him and kissed her tenderly. He ran his amazing tongue along the seam of her mouth until she opened for him. His tongue was long and strong as he probed her mouth. She was reminded of how well he'd used it earlier.

He chuckled.

She pulled back. "Did you read my mind just now?"

"We don't have much time," he said, not answering her question. He lifted her, and she wrapped her stocking clad legs around his hips.

In two steps, he had her backed against the wall as he humped into her. She hadn't replaced her panties or bra from their earlier encounter. In the next instant he worked at undoing his pants with a single hand while holding her with the other.

His cock probed along her channel, but she couldn't reach to help. Then he was there…plunging inside so hard and fast she nearly came. Buried to the hilt, he stopped and allowed her to adjust to having him so deep. She'd never understand how he fit, but he did, stretching her tight and so very full.

He pulled slowly back and plunged deep again and then again. "I can't lose this…lose you." He moved faster and then harder. She prayed he'd never stop. The pleasure ratcheted with every thrust until she didn't know if she'd survive another. The bliss became so perfect it almost made her cry. She fought to control her breathing…nothing could slow the white-hot desire barreling her toward…she exploded with such force she could see stars. His shuddering groan told her Daken came with her.

The pleasure ebbed and then peaked a second time and then a third as he pinned her against the wall, buried inside her.

So many emotions flooded her as her energy

waned.

A knock on the door startled her.

"I don't know who it is." Daken said to her unspoken question. "My men don't knock."

He lowered her to the floor and took a step back. His cock was still hard and he had difficultly zipping his pants. *The Korin are here.* Jenny heard Peck's message in her head and the way Daken increased his step, told her he'd heard it too.

Daken gave a poignant glance over his shoulder to Jenny before he opened the door. "Where? Why would they be fool enough to come here?"

Peck walked inside. "I don't know, but they are. We need to take advantage of our good fortune. The other four are watching the door of their room. Do we bring Jenny or do you want me to handle it without you?"

Jenny didn't want to be the cause of keeping Daken from his men. "I'll stay out of your way. I've had practice."

"It seems to me, both times you stayed out of the way, yet somehow you managed to put yourself right in the middle of it. No you'll stay by my side this time, not wait behind."

Daken drew his sword and waved his hand in an arc. She'd seen both Daken and Peck do this. What exactly it did, she wasn't certain, but she experienced a pressure in her head.

"Let's go."

They found the rest of the team waiting on the second floor. Daken made another signal with his hand, and Kaze rammed his shoulder into the door. It split open and Chiron, Peck and Jargon went over top of Kaze, who scrambled to his feet and activated his sword.

Jenny couldn't see inside the room over Daken's wide shoulders, it surprised her not to hear the eerie pitch of their sonic swords slicing through the air. With all of his men in the room, Daken followed with Jenny on his heels.

"What the hell?"

Jenny leaned over to see what had Daken's attention. Four large Korin sat on a king-sized bed, none of them moving a muscle. "If it's this easy, why do you slice off their heads?"

Daken jerked around to give her a dirty look. "It's never this easy. Not even close."

Jenny was about to congratulate him when a pain pierced her skull. Her legs moved backward without her consent. When she collided with a human wall, she understood. "Lawzard."

"Don't twitch or she dies."

"What do you want, Lawzard? I didn't think hiding behind a woman's skirts was to your taste."

"Colonel, you mock me. Aren't you pleased with my gift?"

"Why?" Daken demanded. "Why are you sending your comrades back to be punished?"

"That's a supposition right now. We can't be certain of anything. Perhaps they'll get a slap on the hand. Take Seto there. His father is in control of the treasury. Seto's father sets great store in his son. Or Hood, his father is an elder and on the council. Do you think he'll allow his son to be interred?"

"What do you know of what's happening?" Daken moved a fraction closer and Lawzard activated a sword.

"I thought you said the Korin are afraid of swords?" Jenny demanded of Daken.

Lawzard gave an evil chuckle and Jenny shivered. "I don't fear swords. I fear ignorance and greed." He waved the sword in an arc, shooting a mist of glistening particles into the air. A sensation of being burned alive and smothered at the same time hit Jenny. She looked to Daken who was doubled over. Sounds of choking and gasping told her everyone was affected. Lawzard moved away from her, but she couldn't see where. The mist grew so thick, she couldn't see much at all.

Just when she wondered if she was about to die, the mist lifted. She searched out Daken who stared toward the bed. She turned to see what had his attention. The bed was red with the blood of the four Korin, who lay in a headless heap.

"I couldn't allow them to go back alive. Not these...they knew too much."

Daken deactivated his sword. "If you touch her, I'll kill you with my bare hands. The Korin don't kill each other."

"Not only do the Korin kill, they do it like the cowards they are. Two of the men I killed came here to kill a new born child."

"Elder White."

Jenny felt Lawzard grow tense and silently communicated it to Peck and Daken.

"How do you know this?" Lawzard demanded.

Peck moved nearer. "We found evidence they wanted to seek John and Amy White, the parents of Elder White. We assumed it was you, although we didn't understand how this would further your case."

"The elder council has been mismanaged by greed and corruption. The elders who wish for reform are in fear of their lives. My father is one of them. Only my reputation as the most evil of the secret society has kept him safe. Now I've been compromised. It's suspected I'm a rebel sympathizer." He laughed. "I have two choices, kill all of you so my reputation will be safe, or somehow convince you not to return so it will be believed I've killed you."

Daken and Peck looked at each other in disbelief.

"You don't think I can? Were you able to stop me from killing the Korin pigs?" Lawzard moved away from her.

"I have newfound appreciation for your power, but you're too late."

"Too late?"

"We can't return. The rebellion has started and we're to be placed in suspended animation. We've already disobeyed orders to return."

Lawzard deactivated his sword and threw it against the wall. "Damn Korin morons. They won't be happy until they've killed all of mankind."

Jenny couldn't help it. "But you are Korin!"

"I may have been born Korin, but my heart is Borka."

Chapter Seven

Lawzard paced. The large muscles in his neck bulged and he flexed his hands in almost a nervous gesture. He shook his beautiful blonde head and stopped in front of Daken. "*You* must go back. No one else can do what needs to be done. The Korin would never listen to Peck or Jargon. I certainly can't show my face. My father would lose any chance he has to gain the people's trust."

Peck sat on the bed next to Jenny and patted her hand. "Lawzard's right. Daken is the only one who can do this."

"I'll make you pay in ways you can't begin to imagine if you are trying to deceive us." Daken said. "If I go, I can't return. Ever." He turned to look at Jenny.

She wanted to scream for him not to listen. Did she dare? She wanted him to stay for selfish reasons. She wanted him to stay for her. "Don't think of me. This is about saving all mankind, not about us."

"More Korin will come if you don't do something. Maybe my father will have the answer. Maybe not, one thing is certain. Someone…one of the elders planned to murder Elder White as a newborn. There are other elders on the council who believe as Elder White and my father. Good men, who believe in the equality of the human race, and who are willing to take a stand. If we don't alert them to what is happening here, there's no chance."

"I never thought I'd find myself agreeing with Lawzard, but he's right. I'm the only one who will be listened to. My stalwart position, never wavering from my orders and blindly believing the Korin knew what was best, will come to good use. They know I don't have a political agenda."

Peck smiled. "Don't be so hard on yourself. Your men would follow you to hell and back and never question your orders. It's a gift."

"I'll go, but I need some time. Time to say goodbye to Jenny."

Jenny started to cry. Right in front of the warriors, she cried like a baby.

"You sure know how to clear a room," Daken said a second later. She dabbed her eyes and looked around. Everyone had gone.

"I'll never see you again, will I?"

Daken turned away. "No. I won't be able to return. If all goes well, the elders will send someone in my place to lead my men."

"I don't care who leads your men. I only care about you."

"Just once, I'd like to feel you naked against me."

Jenny gulped, her heart in her throat. "I was right. I told you I risked having my heart broken. Just thinking I'll never see you again, hurts so bad I can't breathe, can't think.

"Remember I told you I risked creating a moment of time to snare me forever. A moment so perfect, I'd never want to leave. I've already done that, but I'm willing to create another, one I'll carry with me as long as I live." He began to undress.

He was so much braver than she. The pain she knew would follow almost made her say no. She pushed her fear back. "I love you. You should know that."

He stopped, freezing in place. His eyes brightened to sapphire. "I love you. I've never loved anyone before, nor will I ever again."

Jenny ran to him, throwing her arms around his neck. "Show me."

He caught the back of her head in his large hand and kissed her slowly. His breath hot upon her lips caught

her in a whirlwind of sensations as she met the thrust of
his tongue.

Time stopped for them.

No thieves could steal the timelessness they
discovered in each other's arms. Jenny knew she'd made
the right choice. She pulled away to tell him. "I'll never
regret this."

He helped her out of the beaded dress, allowing it
to fall to the floor where she stepped out of it. All she
wore was a garter belt, nylons and heels.

Daken's breathing quickened to a raspy drone.
"Everything I do with you is my first and last time. Even if
I live through this, I won't take another woman into my
heart." Daken's eyes darkened and he reached both hands
to cup her breasts as if testing their weight. In the next
instant, he captured her nipple in his mouth, swirling his
tongue around and over her. His magic tongue. His
mouth strummed an invisible cord connected to her core.
The pull of desire from her breast to her sex was so strong
a rush of moisture dampened her thighs.

He raised his head while his long strong fingers
plucked both nipples. "There isn't enough time...never
enough."

She stroked his chest and worked down. "Let me
help you with your boots."

He let go of her to perch on the edge of the bed and
she turned her rear toward him as she pulled his boot off.
The sound of him sucking in a harsh breath told her he
appreciated the sight of her ass as she bent in front of him.
He ran his hot hand over the curve of her backside and
then down.

"Your other boot. Don't get distracted. I need to
see you naked too."

Once she helped him out of his second boot, he
wrapped his arms around her and laid his face against the
small of her back while he ran his hands down to her

garters.   And then he stood, grinding his hard-on against her ass. He brushed the backs of his fingers over her cheek and down her neck.

"Your pants," she reminded him.

He chuckled and moved away. She turned to see him peel the leather down over his slender hips. When he stood after removing them, his massive satin cock, fully erect and ripe as it jutted into the air, so proud and magnificent, nearly brought her to the brink.

"I'm yours to command," he said before stretching out onto the bed in front of her.

Nothing she could think of would feel better than having him buried inside her. She followed him onto the bed and straddled his hips. She went up onto her knees and guided him to her core. His eyes smoldered. The tip of him, plump like a peach, plunged into her.

Icy prickling sensations seared along her ass while she lowered herself along the thick length of him. Slowly at first and then faster as she watched the straining cords of his neck under the lightning bolt tattoo. His cock jerked and throbbed inside her. She shattered, coming in a rush. He rolled her and began to pump.

She let go of every thought and allowed the pleasure to overwhelm her, feeling centered and at peace as she floated on the almost too delicate sensation.   It carried her in waves, ebb and rise, ebb and rise, each time a little higher and longer.   And then in an instant the sensation became like a tidal wave, taking her higher than she ever been. She hung there on an invisible thread of pleasure, on the brink of something incomprehensible.

Daken stroked his shaft inside her, long slow thrusts, stoking a fire, lapping at her core and never allowing her to cool. She shattered a second time, so utterly she wondered if she'd ever be the same.

Chapter Eight

Jenny hadn't been to visit her mother since Daken left, almost two weeks now. She tried not to resent the fact he hadn't kept his promise to help her mother. She thought about approaching Peck, if she could find him. He'd disappeared with the rest of the Borka, right after Daken returned to the future.

She found her mother asleep in her chair by the window. Jenny moved into the room avoiding the mirror she passed. She knew how bad she looked and didn't need reminding. She'd barely slept and hadn't eaten in two weeks. At this rate, she'd be dead long before her mother.

"Your young man said I'd see you today."

At the sound of her mother's voice Jenny looked up. Nothing her mother said ever made sense. Did she mean Jenny's brother? "Has Paul been here? He didn't say anything to me."

Her mother laughed. The sound reminded Jenny of her childhood. She'd been so close to her mother. Alzheimer's was worse than death in some ways.

"He said I can come home. Not our old home, but a new one, in an underground cave. It even has a swimming pool and a bowling alley. He said it's big enough for an entire community of Borka.

Jenny almost fell as her knees weakened. "Daken?"

"What's that dear? What's that mean? Who or what is a Daken?"

Jenny's heart plummeted. For a second she'd believed her mother had seen Daken.

"Peck," his name is Peck. Strange name. He says…"

"Peck was here? Who am I?"

"Silly girl. You're my Jenny."

Jenny started to cry. Peck had healed her mother. Daken had made certain Peck helped her mother. A knock on the door startled her. Jenny turned expecting to see Peck.

Her mother's doctor stood in the doorway smiling. "I was going to call you. Since your brother and fiancé are here, I didn't think it necessary. They said they wanted to surprise you."

Peck was here with Paul? More than likely he'd concocted a plan to fool her brother into believing her mother had a spontaneous recovery. Also more than likely, by tomorrow, her mother's doctor and everyone else associated with the nursing home would not recall Mary Bender ever having been a resident.

Jenny hugged her mother and tried not to cry harder for fear it'd worry her. Paul stuck his head in the door. "Jenny, I didn't expect to see you until later. See you tomorrow, Mom."

"Bye, dear."

"Peck's giving me a lift to the station. Hell of a guy."

Jenny stomach roiled as she fought to understand what was happening. Had Daken's warriors adopted her family while she moped over losing Daken? And she'd thought they didn't care, that they'd be glad to be rid of her.

"I didn't expect to see you until later."

Jenny nearly fainted at the sound from over her shoulder. "Daken!" She jerked around and jumped into his arms. "Daken."

"I wanted to surprise you. I was bringing your mother to pick you up."

"This is a Daken?" her mother said.

Her heart pounded as she clung tight to him. So

many feelings and thoughts bombarded her, she didn't know where to start. "Yes, Momma. This is Daken. My warrior...my love."

"I thought your name was Colonel Parker. My mind isn't what it used to be. Forgive me if I'm a little slow."

It was difficult to concentrate on her mother when Jenny wanted drink Daken in...to stare at him, touch him and more. "Oh Momma, you're fine. Daken *is* Colonel Parker."

"Mom Bender, I'm going to take Jenny for a little walk around the building. We'll be back in a few minutes."

For the first time since Daken had left, Jenny had hope for a bright future.

"Take your time. I'm not going anywhere," her mother said.

Daken took Jenny's hand and led her from the room.

"How?" Jenny's excitement couldn't be tamed. She wanted answers.

"When I got back, I played dumb. Not hard since I already felt like an imbecile. Peck, Jargon, and Lawzard, all had me fooled. Nobody was what I believed. However, I'm proud to say, I took control upon my return to the future.

"It became clear the best course was for me to allow the council to believe my entire team perished at the hands of Lawzard. His secret is safe and now he's more feared than ever. I also discovered the two members of Shadow Team Twelve Lawzard beheaded were traitors. They were in the pocket of the Korin who is trying to gain control for evil intent."

"It must be hard for Lawzard...everyone believing he's evil and debauched when he's really not. He's like a man with no country...no friends."

"I spoke to his father. A segment of the Korin is trying to set the world straight. Only time will tell. Lawzard's father and Elder White know the truth about what happened here. They believe we can do the most for the cause right here in the twenty-first century. I'm assigned to lead the twenty-first century Shadow Team Eight.

"Eight?"

"Peck, Chiron, Kaze, Jargon, Orion, Lawzard, me and the first woman warrior ever in history, Jenny Bender. Who I pray will consent to becoming Jenny Bender Parker."

Jenny's heart slammed in her chest. Could life get any better than this?

As they walked by the open door of a linen closet, Daken jerked her inside and closed the door behind them. He lifted her against him and kissed her.

She wanted him.

Needed him.

"Put me down, so I can take my pants off."

Daken did as she asked, as she bent to lower her jeans, his cock probed her from behind. She leaned forward, her face pushed against the door while he lifted her, separating her legs. He found her core right away and as he thrust inside, her clit clenched and hardened. He was working his special brand of magic on her!

"I wanted you too badly," he moaned. "I can't last."

"Give me what you have, warrior. You can make it up to me later…forever."